I0574964

TOURIST

TIMOTHY STRONG

Black Rose Writing | Texas

The author grants the final approval for this literary material.

First printing

This is a work of fiction. Names, characters, businesses, places, events, and incidents are either the products of the author's imagination or used in a fictitious manner. Any resemblance to actual persons, living or dead, or actual events is purely coincidental.

ISBN: 978-1-68513-244-6
PUBLISHED BY BLACK ROSE WRITING
www.blackrosewriting.com

Printed in the United States of America
Suggested Retail Price (SRP) $22.95

Tourist is printed in Book Antiqua

*As a planet-friendly publisher, Black Rose Writing does its best to eliminate unnecessary waste to reduce paper usage and energy costs, while never compromising the reading experience. As a result, the final word count vs. page count may not meet common expectations.

Praise for
TOURIST

"A fine example of the American novel."
–Christine Shepps, Business Director

"An exciting ride — a real page turner."
–Joey De Grandprix, Teacher

"A novel of conviction and truth exposing the stigma of mental illness."
–Barry Norton, Insurance Business Owner

To mom who gave it all to me.

TOURIST

CHAPTER 1

"Boy oh boy it never felt so good to see this old beat-up trailer," Jake said, when his mother stopped the car.

"The first time you stayed over a month," she said. "This time less than three weeks."

"That's right," Jake said. "Welcome back to Hollywood! No more nuthouses for me." He opened the car door a few inches. "And I didn't miss the height of fall." He got out of the car, stretched a little, then opened the back door and dragged his father's sea bag across the seat.

"You're coming over for cake, aren't you?"

"Sure thing. As soon as I start a fire."

From the trailer steps, he turned and waved as his mother backed the car out of the yard, then reached for the key under a lip of the steel door frame, and opened the door. The trailer smelled musty from the hay bales packed around its sides, and a thin layer of pollen coated its windows. He rested the sea bag against the couch. The wood stove door creaked, and the noise, as he wadded up newspaper, crackled oddly in his ears. The trailer walls seemed narrower than he remembered. He picked up a handful of cedar kindling, and said, "I don't ever want to go back again."

The fire began to snap, and he gazed out the window behind the couch and remembered his friend Barney's crooked smile, his deftness with a pool cue, and other things.

"Barney is gone," he whispered.

A young maple tree's crayon-orange leaves rubbed against the window, and below, a fresh layer of shiny rust pine needles covered the ground. He studied them, trying to discern a landing pattern in their flight to the earth. Most, he decided, seemed to rest pointing their needle ends toward the trailer. He stared into the dusty bars of sunlight that came through the pine limbs above, then turned back to the stove, added a few chunks of hardwood, and shut down the drafts. Through the window above the stove, Jake saw that a section of stove pipe was cocked off to one side, and when he opened the door, he heard the back-up alarm of a loader working at the new Olympic Arena on the hill a few blocks away. How much work had been done in three weeks?

After he tightened the stove pipe wire, he started off to his parents' house, and the well-worn path, lined with beer cans and empty McDonald's boxes, and the back yards, each with a sagging clothes line, burning barrel, and assorted clutter, seemed dingier than ever beneath the fall colors. Good old Hollywood, Jake thought. But it's better than where I've been.

Behind the Jessels' house, two down from his parents, he saw Randy, his friend Chad's younger brother, near a grease-caked transmission. He was swearing and kicking the ground.

"What's wrong?" Jake asked, noticing he had a cowlick similar to Barney's. Randy looked up and stared like he didn't recognize him, and Jake touched the new growth of his beard.

"Oh. How are you, Jake?" Randy asked. "When did you get home?"

"A little while ago. Where's your brother?"

"Hard telling. It's Friday. Probably at the Grill." He scuffed the ground. "Chad will kill me. I lost one of the torque bolts."

"Tell him I'm looking for him if he stops here."

"Sure. Goddamn transmission anyway."

Jake's mother was pulling dead flowers out of a tractor tire flower bed. She pushed herself up and Jake saw the black marks on the palms of her hands from the tire as she wiped them on her apron. She said, "Now I can really hug you. I'm so glad you're home." They hugged and he squeezed her awkwardly.

"Come in and have some cake."

He followed her inside and asked if she'd paid his rent.

"Didn't I tell you that on the phone? The day Rich dropped off your check I cashed it and paid Phil the rent. It's easy to sign your name. I'm used to it."

She must have called during the time he'd lost at the hospital. Only tiny bits of time remained, and he wanted to ask her what else she'd said that day but didn't want her to know. She opened the bread box and took out a cake: his favorite, chocolate with white icing.

"Are you okay now?" she asked, and placed a saucer in front of him, nearly covered with cake.

"Mom, I'm getting fat as it is, sitting around that nuthouse all day long."

"Don't call it that," she said.

"You saw some of the people there, how bad they were. '

"The staff helped the last time didn't they? Want a cup of coffee?" she asked, putting the tea kettle under the faucet.

"Okay. The cake is good," he said.

She lit the gas stove with a match and put the kettle over the flame; she always put too much water in for what she needed, but it didn't do any good to tell her. She told him his father was laying linoleum and she expected him home soon.

Jake stared out at the bathtub Virgin Mary she'd been after him to paint since summer, and the legs of the vinyl-covered, aluminum chair wobbled; it seemed like he'd tightened them not long ago. He stood up, walked into the living room and stared out the window, then at a picture of him and his parents at his high school graduation, and wondered why he was so much taller than them, nearly six-two. He scratched the new whiskers that hid the dimple on his chin and saw that he looked much more like his mother. Dark brown eyes, straight hair, and big boned like her, but he had his father's strong chiseled-type nose and full lips. He shook his head. That picture was taken eight years ago.

Back in the kitchen, he watched his mother stick a finger into an edge of the white icing. "Why don't you call Rich and see when he wants you to work?" She looked at the clock. "It's after four," she said. "Maybe he's home."

"Later, Mom." He placed his palms on the table and licked bits of icing from his lips. He sensed his mother's nervousness, knew he caused it.

"What did the doctor tell you?"

"Not much." He stared at the crumbs piled up around the toaster oven.

"Well?" she asked. "You hardly said anything on the way home." The tea kettle started to groan and rumble. "You don't know how I've prayed and prayed you'd be better this time."

"They helped me understand the depression and Barney's death. It's almost like the first time was a trial run," Jake said. "I'm sorry I didn't say much on the way home."

"Do you have an appointment to see someone?"

"Give me a break, Mom. I'm twenty-six. I can make a few decisions alone." He reached for the tea kettle.

"The water's not boiling," she said.

"It won't be for ten minutes with all the water you have in here. It's all right." He stared out the window over the sink. Chad's log truck went by, a long shadow in front of it. "I'm sorry, Mom, but I know what I need to do. I need a little time. People treat you different after--"

"I want you to be okay," she interrupted. "I want to help."

"I know," he said, and poured half the lukewarm water down the sink, then thought about getting a beer from the refrigerator to take with him. "The money left from your check Is in the drawer," she said. He opened the top drawer next to the sink and took out an envelope with his name on it. Inside were four twenty-dollar bills. "How much was the check for?" he asked.

"Two-hundred," she said. "I told--"

"I know." Jake interrupted. "My memory--" Then he asked, "Did Phil say anything about raising the rent when you paid him? Everybody thinks this town is a gold mine since the Olympics."

"No," she said. "He's not like that."

"I'm going back to the trailer," he said. "Tell Dad I'll be over later."

"Aren't you going to call Rich? Stay for supper?"

"No thanks," he said. "I'll probably see Rich downtown."

"What did the doctor say about drinking?" she asked.

"Don't worry." He leaned against the door and didn't want her to irritate him with questions, wanted her to hug him again. She'd had problems before with her nerves when he was in college and he didn't want to cause more. "Thanks for the cake, Mom. And thanks for saying prayers."

The lawn, yellowing and lightly covered with maple leaves, was hard under his feet. Before he left, there hadn't been a frost. He heard someone coming down the path; it was Chad.

"What's doing?" Chad said and slapped him on the back. "Beard looks good."

"Thanks, I'm home." Jake started down the path and Chad walked to one side of him.

"That place better than the last time?" Chad asked, past a wad of chewing tobacco.

"Maybe," Jake said. "The hardest part is what people around here think."

"It's nothing. Besides, everyone is worked up about the Olympics. This whole town is nuts, and it's still October."

Jake walked a little faster. "Is the new arena open?"

"Yeah. Since you left, they've been hauling in fill for the back parking lot. Wait'll you see Stoddard Street," he said, and spat a stream of tobacco juice at an empty beer can. "Two days ago a dozer pushed over a boulder that almost rolled into the Foster's house."

"Let's go for a ride." Jake said.

"Sounds good. Your pool arm rusty?"

"They had a bumper pool table at the hospital, but I don't know if I want to go to the bar."

"C'mon," Chad said. "People been asking for you."

"I'll bet. I want to see more of the mountains." He stopped in the path and turned around, looking in every direction at the almost flat depressions and wet areas that made up the land where they lived.

Chad said, "It sucks that you can't see any mountains from Hollywood. But if you could, it would be packed with condos."

"I guess you're right."

At the trailer Jake put more wood on the fire, dropped his Swiss Army knife into his pocket, and opened one of the louvered windows over the sink a crack. He took the car keys out of a drawer and tossed them to Chad. "Start her up, would you? You drive." He went into the bedroom and patted the old quilt on the loft he'd built out of four-inch birch logs, then rested his head on the quilt. He heard the car turn over a few times and then start; headlights shone through the frosted glass of the bedroom door. After straightening the quilt where his head had wrinkled it, Jake tapped his back pocket to see if his wallet was there. It seemed strange to have his pockets full. At the hospital all personal belongings were kept in a safe.

A barren, almost sealed existence.

He got in the car, and Chad raced the engine a little and said, "Let's go, buddy. It's Friday."

Jake rubbed dust off the dash and glanced at the oil pressure gauge. "Everything seems new," he said, as Chad let out the clutch.

"This thing runs good," Chad said.

"Take it easy. It's got to last."

Chad backed the old '53 Ford out of the driveway into the narrow street. He said, "It rides like a boat," and beeped the horn lightly.

After a block Jake could see the roof of the new arena and behind it a tall brick chimney from the old one. The road dipped, and both sank out of sight. Jake stared at the rows of shingle-sided houses and paint-chipped trailers.

"Hollywood hasn't changed since you left," Chad said, and rolled down the window to spit.

"It never will," Jake said." Even the dogs and cats look dirty and hungry."

At the bottom of the dip, Chad shifted into second gear.

"See what I mean," Chad said. "They must have brought in a hundred loads of fill – no, more than that."

"Holy shit," Jake said. He didn't recognize it. What used to be a gradual hill, covered with birch and maple trees, was a steep dirt bank at least seventy-five yards long and a hundred feet high on which boulders lay half-buried.

"There's the boulder that almost went through the Foster's house," Chad said. "I guess the old lady heard it coming and almost had a heart attack. They haven't even bothered to move it." He stopped and shifted into first, let out the clutch and started up the hill to the arena.

"I'd have shit my pants if I heard a rock that big coming toward my trailer," Jake said.

Chad laughed, "Progress my boy, all in the name of progress."

Halfway up the steep hill, the white superstructure stood out sharply against the deep blue sky. More and more of the huge building filled the windshield.

"Something, isn't it?" Chad said.

It was whiter and bigger than Jake remembered. He turned around. Behind them the sun was setting over Hollywood; smoke from wood stoves hugged the tops of the brightly colored trees. Black telephone poles and wires connected the houses.

Chad stopped at the top of the hill, next to the long, curved line of stainless-steel flag poles. On the left, two shiny yellow bulldozers sat, their work day ended. The arena's outside lights came on as they sat parked next to the curb; Jake couldn't tell if it was day or night, except by turning toward Hollywood.

"Drive up a little," Jake said. The speed-skating rink came into view on the right, with the high peaks of the Adirondacks behind it. Jake gazed into the purple-tinged mountains and focused on the passes and peaks where he'd hiked and hunted with Barney.

"Let's get a beer," Jake said.

"Okay." He drove forward. "You okay?"

"I don't know," Jake said. "I hate all this fancy shit when so many can barely make ends meet." He scratched the side of his nose. "Not used to being home, I guess."

"You still think a lot about Barney's dying?" Chad asked.

"They helped me at the hospital with that," Jake said. He turned in the seat towards Chad. "Let's get one thing straight. Okay? It hit me hard.

Do you know how you'd react if your best friend fell off a five story roof and you were working in one of the rooms on the first floor? Christ, Chad, I heard his body hit the dirt." He stared at Chad's pine-pitch blackened hands on the wheel. "I've been to the hospital twice now. I'm finished with it. It's over."

"I don't know what I would have done. You guys were like brothers."

"Because I couldn't take his death I went to that damn hospital. People treat me like some kind of freak. They did when I came home the first time this spring. It won't be different now."

"Your friends don't think that way. To me, it's like breaking a leg," Chad said, and pulled into the Arena Grill parking lot. "You went to have it fixed and now you're home."

"More like cancer," Jake said. "You never know for sure if it's gone. And people don't forget. They'll remember the cops had to take me off that roof Barney fell from the night we buried him."

"C'mon. You can't relive it." Chad shut off the car and handed him the keys. "Bet a beer I win the first game."

"We'll see," Jake said. Directly behind the front of the small bar the stark whiteness of the Olympic Arena rose.

In the crowded bar a Dolly Parton song, Barney's favorite singer, blared from the jukebox. While they waited for the bartender Jake asked

Chad if the Hilton had opened. He tried to shut out everything but Chad's voice.

"They've had more foul-ups there than you can count," Chad said. "That swimming pool they built on the second deck leaked into the cocktail lounge." He laughed. "That'll cost them some money."

Jake smiled, then walked over and put two quarters on the pool table. A set was already up. Several people sitting at tables said hello, and Jake nodded, and kept going.

He wanted to go home. All the noise reminded him of the crowded cafeteria at the hospital where all the patients came to eat – a group of the strangest, saddest people he'd ever seen. You're one of them, he thought, and felt like he'd escaped, that they'd come to take him back soon. At a table in the corner, against windows that faced the street, his boss, Rich, the surveyor, sat with his girlfriend and her older brother. Rich motioned him over.

"Good to see you, Jake," Rich said. Have a seat." They shook hands.

"Working hard?"

"Pretty much. Can you give me a couple days next week?"

"Sure. It'll seem good to get out in the woods."

"Monday, for sure. Pick you up at seven."

"Good. Thanks, Rich." Jake took a few steps toward the bar, and when he looked back toward the table, he saw Rich's girl friend whispering something to her brother.

Chad handed him a beer. "Cheers. Glad you're home." He raised his mug and clanked it against Jake's.

"Thanks," Jake said, and tipped the foam into his upper lip. "That's good. You know something, Chad?" Jake leaned a little closer. "I met some nice people at that hospital, and now I feel like a tourist in my own home town."

"You working next week?" Chad asked, avoiding that thought. "I saw you talking to Rich."

"Monday." Jake took another long swallow.

"Think you'll ever go back and finish your degree in surveying?"

"Maybe," Jake said. "They're playing partners." He turned toward the pool table and watched a fat construction worker sink the cue ball.

Karen, the afternoon bartender, came over and asked Jake how he was doing.

"Fine," he said. "How goes it with you?"

"Busier every day," Karen said. "Missed seeing you around."

"I'm back," Jake said. "For good."

A customer down the bar called her name. She waved and walked down the raised wooden platform.

"She's nice," Jake said.

"Her brother was in the hospital years back. She told me the other day."

"Where?" Jake asked.

"Same one as you."

"Oh." He buried his hand in his left pocket, wrapped his fingers around the fat Swiss Army knife. Barney's mother gave it to him the day after the funeral.

A guy in a plaid shirt at the end of the bar motioned to Chad, and he walked over. Jake glanced around the room and noticed the new Olympic posters on the wall over the jukebox; a chalet perched on a hillside looked more like Sweden than Lake Placid, and Jake smiled. He hoped they didn't get six inches of snow this year, as happened one winter when he was a kid.

Their quarters were up. He went over to the table, popped them into the slots, and rammed the coin lever in. The balls dropped into the bottom of the table and he picked them up, three in each hand, then placed them in the rack.

Chad came over and chalked a cue. "Let's do it," he said.

A big construction worker broke the balls. His Carhart overalls were grease-stained and frayed, and Jake wondered if he was one of the bulldozer operators.

"Nice rack," he said.

Jake didn't know if the guy meant he'd racked them loose and was mad because he didn't make any or was kidding. Jake shrugged his shoulders.

"You shoot first," Chad said, and handed him a cue.

"I can't use that short thing."

"If I was six feet tall, I'd have picked the pole vaulter's cue," Chad said, and reached behind him for the longest cue the bar owned.

"Thanks. You and Barney always used that short one."

Instead of playing partners with Chad, for a moment Jake imagined Barney in front of him. Short, a little over five-five a layer of baby fat still on his frame and his brown hair cut like someone had placed a bowl on his head: Beatles style. Jake chalked his cue as he remembered all this and more. Barney's full mustache that needed trimming, and his blue eyes that lit up so often as he smiled or gazed at a good-looking woman or laughed at a joke. Jake rubbed blue chalk into the insides of his shooting fingers.

"Six in the corner," he said, in the general direction of where the construction worker stood.

"Name's Tom," he said and offered to shake.

"Jake." They shook hands. "And that's Chad."

Chad waved.

Jake sank the six, the one, and missed the four. He took a long drink, finishing the beer, and noticed that his hand shook a little. Chad grabbed

Jake's mug and finished his own on the way to the bar.

The door opened and a good-looking woman came in. That's something I missed, Jake thought. Very nice. She reminded him of his first girlfriend, Laurie. Very attractive.

Tom's partner came over from the bar and shot in five of the stripes before he missed.

Chad put the new beers on the table, shot in two balls, and missed a set-up. Jake threatened him with his stick and took a step closer.

"See that woman that came in a few minutes ago?" Jake pointed to where she stood at the bar, then took his beer from the table.

"That's Karen's relief," Chad said. "She's early. It's not six yet."

Jake stared.

"Down, boy," Chad said, and stroked his chin. "She's married. Only someone as smooth as me might tangle with her." He punched Jake on the arm.

"You should talk. You're married."

"Yeah. Well. You know what they say. Us people that lives in Hollywood gots no morals anyways. Shoot," Chad said. "You're holding up the show."

"You're right. I'm supposed to be home for supper." Jake started toward the table, and Chad asked if he was staying in that night.

"Probably," Jake said, and bent over to take a shot. He missed and left the construction worker a clean run.

"Looks like you're buying," Chad said.

The construction worker sank the rest but left himself a terrible leave for the eight. He called a bank shot in the corner and made it.

"Nice shot," Jake said, and swallowed more beer.

"Luck," Chad said softly.

They all shook hands, and Jake headed for the door.

"I thought you were buying," Chad said.

"Rain check. I owe you," Jake said. "You coming with me?"

"Yeah," Chad said. "Let me finish my beer."

Jake walked toward the door, took a closer look at the new bartender and finished his beer. Chad walked past him and out the door.

"What's her name?"

Jake got in and paused as he was about to turn the key. He looked at Chad, then at the Arena directly behind the bar.

"Amy," said Chad.

"How long she been working?"

"Who cares? She's married," Chad said.

"Yeah, yeah," Jake said.

He drove around the back way to drop Chad off.

"What are you doing tomorrow?" Chad asked.

"Who knows?"

"I have to cruise a lot over in Essex. Come along?"

"Sure," Jake said and stopped in front of Chad's tar-papered house. "I thought you were having Grant saw out siding."

"I'm waiting to win the lottery." Chad slammed the door and waved, then walked around the front of the car. Jake raced the engine and he jumped out of the way.

The road home headed toward the Arena and the glow around it was brighter than he remembered. At the trailer, he rolled down the car window, inhaled the odor of pine needles and listened to the leaves fall.

CHAPTER 2

Jake fell asleep reading Gray's Sporting Journal, a snobby fishing magazine his friend Dave had found in the trash at the Lake Placid Club. He woke up at five, went back to sleep, and was up again at seven-thirty, wide awake. The bed felt good after the thin, plastic-covered mattress at the hospital, and it was nice not to be awakened at seven; he never could understand the therapeutic value of that. Jake remembered a phrase the doctor used. "Look out for your own best self-interests." She'd said it to him in several of his last sessions. Probably says that to everyone that's leaving, he'd thought and told her that he didn't want close friends anymore; he was afraid they might die like Barney did. They'd spent a one-hour session discussing why his reaction might be valid and why it was all right, or not all right, to feel that way.

Jake stared at the ceiling and knew, by his thoughts the day before with his mother and at the bar with Chad, that he'd already forgotten that therapy session and others. At the hospital, he'd sworn to put the advice they gave him into practice; to think and consider his emotions against experience and not let his nerves guide him. Easy to say. What he wanted to do was hole up like a toad in a rotten log, as he'd tried to do before going to the hospital this last time. He rolled onto his side and stared out the translucent pane of glass in the bedroom door.

He threw off the covers, slid out of the loft and put on his thick maroon bathrobe. It would be fun to cruise a woodlot with Chad. He stood by the window staring at the layers of crisscrossed pine needles and tried to remember the last time he'd had fun. He knew Chad wanted to help but told himself he had to recover on his own.

It was chilly and the fire was almost out. When he first moved out of his parents' house and rented the trailer, a few months after Barney died, he'd set the oil furnace thermostat at fifty and hadn't changed it since. He stirred the ashes and small coals, tossed on slivers of cedar and glanced at the clock over the refrigerator. Almost eight. He added bigger pieces of kindling and blew on the flames. Barney had never been in this trailer. The fire caught and he closed door, leaving the drafts open to burn out any accumulated soot. He wondered when Chad would show up. The sky was pale blue. He didn't need a pass now to walk outside and he didn't have to listen to the moans and cries of the old men in the geriatric ward next door or hear the complaints of the people he lived with. Adjustment. He walked over to the sink and rested his hands on the cold, blue Formica. "It's behind me," he whispered and pushed hard on the counter. "I'll never go back again." He started a pot of coffee, stepped outside and walked around the yard swinging his arms in the morning breeze. Behind the trailer, he gazed at his reflection in the living room window. For over three weeks, he hadn't shaved and liked how his beard looked and felt. It came in blacker than his light brown hair and covered the dimple on his chin. The doctor at the hospital hinted that she thought he should shave and asked why he didn't. He told her he didn't like the electric razors they provided and that he usually grew a beard during hunting season anyway. It seemed to satisfy her.

Jake heard the bang and rumble of Chad's log truck and walked around front. Chad stepped off the running board and slammed the door of the rusty Ford.

"How's it going?" He rested an arm on the fender and pulled a pouch of Chattanooga chew from his wool shirt.

"Good to be home," Jake said and rapped his knuckles on the side of the trailer as he walked past.

Chad stuffed a wad of tobacco in his mouth and arranged it with his fingers and then his tongue before he spoke.

"Got time for coffee?"

"Sounds good." Chad spat and walked toward the trailer. "You going to bank the trailer up with new hay? This stuff looks kind of moldy."

Jake bent down and felt one of the bales he'd put in last fall; it was soggy and half frozen.

"Probably should."

"Maybe we can find some today," Chad said.

They drank coffee and Chad filled him in on the local gossip. He finished the last of his coffee.

"Let's go. You can drive if you want to. I've had a long week."

"Why are we taking the log truck?"

"Transmission's gone in the pick-up and the old lady needs the Vega for work."

"How's the nursing home these days?"

"She says it's a lot of shit work." Chad laughed and said he was going out to check the oil. Jake put on his Red Wing boots. He sat on the couch and watched Chad walk around the truck checking tires, not knowing if he really wanted to go, or spend time with the same person for most of the day. Why? he asked himself. Is it Chad? We always had a good time together. At the hospital, he'd imagined Chad losing his brakes with a full load of logs on the steep hill going into Port Henry. He'd thought of at least one way every one of his friends could die unexpectedly. He put on his Ford hat and closed the trailer door.

"I already fueled up," Chad said. "Head her out the back way."

Jake backed out of the yard using the mirrors and beeped the horn as they went by his parents' house. The truck tattled along: it rode like a stone boat when it was empty, which was the only time Chad let him drive. Jake didn't use the split gears either; Chad had told him one miss might blow the transmission. It didn't matter. Jake felt important when he drove the truck. "Big lot we're going to?"

"Not bad. Keep us out of town and away from these damn Olympics for the winter. It took me twenty minutes to get through town the other day. Damn tourists. He spat out the window. They rode past the road to John Brown's grave, then the empty horse show grounds where the Olympic torch would be installed, and on toward the Olympic ski jumps. Jake shifted into third and tapped the brakes. At the dip near the jumps, as usual, cars were parked in the No Parking zones and people walked around or took pictures through the two-tiered chain-link fence.

"Go buy a postcard," Jake said and tooted the horn.

"It'll get worse," Chad said. "Nothing in it for you or me. That's for sure. Some of the people in Hollywood will get jobs but not many and not for long. I'll never work for the bastards."

"Amen." Jake shifted into high, gave it the gas for the hill leading past the trail head road to Mt. Marcy. Yesterday, he and his mother had come in from the opposite direction. Jake stared at the high peaks as if he'd never seen them before, their colors brilliant against the blue sky. The open fields at the base of Marcy reminded Jake of the flat and boring countryside he'd been in for the last three weeks. "A beautiful fall," he said. "Glad I didn't miss it."

"Hunting season soon," Chad said. "We get a hard freeze and the leaves will soon be gone."

"Lots of deer sign in the woods?"

"Some. You got relations in Essex?"

"Aunt and uncle."

"Maybe your uncle knows where we can get some cheap hay."

"Might." Jake took it easy on the curves through Cascade Lakes and enjoyed the rugged cliffs and bright yellow birch leaves. The sun was barely up on the first lake and on the second one, the white birch trunks and sprays of yellow reflected in the water. He started to say something about how beautiful it was but stopped. Chad had been in the woods since he was old enough to go with his father and saw them more for their usefulness. It wasn't that the beauty Jake saw was wasted on Chad; it was a part of him. Jake never understood that until he spent a year in forestry school at Paul Smiths College with people from Long Island and New York City who complained about the cold and desolate surroundings. From then on, he thought of Chad and many other natives as having the truest knowledge of the woods and the greatest appreciation for them. Even the professors at the college didn't know diddly compared to Chad or his own father. Once a professor had shown him a geode from Canada: hard gray, lichen covered rock outside, pure olive colored crystals inside. Jake thought most of the natives were like that: rough exteriors hiding a deeper purity. Something born into us.

"Lots of people getting lost lately," Chad said, and rubbed tobacco juice off his chin with the back of his hand, then wiped it on his green work pants. "Took them three days to find a guy, his wife and eight- year-old kid up near Marcy." He waved to an oncoming loaded log truck and reached over and touched the horn.

Someone Jake didn't know.

"They lost the trail coming off the side of Marcy, trying for the trail to Marcy Dam. Hard to figure. The trails are marked better than this road." Chad shook his head and slapped his knee. "Damnedest thing. A Conservation Officer told me the mother was trying to breast feed the kid when they found them. Said she'd heard she could produce milk if the kid nursed long enough. Can you believe it?"

"Weird or what?" Jake said.

"Stop when you get in Keene. I'm thirsty."

"Yeah. I could use a soda," Jake said. "Maybe some cigars, too." He paid more attention to the road than the foliage as he drove around sharp corners down the steep grade into the valley. He wished it was warmer so he could go swimming and scrub off the hospital he felt clinging to his skin.

At the store, he bought a Coke and a pack of tipped Swisher Sweets. The lady smiled at him as she handed him change and said, "Thank you. Gorgeous day."

"Beautiful," Jake said. "Makes you glad to live here."

Chad came up to the counter, a quart of Pepsi under his arm, and asked for a pouch of Red Man.

"What? No beer?" Jake said.

"Not until four. New rule."

As they drove out of Keene, Chad untwisted the Pepsi cap, removed his wad of tobacco and threw it out the window. He cleared his throat and took a drink.

People were out raking and burning leaves, and many of them waved at the old log truck. Jake smiled and checked the mirrors. Color filled the two side mirrors most of the time and swirling leaves kept crossing the rear view.

"Your dad working much?" Chad asked.

"I haven't seen him yet but the last time I talked to him on the phone he was working every day. It's hard to talk to him." Jake moved over to let a car pass. "He's like your dad; won't admit his age, refuses to slow down even a little."

"I know. Stubborn old farts. The old man wants to cut and skid, instead of load. This winter, he told me the other day, if the snow gets too deep on this lot we're cruising today, he wants to rent a team of horses from someone he knows over here. He'll be sixty-three by then."

"Doesn't do much good to say anything," Jake said. "To them we'll always be kids. We're twenty-six and they still act like we're raising hell in high school."

Jake shifted for the turn up Simon's Hill. From the bowl of the valley, the high peaks glowed a smoky burnt orange. In the middle of a hay field on the right, elm trees in a humped-up Indian burial ground reminded him of Barney lying under fresh fallen leaves. He shifted into second gear and stopped, waiting for an oncoming line of cars to pass.

"Look at all the leafers." Chad said. "Spending money to look at trees."

"And this year the tourists have the added bonus of saying they were in Lake Placid the fall before the Olympics," Jake said. He let the truck roll along easy in third gear up the long steep hill. "Seen Grant lately?"

"Stopped by last week. He's not sawing much. More drinking than anything."

Jake tooted the horn as they passed the house. It didn't look like Grant was up yet.

"You should be making boxes like you did with Barney," Chad said. "Think of all the tourists this year."

"I know. Everything is still set up in the shed out behind Mom's house. I don't like … I haven't been in it twice since he died."

"Let's stop at Grant's on the way back and see what he's got for red cedar," Chad said. "You guys made nice boxes, especially after you set up that rig for burning in emblems."

"I'll think about it."

"Jake, it's none of my business but you can't go on, in and out of that hospital."

"I'm done with it."

Chad put in a fresh chew and Jake asked him to steer while he lit a cigar. Smoke got in his left eye and stung. He rubbed it and saw the brilliant colors through a watery haze.

A few miles later in Elizabethtown, they turned at the Wadhams Road toward Essex.

Chad spat a long stream of tobacco juice.

"Shit," Jake said. "I wish I could have done something the day he fell."

"No one could have," Chad said and stared out the windshield.

Several miles out of Essex, Chad told him to turn down a dirt road and, after a few miles, he said, "This is it. Pull over anywhere."

Maple branches interlaced overhead and the quiet seemed unnatural after the engine noise. Jake stepped out and latched the door quietly. Chad walked back on the road a short distance, found a surveyor's corner mark next to a stone wall and stepped across the ditch. Jake followed. On the lower trunks of the maples, scars from years of tapping showed as lighter colored circles inside the gray bark.

"You cutting everything or just soft wood?"

"Spruce, pine and hemlock," Chad said. "Maybe a little beech. The guy that owns this makes maple syrup every year."

"Good. Be a shame to cut these maples. This is a nice sugar bush."

"You going to make this year?" Chad asked.

"If Dad's able and I have the time," Jake said. "We didn't this spring and there's not much syrup left."

Chad headed away from the boundary line they were following and, as the maples thinned out, pine forest began. Under the biggest pines, pure white mushrooms grew and squirrels chattered at them from high limbs.

"How many acres?" Jake asked.

"Little under five hundred, the owner said. It's a pie-shaped piece, the bigger end up top. We'll go up there and follow the back line over."

They came to the top of a small knoll and Jake turned towards the town of Essex to the east: Lake Champlain and, in the distance, the Green Mountains of Vermont. Jake tried to take it all in. Colors, up close, just beyond the tops of the pines were focused, the lake azure blue. It sparkled in direct sunlight and the highest Green Mountains were hazed with bands of yellow and orange across their sides, blending into the pine and spruce forests on their peaks. Jake turned to say something to Chad, but he was looking off toward the western boundary line. A steep hill blocked out the Adirondack peaks.

"Tough skidding over there," Chad said. "But looks like good timber." He started off.

Jake stared to the east for a moment longer, then hurried to catch Chad, who could move for a guy his height. Jake stretched his long legs in big strides to catch up.

It warmed where the sun shone into the gut between two hills and Jake took off his red flannel shirt. He tied the arms around his waist. At the bottom of the gut, Chad stopped. "Stay here if you want," he said. "I'm going to scout out a road. This might be a good place to load if there's a way around." He pointed to a spot on the bank that would be perfect to build a platform for a header.

Jake snapped off an armful of boughs and dropped them on a flat rock under a big spruce, then sat and leaned against the trunk. After a few minutes, he felt his muscles relax and stretched out his legs. Squirrels chattered around him. A fat gray ran across a fallen log, almost out of sight. Beech nuts, knocked off by the squirrels, pecked the ground and Jake dozed in the shadowed sunlight until he heard Chad coming through the leaves up the gut.

"Nothing there," Chad said. "Steep stuff. We'll walk the other way when we come down."

"Okay." Jake got up, brushed off the back of his pants, then watched Chad step from a log onto a rock and around a beech tree. Jake's calves ached as he started out. The second hill was steep, almost a cliff, and Jake was glad he wasn't carrying surveyors' tools as he pulled himself from tree to tree and rock to rock.

"Little out of shape?" Chad asked and spat toward a boulder.

"Some. Sitting on my butt for almost three weeks didn't help," He stood next to Chad, gasping for breath.

Chad squatted beside a downed log and looked over the country they'd covered. "Can they help?" he asked and picked up a small stone and watched it roll around in his palm. "I mean at the hospital?"

Jake followed the stone in his palm and said, "What helps as much as anything is seeing the people that have totally lost their minds. I mean totally. It makes you want to get better, fast. Especially the second time around."

Chad stood up. "We're almost there. Oh, I meant to tell you. On the edge of the gut there's a small stand of red cedar in a little swamp. If we get the lot, I'll take a load over to Grant if you want." He tossed the stone down the steep hill, turned and walked straight up it. Jake scratched the back of his neck and started out. Chad was probably right; he missed building boxes. It didn't seem so long ago that he and Barney bought fifty dollars-worth of red cedar from Grant and made small jewelry boxes and after they sold well at a store in the village, they'd gone out with Chad, cut down ten trees, taken them to Grant's, helped him saw them out and stacked them to dry. At one time they'd talked about making it a big thing, but never did more than work in the shed behind his parents' house whenever the store sold what they'd built. It kept them in drinking money and paid for the tools.

Jake put on his shirt. He heard Chad cruising around in the steep stuff off to his right and headed for the top. He found the survey line that ran along the top of the hill; stones placed in pyramids every fifty feet along a line. On the other side of the line, the beech trees were marked with State Forest Preserve posters, and the bottom of each sign read 'Primitive Area.'

Chad came up to Jake, laughed and pointed at one. "That's the area for us. We're the only primitives around here. Damn the state." He walked over, ripped one of the tin signs off the tree and threw it into state land.

"They're hogs." Jake said. "The Adirondack Park Agency won't be happy until all the Adirondacks are owned by the state. Just think of all the tax money the towns have lost over the past few years. All for one big happy park for the city slickers to play in."

"You mean get lost in, garbage up and start on fire." Chad walked over to another tree and ripped the sign down. "I won't cut on their land, but I won't look at their damned signs either." He flipped the sign away from him. It side-slipped for a second against the bright orange of a small oak, then fluttered to the ground, shiny side up.

They walked to the highest part of the hill and looked toward the Adirondack Peaks; they were shrouded in clouds. Toward Vermont, the clouds, shadows moving up the lake – patches of bright blue between them – hid all but the peaks of the mountains.

"Nothing we can do about it. Let's go," Chad said. "It's a good lot."

They walked down the mountain toward the other line and found a good place to load. When they were almost out of the woods, Chad said, "We'll ride over to the owner's place and I'll firm things up." He scratched his chin. "You know. He might have some hay."

Chad drove two or three miles down the road and stopped at the first farm they came to. The first thing Jake noticed was a sugar house out behind one of the barns: a nice one, with a vented cupola on top, and large galvanized holding tanks on the side. Chad pointed to a barn; bales of hay visible through the barn boards. "Maybe he's got some old stuff," Chad said. "How much you willing to pay?"

"No more than fifty cents a bale. I need thirty."

"Stay here. I'll go talk to him."

Jake rested one foot on the dash and pushed the other one into the floor boards. He hoped his father wanted to sugar this year and thought of all the years he'd made syrup with his grandfather. Deep snow when they first tapped and the sweet steamy smell as they boiled late at night. His grandmother baked them peanut-butter cookies to dip into the thickening boiling sap.

Chad called his name and Jake looked away from the sugar house. "Back the truck up to the barn door. He's got some stuff he was going to throw out. It's yours."

Jake waved and moved over to the driver's seat. He drove the truck forward and backed around to the door. Chad and the farmer walked beside the truck. When the farmer said, "Good,"

Jake stopped and shut the truck off, then stepped out and introduced himself.

The farmer leaned against the barn door hands in his overall pockets. "Mason. You any relation to Dewey and Jane Mason?"

"My aunt and uncle," Jake said.

"Good people," he said, and looked at Jake as if he expected the same of him. The farmer opened the barn door, propped it open with a length of pipe, and pointed to forty or fifty bales of hay stacked at the back.

Through spaces between the barn siding, as Jake stepped farther inside, he could see the stand of maples and birches that lined the edge of the pasture. In the dusty light of the barn, the orange and yellow brightness contrasted with the dull gold hay bales.

Chad walked over and picked up two bales by their strings. "These okay, Jake?"

"Fine."

The farmer stood with his hands in his back pockets. "Help yourself," he said. "All they're good for is bedding, and I quit keeping cows two years ago."

Jake grabbed two bales and walked to the truck. "Nice sugar bush where we walked today," he said, on his way back.

"Been tapped a good many years. Don't know about next season, though."

Jake grabbed two more, and Chad stayed at the truck, pulling out chain from behind the seat to secure the bales.

"Nope," the farmer said. "My back's been poor this fall and if it doesn't get better by spring, I'll make do with what I have left from last year."

"My dad and I make every year," Jake said. "Much smaller operation than yours, though."

"Something to do in the spring," the farmer said.

When Jake went to the truck with two more bales, he whispered to Chad, "What's his name, again?"

"Farnsworth."

"I appreciate the hay, Mr. Farnsworth. It'll help keep me warm this winter."

"All those folks coming to Lake Placid ought to keep you warm enough," he said, and laughed. "Glad I don't live there. Probably more politicians and city slickers than you can shake a stick at."

"You know it," Chad said.

When they'd loaded a few more than thirty, Jake said, "Guess that's all I need."

Mr. Farnsworth motioned with his arm. "Take them all," he said. "Cover em' up with a piece of plastic. They'll last till next year."

"Might as well," Chad said, and winked at Jake. "Can't beat the price."

After they loaded the rest, Chad threw the chains over the top and tightened down the chain binders.

"Thank you very much," Jake said, and shook the farmer's hand.

"You're welcome," he said. "Stop by this spring and let me know how the syrup business is doing your way. If I had some young fellas like you to help, I'd make for sure."

"I'd be glad to come over and help tap," Jake said, as he started the truck.

"See you in a couple of months," Chad said.

On the way home, they talked about all the old timers they knew in the Adirondacks, and Jake told Chad he'd like to live on a farm like Mr. Farnsworth's, out in the country, with nice fields to raise a few head of beef, and plenty of maples for syrup every year.

CHAPTER 3

After they unloaded the hay, Chad asked Jake if he wanted to start dragging out the old stuff. Jake leaned on the bales stacked three high, told Chad his body felt like putty, and that he'd do it tomorrow.

Jake went inside after Chad left and saw a note from his father on the kitchen table: Stopped by to see if you wanted to go fishing, Dad. Ten-o'clock was written in one of the upper corners. Jake looked at the kitchen clock, almost two thirty, then he opened the window over the sink a little more.

His father must have put wood on the fire. He didn't know why he hadn't gone to see him the night before. Jake stood by the stove and looked out the window facing the road. He was tired and sore, and wondered if he was just out of shape, or if residues of the drugs they'd given him at the hospital still sludged around his veins. He reached into his pocket for the knife, took it out, and placed it on the end table under the window next to the couch, and put his wallet beside it. He wanted to remember everything about his friend. But they'd helped him at the hospital understand the impossibility of that. At least to a certain extent.

The pine needles looked dusty. He opened the window above the couch, smelled their pitchy odor, and wondered when it had last rained, not liking that he didn't know. He did know why he hadn't gone to see his father. Shame. His father was ashamed that his son entered a mental institution and Jake didn't blame him. "I'm ashamed, too," he whispered, then sat on the couch and took off his Red Wing boots. They cost sixty-five dollars and he wouldn't have bought them if Barney didn't swear they were the best boots made. He liked to remember.

His father never understood why he couldn't leave Barney's death alone. As he lay back on the couch and arranged the pillows, he thought about turning the overstuffed couch around to face the windows, away from the door and wood stove. Isolation. The carpet of rusty orange pine needles stayed with him as their smell wafted in through the window and he fell asleep.

Aching muscles woke up him up and his mouth tasted like stale cigar tobacco. He rolled his tongue around in his mouth and sat up, wondering if his mother planned on him coming for dinner. He added wood to the fire, brushed his teeth, and drank a big glass of water in the tiny Formica-pink bathroom, then splashed water on his face and scrubbed the growing bristles dry. He shut off the bathroom light, put on his hat, and started out for his parents.

"Hello, stranger," his father said, when Jake walked in. His dad stood and they shook hands.

"Good to be home," Jake said, his father's hard calloused hand in his.

His mom came in from the living room. "Staying for supper?"

"Is there enough?"

"I made a big pot of venison stew." She started to set the table.

"Where did you go fishing?"

"Lake Placid. It's mobbed with leafers ogling the trees. So many boats spoil the fishing. But

I think the lake trout are coming into shallower water. Want to give it a try tomorrow?"

Jake sat down at the other end of the table from his father. "I went to Essex with Chad today. A farmer gave me some hay for under the trailer. I should do that tomorrow, and I'm working with Rich on Monday."

"You saw Rich?" his mother asked.

"Last night at the Arena Grill."

"Do the bales in the morning, and we'll fish late afternoon till dark."

41

Jake didn't know if he wanted to go; like most things with his father, it was more of an expectation than an invitation.

"When's the last time it rained here?" he asked. "Seems pretty dry."

His father leaned an elbow on the table and rubbed his bald head. "Was it last week, Joany? Middle of the week?"

She looked up from stirring the stew and tapped the wooden spoon on the edge of the crock pot. "Last Tuesday. I remember I took in Monday's laundry after dark because of the forecast on TV."

"Speaking of laundry, Mom."

"Bring it over tomorrow," she said

"Got a good deal on some Lake Clear wobblers and Christmas trees lures the other day," his father said.

"Where?"

"From a woman in Saranac Lake. Her husband died, and she's selling out the stock in his tackle shop to pay the bills. She has no idea what the stuff is worth."

His mom put a steaming bowl of stew in front of Jake and went back for another.

"Well, I see the prodigal son is home," his father said. "He gets served first."

"Oh, Doug. Relax. I'm glad he's home."

Jake watched his father laugh, pick up his spoon, and fill it with stew as soon as she placed it in front of him. He raised the spoon toward Jake and said, "I'm glad, too, and this time for good. Right?"

"You bet." Jake knew his father's attitude hadn't changed since the last time he came home from the hospital. A kind of sadness combined with anger at Jake's predicament. Jake spooned up a chunk of venison. Do parents forever take responsibility for their kids? If so, he didn't want to have children.

While they ate, his father told him the Farmer's Almanac forecasted a cold winter and not much snow. He said the Olympic committee was planning on stockpiling the stuff for the cross-country trails starting in January, if they didn't have enough snow by then.

"Where would they get it?" his mom asked.

"Oh, there will be some snow," his father said. "They might skim it off the fields or the Lake if it's frozen, then put it in dump trucks, and haul it to where they need it."

Jake got up and turned the burner on under the teakettle for coffee, then lifted the pot and poured out three extra cups of water.

"Don't anyone say the stew's good," his mother said.

"Mom. It's great. No comparison to what I've had lately."

"Your stew is always the best," his father said.

"I'm glad you think it is," she said, and took their bowls to refill with big chunks of venison, carrots, and potatoes swimming in a light brown gravy. After dinner they had coffee and apple pie.

"Good crop of apples this year?" Jake asked. "The pie sure tastes great."

His father said it had been an average year.

Jake helped with the dishes, and his father went into the living room to read and watch television.

When Hee Haw was over, Jake's father asked why they'd gone all the way to Essex for hay. Jake rocked back and forth in the platform rocker that had been his grandfather's and told him Chad asked him to cruise a wood lot over there, and the owner had some old hay.

"Much deer sign?" his father asked.

"Hard to tell with all the leaves," Jake said. "I'd say it's a little past the height of fall over there."

"This weekend's supposed to be height here," his father said, "but I think they say that for the tourists. It was probably last week." He closed the Field & Stream magazine in his lap. "Do you know whose property you walked?"

"Farnsworth. He gave me all the hay I need, and more. Nice old guy."

"Don't know him. Probably Uncle Dewey does. You should have stopped and said hello."

"We took the log truck. Didn't go into town."

"Why didn't you take your car?"

Jake stared at the knotty pine walls, aged almost black in places, and stopped rocking. "I don't know. I never thought... I should have offered."

"Chad knows you like to drive that truck," his mom said.

It bothered Jake. He didn't want anyone doing him favors; but they wouldn't have been able to get the hay. Chad didn't know about the hay, though. He stood up. "Thanks for dinner, Mom."

"One o'clock tomorrow?" his father asked.

"I can't. Too much to do. Sorry."

Jake stopped several times on the way home, and looked at the high, gray, stationary clouds, and the orange glow from the lights at the arena, more intense than ever before, reflected off their undersides. The low brush seemed caught in the still light. He wanted to clear things up with his father, wanted him to be proud of his only son. He stepped on a tin can and the noise startled him. Jake knew he was unwilling to take orders from his father, always see and do things his way.

When he reached the trailer, he walked around it twice, as quietly as possible; a thin ribbon of blue smoke and heat shimmers drifted straight up from the stove pipe. Maybe, sometimes, he thought, the hospital wasn't such a bad place to be, and knew he didn't want to believe that. What in hell is going on? Inside, he lit candles instead of turning on the lights, and the small pile of coals in the stove flickered and winked under gray ash hairs. He wanted someone warm to hug and hold him close.

"Good God," he said, into his reflection from a window. How in hell could he even think of going back to that place. In the bedroom he took out his wallet and flipped through the cellophane pockets to Barney's graduation picture. Formal. Cowlick slicked down. But more of a smirk than a smile. His light blue eyes seemed to stare out at Jake, and he closed the wallet.

After he put wood on the fire, he took a shower, and got ready to go out and see Laurie, his first girlfriend friend from high school who worked at a bar on the other side of town. She'd written him a short note both times he'd been away; more than most of his other friends had done. He put on a clean pair of jeans, and an old Lake Placid High School sweatshirt. It still smelled fresh from hanging on his mother's clothes line.

He drove down the main drag of Placid, and saw people stare at his '53 Ford. At the new Hilton, he took a left onto the road leading to Saranac Lake. Two miles out of town he turned down the narrow-paved road that ran beside the closed up Thousand Animals tourist trap. He never drove by the place without looking for the black bear that climbed up a red steel pole from his cage and stared down at the people with a sad look. Jake had never liked zoos and was glad when it closed for good a few years back.

Laurie worked at an old country inn that sat on a hill above the shore of Lake Placid. It was open to the public, and on weekends, students from North Country Community College in Saranac Lake came over to dance and drink beer. Not many people from Hollywood ever went there, and the bar, called The Professor's Mustache, reminded him of his year at Paul Smiths College. He parked next to a new black Camaro, and when he got out, compared his forest green brush-painted car to the deep, glistening black. He smiled and kicked one of his rear tires.

The bar was smoky, the bluegrass band loud. He paid the dollar cover charge, and Laurie waved and winked at him when she looked up from the pitcher she was filling. He gave her a mock salute and looked over the crowd. As usual, more guys than girls. Jake went over by the wall to the right at one end of the bar and waited for Laurie to bring him a beer. She came over, wiping her hands-on a bar towel, her long strawberry blonde hair tied up in a blue ribbon, loose strands curving back from her high cheekbones.

"Hello stranger," she said, and arched her eyebrows. "What would you like?" She laughed and touched his forearm.

"Coldest draft you got, and thanks for the letters."

"Not necessary." She opened a nearby cooler and reached all the way back for a frosted mug. He watched her walk toward a line of moisture-dotted, silver spigots, and a guy waiting next to

Jake said, "That's worth coming here for." Jake stared past him as the band started to play and placed a dollar bill on the bar.

Laurie put his beer down and dropped a quarter beside it. "Busy night," she said, and turned as someone called her name. Jake didn't see her boyfriend, Jeff, who was usually the bouncer, and then someone tapped him on the shoulder; it was Jeff, holding a thick, mustard- smeared ham-and-cheese sandwich. "How are you, Jake?"

"How about you?"

"Busy bouncing,'" he said, and laughed, moving toward a bar stool inside the door. The guy who'd taken Jake's dollar at the door moved away.

Lots of young girls. Jake saw a few he'd like to take home and took a long swallow of beer. For over an hour he sat on a bar stool, his feet propped on the rungs. Laurie was too busy to talk much, and he wondered why they didn't hire extra help besides her and the one other girl who waited on tables.

The band was good. They played a mixture of bluegrass and rock and roll, some of it their own stuff. One original tune, announced as, "Pretty Lady of the Valley," made Jake want to dance, but he didn't dare ask anybody. He tapped his feet on the chrome rungs of the stool and listened to the words, "Pretty lady, take me in your arms, for the past is but forgotten truth, the future lies so far."

Nice, he thought, and wondered if one of the band members had written it. The next time Laurie filled his beer he asked her where they were from.

"Plattsburgh," she said. "They're cutting an album of their own stuff."

Jake walked outside during the next break. The sky was clearing in the east, and the backside of Whiteface Mountain cast a shadow over the lake. He sat on a big rock, away from the other people milling around or standing in small groups smoking pot. The smell of marijuana mingled with decaying leaves smelled good. He considered going over to the arena to look at the new bartender but decided to stay for another set. The lyrics were good, but he couldn't always follow them, and now wished he had a written guide to follow. A guide of some sort would have been handy at the hospital, where the majority of patients were lifetime residents. He remembered saying hello to a cute girl. She'd looked at him hard and intensely for several seconds, then ran up a nearby staircase laughing hysterically. He imagined her mind as a tight knot of confusion and mistrust. An anxiety attack had overwhelmed him, and he'd gone back to his own ward, and rested on a couch doubled up like a snail in its shell, insides quivering.

He walked back inside the bar, sat and drank another beer; it tasted good, and he wished he could forget where he'd been last week at this time. Laurie came over to refill his mug.

"Jake," she said. "It's none of my business, but should you be drinking much while taking medication?"

"No," he said. "They decided I don't need it."

She looked skeptical.

"Honest. I wouldn't lie to you.

"I believe you. That's good." She took a mug from the cooler and poured him a fresh beer. "On me," she said, and pushed his dollar away.

"Thanks, Laurie." Sometimes he wondered why they ever stopped going out.

While the band got ready to play, Jake thought he saw a girl staring at him. He turned, looked behind him, then to the left toward the kitchen, and when he glanced in her direction again, she was talking to the girl beside her. Wishful thinking. She was cute: dark-brown hair curled in toward her ears, full lips, and clear tanned skin. Probably nineteen, twenty at most. At the end of the next song she came up beside him and put her empty glass on the bar. Jake looked at her profile; she was pretty all over, and young. He wondered if she was eighteen.

She ordered a vodka and cranberry juice from Laurie, then turned towards him. She stared directly into his eyes.

"Why aren't you dancing?" she asked.

Jake took a drink of his beer and felt a little slide down his chin. Smooth, Sherlock, he thought. "I don't know," he said, and wiped his chin with the back of his wrist.

"C'mon," she said.

Before he could think of what to say, he was following her to the dance floor, and on the way felt his legs wobble and decided he was getting drunk or dreaming, or both, and wondered if she was drunk. He didn't remember a girl ever having asked him to dance.

She didn't dance like she was drunk, moving to the rhythm and beat from foot to foot, hips swaying. Jake leaned close to her when she looked at him. "What's your name? Where you from?" he asked.

"Terry. From Saranac. You?"

"Lake Placid."

She nodded and the band moved from John Denver into a fast bluegrass tune. The dancers spread out a little more, most of the partners taking hands, twirling and spinning each other. Jake saw Laurie watching them from behind the bar and waved.

Terry knew how to dance, and he wondered if she came here often. He took both her hands in his, and spun them both around, their hands re-gripping as they came around to face each other. They pulled away from each other, arms extending straight out, and Jake felt a pleasant tug in his shoulder muscles, and then he held her around the waist and smelled her perfume. She smiled at him as the song ended with a flourish from the banjo.

"Thank you," he said.

Terry followed him back to the bar for her drink, and he offered her his seat.

"I should keep my friend company," she said, looking over to where the girl sat by herself.

"Can I ask you a question?" he said. "Why did you ask me to dance?"

"You looked like you wanted to, so I did." She pushed her glass around in the moisture on the bar, and started to say something else, but Laurie came over. Terry smiled at him and walked over to the table where her friend sat.

Laurie wiped off the bar in front of him. "Think she's eighteen?" she asked.

"Huh?" His gaze followed Terry back to her table. "Who cares?" he said and frowned at Laurie. "You're the bartender."

"Oh, she has proof." She walked back down the bar, and Jake wondered what the hell was going on. Were the beers he'd drunk fuzzing up his brain? Did Laurie come over and scare her off? He leaned against the wall and scratched his cheek.

The band played a slow song, and Jake stared at Terry, wishing her to look up. She did, for a second, but towards the band. He didn't want to go over and be refused. She looked up again, towards him, and through the smoke and noise, he nodded toward the dance floor. She smiled.

When he came up to her, he took her hand and led her into the crowd of dancers. "Thanks again," he said, and put his arms around her waist. She rested her head against his shoulder and Jake saw goose bumps on his arms and stared down at the spot where her hair parted. It's like being back in high school, he thought, and his legs wouldn't do what he wanted them to. She leaned back and looked up at him.

"Hi," he said. "How's the weather down there?"

"Nice." She smiled and rested her cheek against his shoulder.

Jake felt warm, moist heat through her beige sweater, and raised one hand a little higher, and held her tighter. She held tighter, too. As the song ended, he looked into her eyes. She was crying.

"What's wrong?" he asked.

She brushed off the tears with a sleeve of her sweater. "Not here," she said.

"Let's go for a walk."

It was colder out, but he didn't know if he should put his arm around her. She stopped in the middle of the lawn and stared at the lake.

"What is it?" Jake asked.

"I broke up with my boyfriend a few days ago. He said he'd beat up anyone I went out with."

"Is he here?" Jake looked back through the windows.

"No."

"How old are you, Terry?"

"Eighteen."

"You go to Saranac High."

"No. The Catholic High School."

He took a step closer to the lake and thought, this is wonderful. I'm hanging around a teeny-bopper.

"Don't go," she said.

He kept walking and couldn't hear if she followed him across the frosty grass. He stopped where the forest began and turned around. She was still standing there, arms hugged across her chest.

"Wait," she said, then turned and walked into the bar.

Jake sat on a fallen log and checked his watch. Almost one-thirty. Just what he wanted to do, get in a fight with some high school kid. She was pretty, though. But eight years difference? He remembered when he was in high school. He'd never known what he wanted. Did he now? He wished he hadn't drunk so much. He pushed his heels into the ground, and the smell of cold cedar rose up.

She called his name from the top of the hill and he turned and waved. When she sat down next to him, he said, "What's up?"

"My girlfriend wanted to leave. I told her to go ahead."

"Oh."

"You have a car. Don't you?" she asked.

"Yeah."

"Are you mad I stayed?"

"No." He moved back a little on the log, and before he could catch himself, fell off onto his back, and started laughing. She laughed too, and he grabbed her coat at the elbow and pulled her off beside him. He kissed her, and said, "It's not often a young girl picks me up."

"Who asked who to slow dance?" she said and pushed hair back behind her ears.

"Okay. Okay."

"I knew you'd be nice."

After everyone had left, they walked up to the parking lot. Laurie had thrown his coat into the car. "This is yours?" she said.

"Yeah. My limo is in the garage."

He drove her home and she sat in the middle.

"I'm pretty glad I met you," she said.

"Me, too." He put his arm around her, surprised he felt so comfortable with her, and wondered how much the beer had to do with it.

"Where do you live?" she asked.

"In Placid. I said before."

"But where."

"What's the difference? You must know from my car; I don't live in one of the mansions on Mirror Lake."

"It doesn't matter."

"Where do you live?" he said, as they entered the town of Saranac Lake.

"Beech Avenue." She told him to take a right at the Y and another right two blocks down. "It's the next house," she said. "Drive by a little ways."

The houses that lined the street weren't real high class, but they weren't trailers either. Jake sighed.

"What's wrong?" she asked, as he parked, and shifted into neutral.

"It's been fun," he said, "But..."

She interrupted. "You live in Hollywood. Right?"

"Hm. Hmmm."

"So what?"

"Terry. I'm eight years older than you. How would your parents like that?"

"I won't tell them."

"C'mon," he said. "Be realistic."

She stared out the windshield. "Do you have a phone?"

"No."

"I'll be here next Friday and Saturday." She opened the door and walked around to his side. He rolled down the window, and she kissed him good night, almost climbing back into the car.

"Don't forget," she said.

Jake drove away, and as he shifted through the gears, he shook his head, the smell of her rising from his lips and mustache.

CHAPTER 4

All morning Jake pulled the old bales of hay out from under the trailer, threw them into a wheelbarrow, and dumped them in a low spot out back. The muscles in his upper body felt like spring steel, and his feet as if they barely touched the hay-strewn trail as he traveled back and forth. Love. The steam cloud from his breath grew less and less as the sun climbed higher.

He stopped to rest and slapped black strands of moldy hay off his hands and pant legs. In the large louvered window he'd been working under he could see his reflection, cut into several pieces by the blue-green edges of glass where it overlapped.

"You're alive," he said. "And not going back to that place again. No matter what." He wondered if her real name was Theresa, and how she spelled it, then whispered it softly. He yanked out another bale, and for a change it came out all in one piece.

By twelve-thirty all the old bales lay scattered in the brush behind the trailer. He went inside for his knife and fixed a cup of instant coffee from the water he'd been keeping hot on the stove. Outside, he rested the cup on the car hood, and stared at the spot on the seat where she'd sat. Even if I never see her again, it's okay. She'll probably make up with her boyfriend this week, and that will be that. He couldn't ever remember being kissed like that. An orange oak leaf fell near his foot, and he looked up to see where it had come from; the nearest oak was down the street. A high breeze moved in the tops of the trees, and a barely audible rattle of leaves reached him. He picked up the leaf and studied the raised green pattern of bumps on the dark orange surface, wondering what they were.

The leaves have fallen twice since Barney died, he thought. Each tree has one more growth ring since that summer day he fell off the five story roof of that condominium at the Lake Placid Club. Jake tore the fleshy parts of the leaf away from the veins and held the leaf up to the sun.

"I love you old buddy," he whispered, and stared at the brightly lit skeleton. "God knows, I must change, too."

Jake lined up the new hay bales under the trailer, leaving half a foot sticking out, and the work went quickly. Loose bales he tied up with nylon from a roll of twine and clipped the ends off with the small scissors on his knife. Hay dust hovered in the sunlight, sparkling. He peeled off thin sections and packed them on top of the bales to make a tight fit. By two the job was finished. Jake stood back: the trailer looked like a beached whale. The gray and white pattern painted on its sides melded with the dull gold bales. It worried him that a stray spark from the stove might ignite them. He'd found half a roll of tar paper under the trailer and cut this in eight-foot sections, tucked them up underneath the metal lip of the trailer, and draped them down the sides of the bales, then weighted the edges with stones. It worked. He lightly raked the hay off the pine needles all around the trailer, which he preferred to a lawn.

Later that afternoon Jake's father drove in and asked him if he wanted to go out for a beer.

"Sounds good," Jake said.

They stopped at a redneck bar on the other side of town.

"That's Curt Dixon's truck. I might have a job for him hauling old flooring this week."

Jake hoped it wasn't. Curt Dixon was one of Barney's uncles, an unfriendly old redneck who drank all the time.

"Let's go some place else, Dad."

"What for? The beer's as cold here as anywhere else."

"Shit," Jake muttered under his breath. This guy had always accused Barney of not helping his mother enough. Of all times, Jake did not want to see him today.

Inside the bar his father walked up to Curt, and Curt gave Jake a look that said, 'You're not all right, and you can't fool me.'

Jake played pinball and almost chugged his beer while they talked.

When his father came over Jake said he was ready to go.

"Okay. Thought we might have another one, but if you're in a hurry." He turned and walked toward the door and Jake followed.

Jake apologized to his father for wanting to leave and tried to explain about Curt, but couldn't, and they rode home without saying anything more. He didn't think his father would ever understand mental illness, or what he'd been through.

As Jake walked down his driveway, the trailer, perched on the new bales of hay in the dying light, seemed more like home than ever before. It sat back from the road, and brush partially hid it from the other houses and trailers near it. A small pocket of near-isolation. He walked around it once and brought in an armload of wood. Using an old coal shovel that had belonged to his grandfather, he shoveled ashes into a pail and took them outside. After he'd started a new fire, he sat on the couch in the gathering dusk. It's some kind of momentum, he thought. Now, lost momentum. The depression settled over him like a gray rain. His therapist, Elwood, at the hospital, had tried to help him understand that when this happened it wasn't enough to think, I'll beat it. I'm stronger than it is. He'd told Jake to think about why it happened, what triggered it.

He sat and listened to the fire catch hold of the new logs and stared into the fading light. All the experiences he and Barney had had with Curt Dixon were bad ones: confrontations that ended up in shouting matches, leaving anger and bitterness. One time he'd seen them smoking pot behind the Arena Grill. He'd gone to Barney's mother and told her. The next day, at the bar, Barney had told him to mind his own damn business, and Curt told him he'd never amount to anything, like his father, who'd run off with another woman and never came back. Jake had held Barney back, and Barney had screamed at Curt and told him to go fuck himself.

He didn't want to remember anything bad about Barney. But, at least now, it was clearer to him why he felt the way he did, though it didn't make it much easier. He got up, turned the lights on, and fixed lunch for the next day.

On Monday, Tuesday, and Wednesday he worked hard with Rich, traveling miles each day carrying the surveyor's transit and tripod. Jake marked lines with orange spray paint and florescent plastic tape and drove in stakes to mark corners. At night he ate a quick supper with his parents, watched television for a while and went home to bed.

During lunch on Thursday, Rich told Jake he wouldn't need him until the following week. He said, "Real productive week, Jake. Glad you're back." He made out a check and handed it to him. Jake folded it in half and put it in his wallet. "Look at it," Rich said.

"I trust you."

"No. Look." Jake unfolded the check. A hundred-and-twelve dollars seemed a little high, but he never kept track of his time. "I put you up to four dollars. You're worth it."

"Thanks, Rich. I appreciate it."

By two o'clock they were back in town.

Rich stopped at the Arena Grill. "Time for a cold one," he said.

Jake ordered a Coke. In the almost empty bar, strong sunlight filled the section facing the street, and the air smelled like stale beer. After he finished his soda, Jake cashed his check at the bar and told Rich he'd walk home.

Outside, it felt like rain, but was almost cold enough to snow. A small maple near the speed-skating rink had lost all but a few leaves, and the Olympic flags flapped in the wind. Jake walked over to the main doors next to the ticket booth. A little surprised to find them unlocked, he went inside, and up two winding flights of stairs. The newness of the place unnerved him; everything was white, except for the brown rubber stair treads and orange hand railings. He wondered if it was okay to be there. At the top of the stairs, a long concourse stretched out to the left. A sign indicated the gift shop, cafeteria, and offices were in that direction. In the Olympic Authority Offices, directly across from where he stood, a woman looked up from her typewriter, glanced at Jake, and went back to work. He walked to the doors of the main arena: locked. Inside, a worker on the Zamboni machine cleaned the ice.

A man dressed in a black overcoat and scarf came out of the farther left door and Jake caught the door's edge before it closed, and walked in. Cool inside, almost cold, the newly opened arena smelled as clean as the smooth ice surface the Zamboni kept in perfect condition for the skaters. It must be twice the size of the old arena used for the thirty-two Olympics, he decided, and remembered that it wasn't until two years before that the town had finally paid off all the debts for that Olympics. He couldn't begin to imagine how much debt they'd be in this time: new ski jumps, luge run, speed skating rink, renovation of Whiteface, and this, which all meant a raise in taxes for his parents.

He leaned against a steel pillar and watched the Zamboni driver guide the machine down the last strip of ice in the center of the rink, then move off the end and out the back garage doors that faced Hollywood. Jake turned to go and heard the sound of skates on ice. Two girls wearing tights and sweat shirts came onto the ice. One went over to the side and started a tape. Classical music filled the air. The other girl shook her head. Even at the far end of the Arena Jake clearly heard what she said. "No. The Tchaikovsky." Then he heard the clicking of plastic cassette tapes.

She stood at center ice in a pose, waiting.

Jake jumped when the music began. It filled the arena with violins, horns, cymbals, and drums. She skated toward him, and twenty feet from the end of the rink, she jumped, spun full circle, and landed, her arms outstretched toward him for a second. She swerved, and headed in the other direction, skipping and dancing to the music. Keeping in time with the staccato rhythm of the violins, she jumped to touch her toes, skated a few strides farther, and did a double toe loop, his mother's favorite jump. She missed her next jump, faltered, and continued on around the ice.

When she finished a long spin that ended precisely with the music, she skated over to the stands where a woman, unnoticed until then by Jake, sat, her arms crossed. They talked for a few moments while the other girl, who looked younger to Jake, changed tapes. The older woman must be their coach, Jake decided. He wanted to sit down but wasn't sure if he was supposed to be there.

The younger girl skated to center ice and composed herself, chin pointed up. The music began slow, and she waited a moment, like a puppet, then came to life As the music picked up, she skated in long strides, picking up speed. At the sound of cymbals, she jumped, spun around twice, and landed perfectly before their sound had died away. Jake wanted to applaud.

"Excuse me," someone said behind him. "Do you work here?"

"No." It was the man in the overcoat.

"This is a closed practice session. Visitors distract the skaters."

"Okay." Jake left the arena. The man sounded like he had a Russian or German accent.

It had started to rain. Behind the arena he saw piles of ice shavings dumped from the Zamboni. He walked over, packed a snowball, and looked inside the open garage doors. If only he could think like those skaters could jump, land, and glide. Jake tossed the snowball high above the new parking lot and watched it splatter. He walked toward the line of flag poles, and looked to his left before crossing, then remembered it was one way. Cars could only come up from Hollywood, not go down into it. He imagined an appropriate sign, Danger: Primitives Live Below. One Way Only. He crossed and gazed at the speed skating rink. Bare cement shiny with rain.

At home he hid a hundred dollars in a coffee can under the sink. That left him thirty dollars spending money from his last check, but twenty dollars short for next month's rent. He checked the calendar. Today was Thursday, the twenty-fifth. No sweat, he thought. I'll have enough left by the first of November.

He'd been trying not to think of last weekend or the upcoming one, but the warm feeling of Terry stayed with him. What if when he saw her, she wanted to come here? No. He'd refuse. What would she think seeing this after the house where she lived? Her father probably owned a business or something. He found the feather duster his mother had given him and dusted cobwebs out of all the corners. The place needed a good cleaning, no matter what, he decided, still telling himself she'd probably go back to her old boyfriend. The top of the refrigerator was filthy; he wiped it down with Pledge, then did the pine boards placed on cinder blocks he'd used at college for a book case. He put a light coat of Wesson oil on the cast iron wood stove and started in on the bathroom. Where did all the energy come from? When he got to the bedroom, he changed the sheets, and after that cleaned the inside of every window, even the louvered ones in the kitchen and living room.

He lighted a scented candle from last Christmas, cleaned out the wood box, and brought in more wood. By the time he finished it was dark.

He'd forgotten all about supper, and he hadn't done the floors yet.

On the way to his parents, Jake thought about making boxes. The act of constructing them from start to finish had always given him a sense of accomplishment; he had to do something with all this energy. Maybe he was finally getting better, and maybe most of the drugs had left his system. The doctor had said he could make it on his own. Maybe.

Supper was long over when he arrived, and he told his mother he'd had to work late. "Can I borrow the vacuum, Mom?" he asked.

"Don't break it," she said, and put a plate of meat loaf and mashed potatoes she'd tried to keep warm in front of him, then went into the living room to watch television. She didn't like it when he or his father were late; she wanted to get the kitchen cleaned up so she could watch television and relax. She acted more upset than usual tonight.

When he finished eating, he washed the dishes and the pots. It was after seven. He stood in the living room doorway. "I'm going out to the shed."

"Working tomorrow?" his father asked.

"No. No more till next week. You got anything going?"

"Just small jobs. I'll let you know. Material isn't in for a big floor I have to do at the club. Maybe next week."

"Good meat loaf, Mom. I cleaned up."

She was almost asleep on the couch. She hadn't seemed like herself since he'd been home. He took the vacuum out of the hall closet and put it on the back porch. They'd be asleep when he left. He sat in a rocking chair on the lawn and tried to relax. It was as if he was in high school again and he liked that. After a few minutes, he decided to walk over to Chad's. The shed could wait for another night.

CHAPTER 5

No one answered the door at Chad's, and on Jake's walk home the smell of dead leaves crushed by traffic went with him. Inside the trailer he smelled lemon Pledge. He sat on the couch, and his nerves pricked deeper. He unlaced his boots and took off his socks. The conviction to stay out of the hospital remained stronger than ever, but deep down, he knew the possibility of going back existed. As he sat staring at the carpet squares a tremor shook his body. He couldn't figure out what caused the thoughts to crowd in all at once: uncertainty about a girl, about his sanity – his ability to go on improving.

He grasped his hands and pulled as hard as he could. At the hospital, his therapist Elwood had talked about how to avoid confusion. He tried to think, and finally remembered what it was, and wanted to kick himself for not remembering sooner. He always complained that he never had enough time alone to think and sort things out, come to terms with himself, and decide what was best. Interruptions always came along, mostly created by himself. Then he remembered clearly one part of his and Elwood's conversation.

"What can you do?" Elwood, his therapist had asked. Jake even remembered the wrinkles in his forehead and how he smoothed his mustache as he asked, "Where can you go?"

Jake had told him about taking long drives in his 1953 Ford and working in his and Barney's woodshop.

"Do it," he'd said.

Jake unclasped his hands and tried to relax. It was too warm in the trailer, so he opened the door a crack, and remembered something else Elwood had told him. "Don't be afraid to talk out loud when you're alone. It might help you think more clearly." Jake looked outside at the patches of light cast from inside the trailer. "I will," he said, and smiled a little at the sound of his own voice.

He decided he didn't want to go and meet Terry, if she showed up. Probably the best way would be to find Laurie tomorrow, and ask her to tell Terry he'd gone away for the weekend, and if she wanted to leave her number, he'd call her next week. Good idea, if Laurie would do it.

"I will," he said and remembered a Beatle's song by that title he liked. "'I will wait a lonely lifetime. If you want me to, I will,'" he sang, and whistled the parts he couldn't remember the words to. He walked back and forth in the trailer thinking of where he might drive to the next day.

It took a long time to fall asleep. He kept repeating to himself, as he lay on his side, rubbing the silky edge of a blanket, "I won't go back. Won't go back."

In the morning, after coffee, he drove over to Laurie's. She was in the kitchen and yelled for him to come in when he knocked at the side door.

"Hi, Jake," she said, closing the top of her bathrobe and tightening the blue sash at the waist.

"Sorry to bother you this early," he said.

"What's up? Coffee?"

"Sure. I'll get it," he said, and motioned for her to stay sitting.

He took a green mug out of the dish drainer, poured a cup from the percolator, and sat down opposite her. "I want to ask a favor," he said, and wondered if she was uncomfortable, his being there. She didn't look it.

"Well?" she said.

"You remember the girl I danced with the other night?"

"Yeah. Your car was still in the parking lot when I left." She winked.

"Thanks for putting my jacket in the car." He sipped the coffee. "Well, I'm supposed to meet her there, either today or Saturday, but I need some time alone."

"Afraid you'll get stood up?" She gazed at him over the top of her coffee mug. "What do you want me to tell her if she shows up?"

"Thanks, Laurie. Tell her if she wants to leave a phone number, I'll call her the beginning of the week."

"No problem." She sipped her coffee; small wisps of strawberry blonde hair framed her face.

Jake tried not to stare at the space where her bathrobe closed and remembered how jealous he'd been when they were going steady in high school.

"Tell me. How are you really doing? We've known each other for a long time."

"I know." He cupped his hands near the coffee mug, not touching it. "It's gonna take time. I still couldn't face Barney's death after my first stay at the hospital. My nerves were too raw."

"What's better now?"

"I've had time to think and listened more to what they had to say."

"I hope so, Jake. I really do."

"Thanks. Sometimes I'm ashamed I went there for help and think the whole town knows about it."

"Why care what others think if you are better?

"Do you hear anything?"

"Not really." She sipped her coffee and stared out the window toward the street.

"Come on, Laurie."

She placed her hands palms down on the table and looked at him. "You know how people are around here. They live to gossip."

He stared at the backs of her hands, the color of the freckles matched her hair, almost. How many years since he'd held them at high school dances, the prom, or on a blanket after making love under the stars. The first time for both of them. He took a big swallow of the coffee and burned his tongue. "I'd like to know what they say," he said.

"They're curious, is all. They want to see if you're okay."

"Well, I am," Jake said, knowing she was lying to be nice, probably wondering like everyone else what he'd been doing on top of that building the day they buried Barney.

"I'd better go," he said.

"What's this girl's name?"

"Terry." He put his cup in the sink, and almost touched her shoulder as he thanked her. He waved goodbye at the door, and she said, "Keep in touch."

Jake drove away and out into the countryside on the back roads. The heavy old car smoothed out the bumps and as he turned around at the dead end of a dirt road, he decided to visit Barney's grave. He'd put it off too long.

He walked by the grave twice, somehow convinced it was on the other side of the graveyard near the brook. The slab of orange granite with his friend's name engraved in it didn't seem real and he walked away from it toward the steep bank above the brook. The autumn before Barney died, they'd hiked in the Adirondacks for three days, checking out deer signs. The brook below reminded him of the spot where they'd built their lean-to. Tears rolled down his cheeks, unstoppable. He rested his shoulder against a chalky birch tree, then rubbed his forearm across his eyes.

"I'll never see him again," he said, and looked back toward the grave. "I must face it."

He walked down the steep bank, pushing aside the tangled brush, catching his feet on roots, and stubbing his toes on rocks, and his eyes would not clear. He didn't know how far he'd walked, when the sound of a tiny waterfall caught his attention. He stopped to catch his breath, and its musical sound, as it dropped six inches over a small rock lip covered with leaves into a foot-deep circular pool, brought him back to his senses. He looked over his shoulder, back toward the graveyard. His eyes felt clean, and exhaustion pushed into his muscles. He sat down in some green moss and rested his head on a smooth rock and closed his eyes.

He woke up slowly, the sun in his eyes, and moved his head to a more comfortable position. The waterfall splashed and gurgled into the pool. He stood and listened. After over a year I finally cried, he thought. I didn't know if it would ever happen after the anniversary of his death came and went this summer. The pleasant smell of cold water and fall decay reminded him of the awful odors at the hospital. I live for this, he thought, and stared at the waterfall.

The leaves rustled as he walked along the brook looking for a good place to climb the steep bank. When he kicked them, a cloud of this year's still-yellow and orange leaves flew up along with brown ones from years past. Behind him, a wide trail of mostly brown leaves marked where he'd plowed along. I needed this, he thought. The part of me that holds on to too much of Barney needs to be covered by a freshness like these leaves. He knew there hadn't been much new growth since Barney's fall; like a dry year when a tree's growth rings are close together.

Halfway up the bank he rested and remembered that on his and Barney's first night out camping they'd gone to the crowded area where all the tourists stayed. They shared a half gallon of wine with two girls they met. Barney had gone down by the river with one for quite a while, but Jake didn't have much luck with the girl he stayed with by the fire. She wanted to tell him all about her planned career in business when she graduated from NYU and kept moving away when he moved closer on the log where they sat in front of the lean-to. Jake could still see Barney and the girl when they came back from the river, their clothes rumpled, Barney's shit-eating grin and his cowlick sticking almost straight up.

At the top of the hill, Jake heard a crashing in the brush, and looked up in time to see the white tails of two running deer. Maybe he and Chad would come back hunting in a few weeks.

"Love never dies," he whispered, glad that he had finally cried. He rubbed pollen and dust off the top of the grave, still hating the thought of his friend buried underneath the cold, damp earth.

CHAPTER 6

On the way home Jake drove fast, the big six-cylinder engine winding high on the straight stretches. Leaves blew in clouds along the road in the wind kicked up by the Ford's bulk. They don't make them like this anymore, he thought, and patted the steering wheel Barney could barely see over. Jake always kidded Barney and offered to put a pillow in the car for him to sit on. Jake laughed and remembered Barney gave him the finger every time he mentioned it. "Keep the good times, the bad will always hurt too much," he muttered under his breath.

For the rest of the weekend Jake worked in the wood shop and tried not to think of Terry – unsuccessfully. After two nights of hard frosts, fall was about over. Most of the leaves had fallen and Jake looked forward to the first snow. On Sunday afternoon, when he came back to the trailer, he saw a note taped to the door. He unfolded it and read, "Terry felt bad you didn't show up. She left this number." It was signed by Laurie.

Jake let out a whoop that started all the neighborhood dogs barking. He went inside, grabbed a handful of change, got in the car, and drove to the Arena Grill. At the bar he ordered a beer from Amy.

"Thanks Amy," he said, and walked into the phone booth, closing the door. His fingers trembled a little as he dialed the number.

"Hello."

"Hello. Is Terry there?"

"Just a moment. Who's calling?"

"Jake."

The person called Terry's name.

"Hi, Jake. How are you?" she said.

"Good. Thanks for leaving your number. What are you doing?"

"Nothing."

"Can you get out for a while?" He looked at the clock. A little after six.

"I'll ask," she said.

What am I doing? How long has it been since I had to ask a girl if she could go out.

"If I'm back by eleven. School tomorrow."

"Did you tell them about me?"

"Yes. It's no big deal."

"I'll be there in forty-five minutes."

"Why so long?"

"I need a shower."

"Why don't I come over? My parents aren't using the car."

He took a long drink from his beer and said, "Okay. See you in a bit."

"Jake. I don't know where to go."

"Oh. Sorry." He gave her directions, hung up, and finished his beer.

At home he built up the fire, lighted candles, and took a shower. He'd just finished dressing when she knocked on the door. He opened the door and stared. She didn't look more than sixteen, standing on the cinder block steps, three feet below him. She was wearing tight jeans and a wool coat.

"You look nice," he said, and stood to the side.

"This is nice and cozy," she said, turning and looking at everything.

"This is it," he said. "So, what's new? Here. Let me take your coat." He walked to the bedroom and threw it on the chair. Jesus, I'm nervous, he thought, as he walked the few steps back to the living room, not knowing what to say about not showing up, wanting to kiss her.

She turned her face upward and smiled. "Good to see you."

He touched her chin and kissed her.

"I missed that," he said, hugging her close. Then touched her cheeks red from the cold.

"Me, too," she said. "I've never been to anyone's apartment before."

"Really? Let's sit." She sat beside him on the couch, and he put his arm around her.

"This is nice" she said. "Romantic."

"What did you tell your parents about me?"

"That you live in Lake Placid, work for a surveyor, and have your own place."

"What was their reaction?"

"Jake. They trust me. I'll be in college, on my own next year."

"Maybe we'd better talk some more about me." He took his arm off the back of the couch and held her hand. "I like you, you know, and was afraid you wouldn't be there this weekend. I thought maybe you'd hung out with me because you were mad at your boyfriend or something."

"That's not true" she said. "You thought I'd stand you up. Didn't you?" When he didn't answer she squeezed his hand. "Isn't that it?"

"Yes. That, and other reasons, too."

"Can you tell me?" Terry asked.

"Yeah. But I'm afraid to for some of the reasons I didn't show up." He coughed and swallowed a couple times. "But I'll tell you." He got up, opened the stove door, and re-arranged the fire with the poker.

She sat forward, elbows on her knees, and said, "Go ahead."

"Okay." He smiled at her over his shoulder. "Just give me a minute." He walked back and forth from the kitchen to the living room. "I'll make it short," he said. "Over a year ago my best friend fell off a roof and died. I was there when it happened." He stopped in front of her. "I thought I was handling it pretty well until this spring, when I got so depressed, I had to go into a hospital for a month. I got out for the summer and a month ago went back for three more weeks. We met my first full day home." He stared past her shoulder at the reflection of her back in the window.

"I'm glad you told me," she said.

"You want to go out with someone that's been in a nuthouse? C'mon. What would your parents say?"

"I make most of my own decisions," she said. "Look at me." She reached a hand out to him. "Let's talk about you and me."

He sat down next to her. "You're pretty intelligent, or experienced, or something..."

She held up her hand to stop him. "For my age," she finished for him. "I know that's what you were going to say. Listen to me for a minute. We both might as well be honest about our past."

She leaned forward and held one of his hands in her lap.

"Four years ago, when I was fourteen, I got pregnant. My parents are strict Catholics and didn't want me to have an abortion." She paused and turned his face toward hers. "I haven't told many people this. I went to a special home in

Florida for pregnant teenagers until I had the baby."

Jake wiped tears from her eyes and hugged her.

Over his shoulder she said, "I guess I want you to understand why I don't act like a high school senior, or the way you think of them."

"So young," Jake said.

"Young and stupid. Can we go for a walk?"

"Sure." He helped her into her coat.

"Hug me," she said. "Harder."

He picked her up, turned around once, and put her down. She squeezed a lot harder than he remembered she could.

Outside they held hands, her fingers intertwined in his, and walked along the path toward his parents' house. "Different from where you live," he said.

"Who cares? If the people have good feelings about each other."

"Not all."

"I suppose," she said, and kicked a stone off the path.

"That's my parents' house," he said, and stopped. She wrapped her arms around his waist. "Why do you care so much about not living in a great house?"

"I don't know." He didn't want to talk about the bad stuff anymore. Share miseries. "I saw where you live," he said. "What you're used to."

"So, if it was the other way around, and I was older and lived in this part of town, you wouldn't go out with me?"

"No," he said, placing his hands on her shoulders.

"Then what is it?"

"My being stupid, I guess. Afraid, too."

"Of what?"

"That you won't last, like my best friend didn't last," Jake said.

"That's always a possibility," she said. "Is it a good enough reason not to try?"

"No. It's selfish. Something I have to get over." He turned around. "Let's go back to the trailer."

They sat on one of the extra bales behind the trailer and talked until it was almost time for her to leave. It was a dream.

"I'm glad you came over," he said.

"Good times ahead." She leaned against his shoulder. "Right?"

"Yes," he said, and pulled her backwards off the bale onto the soft, pine-needle covered ground. He pinned her arms to her sides, and she laughed, struggling to free herself. "Uncle," she said. He rested his weight on his elbows and kissed her, then rolled on his side.

"Thanks, Terry. I can't remember having a talk like we had tonight. Next time we'll talk about the good things."

"Between us," she said and jumped on top of him and tried to pin his arms but couldn't. He held her hands. "What now?"

"This is fine," she said, and leaned down and kissed him for a long time. He released her hands, put his arms around her, and hugged. Oddly, a part of him wanting to return to the hospital.

"You know I hate to leave," she said. "What time is it?"

She pushed up the sleeve of her jacket. "Little after ten-thirty."

"When can you come over again? I'll cook dinner some night."

"How about Wednesday?"

"How about Monday?"

She laughed, and he watched puffs of steam pulse from her mouth.

"I would," she said. "But I have band practice after school every day except Wednesday and Friday. We're playing at the Olympic opening ceremonies."

"What do you play?"

"Tenor saxophone. Wednesday?"

"I may have to work late. I don't know yet."

"Call me when you know."

He walked her to the car and kissed her good night.

"This could be a nice habit," she said.

"Yes," he said, and kissed her again.

She started the car and rolled down the window. "Bye."

"Bye." He waved and stood in the driveway until he couldn't hear the sound of the car, then put his hands in his pockets and walked in a small circle. He couldn't remember when his lips had felt so good.

He loaded the stove, went to bed and didn't wake till almost ten o'clock. As he fixed coffee and turned on the radio, he noticed the frost had already melted from the sunny patches in the yard, but still clung in the shadows and to the metal on the car. He gazed out the back window and pulled his robe tighter. Where they had wrestled, pine needles and hay formed tiny peaks, and the earth was dug up in several places. He whistled along with a Beatles song on the radio and did a little dance, trying not to spill his coffee. Maybe they'd go dancing at the Professor's Mustache this weekend. He hoped the same bluegrass band would be there and tried to remember their name. Was it Home Corners, no, Home Comfort, that was it. He opened the door and felt a slight breeze that wasn't as cold as he'd thought and decided it would be a good day to paint for his Mom, and work in the wood shop.

On the way over he stopped on the path, picked a milkweed pod, opened it, and blew the white parachutes off into the breeze, and knew, even if Terry left him, he would be happy for last night. He dropped the empty shell and reached for another full one. He wanted to look ahead for what was good, and not worry about every little thing that might happen. He opened the pod and rubbed the tips of his fingers up and down the white, tight silkiness. "I will," he said, and tried to sing that song by The Beatles, as he walked the rest of the way to his mom's.

"What's up Ma?"

She jumped. "God! Don't sneak up on me like that. I'm making an apple pie."

"Great. Any coffee?" He shook the pot and poured the last half cup into a mug.

"You don't want that," she said. "Put some water on."

"I'm fine. It's warm enough. I think I'll paint your statue today." She didn't like it called a Bathtub Mary.

"I've been trying to get your father to do that all summer," she said. "I even bought the paint last time they had a sale at Aubuchons. She brushed away a strand of graying hair from her forehead with the back of a flour-covered hand. "It's in the hall closet. Your clothes are all clean in there, too."

"Thanks." He took down the paint from the shelf: sky blue and oyster white, brought them into the kitchen and set them on the table. "What, no red for her lips and fingernails?"

"Jake. Don't say things like that about Mary!"

"Just kidding. Just kidding." He walked down cellar to look for brushes and turpentine. While in college he'd hesitated to bring home friends, partly because of that tacky statue, and now he was going to paint it. He found several old brushes that would work, and half a can of turpentine.

"I bought sandpaper, too," she said, from the top of the stairs. "It's in the drawer up here."

For the rest of the morning he scraped and sandpapered the statue and bathtub, and by one o'clock finished painting.

She fixed tuna-fish sandwiches and tomato soup for lunch. "You seem awful happy today," she said.

"It must be the weather." He knew she wouldn't think much of his dating a high school senior but wanted to tell her.

"That all?" she said. "Nothing else? I saw Laurie at the store yesterday."

He took his dishes over to the sink. "Good lunch, Mom. What did Laurie say?"

"Something about a girl giving her a phone number for you."

"Yes."

"Is that all?" she asked. "Who is she? What's her last name? You weren't going to tell me, were you?"

"Give me a break. Her name is Terry and I met her at the bar where Laurie works."

"That's nice. Do I know her?"

"No. She's from Saranac Lake."

"I know people in Saranac. What's her last name?"

"I never asked her." Now she'll ask how old she is, for sure.

"Bring her over for supper some night. I think that would be nice."

"Let's go out and look at the statue."

She stood in front of it. "Nice," she said. "I'm so glad it's done. It's not right to have a statue of Mary that needs painting. Have you seen some of the others around here? They're a disgrace." She wiped her hands on a towel. "I'm going to the store. Want anything?"

"No. I guess not. You seem nervous, Mom. Are you upset about something? What is it?"

"Nothing," she said. "Tired lately. That's all."

It worried him.

After she left, he cleaned the brushes and put everything away, then went out to the workshop. The shop had been set up to Barney's exacting standards, using every inch of the sixteen by sixteen space to advantage. Years ago, it had been a chicken coop.

Several days after the funeral, when he'd visited her, Barney's mother told him to keep all the tools they'd bought as partners; she'd even given him Barney's carpentry tools. He hadn't seen much of her since then. Her features, particularly her clear blue eyes, and large cheek bones, reminded him of Barney. He slid Barney's metal tool box under a bench.

Over the weekend he'd started several boxes and now decided he'd better give the place a good cleaning before doing more. Jake whisk-broomed the radial arm saw, table saw, joiner, and work benches. Dust filled the room, and he opened a window and propped open the door, then pushed in the button for the joiner; its roar filled the room. He ran a piece of scrap red cedar through it and checked the cut. The odor of cedar filled the air.

Afternoon sun filtered through the unsettled dust in the shop. Jake sprayed WD 40 on the metal surfaces and stacked the red cedar boards in neat piles. Some of the pipe on the little stove that rested on cinder blocks in the middle of the dirt floor needed replacing. Jake found a piece of paper, and with the stub of a pencil listed the supplies he needed. He wondered if he, or Barney, was the last one to use the pencil. There was still half a box of wood screws, and plenty of dowels for plugs, but he needed belts for the sander, and a new jug of glue. Other than that, and two lengths of four-inch stovepipe, he was ready to go. He hoisted himself up onto one of the work tables. It would take some getting used to, working alone, but maybe Terry would keep him company once in a while.

He swung his legs back and forth and stared at the dirt floor. She's been through hard times, too; she had a kid four years old, living some place she'd never seen. He wondered if she knew whether it was a boy or a girl.

His mother called from the back door to ask if he was staying for supper, and he jumped down and went to the door. "Yeah, Mom. I have to go downtown for some things. Is there time?"

"Don't be late."

The streets were busy for a Monday afternoon. He parked behind a cream-colored Sprite and noticed how people looked at his forest-green Ford.

Inside the hardware store Jake waved to Ben Chaker, one of the clerks he knew from high school, and walked to where they kept the glue. Ben came over and shook his hand. "How are you?" he said.

"Fine. Thanks." Jake wondered why Ben acted like he hadn't seen him since they graduated from high school. Then he knew, just another reaction to someone that's been in a mental hospital. "I need some glue," he said.

"Over here. We re-arranged everything for the Olympics. Going to make more boxes?"

"No. I'm buying the stuff to glue my car together," Jake said, and picked up a half gallon jug.

Ben laughed. Jake could see he was uncomfortable, so he stood and read the label on the jug.

"You and Barney had a good thing going with those," Ben said.

Jake wanted to say, "Eat shit and die," but carried the glue to where the stovepipe was, picked out two sections, and went up front to the counter. Over his shoulder he said, "I need a quart of satin Tung oil."

"Sale on that," Ben said.

Jake hoped he worked this week, or he'd be late with the rent. The bill came to over thirty-three dollars.

"Good luck," Ben said.

"Yeah."

As Jake backed up to get out of the parking spot, he tapped the front of the Mercedes behind and smiled, wishing he had the balls to give it the gas and dump the clutch. He drove by the Arena Grill, saw Rich's truck in front, and pulled in.

Rich motioned to him from his usual spot in the corner and Jake walked over, sipping foam from the top of a mug.

"Howdy, boss," he said.

"Hi Jake. Sit down," Rich said and pulled out a chair. "I was going to call your mom tonight. Work Thursday and Friday?"

"Sounds good," Jake said.

"We're moving to a new job. Got a state contract to survey behind the bobsled run. Should be easy."

"Why aren't the state surveyors doing it?"

"Too busy."

Jake took a long drink. "Yeah. Too busy zoning other people's land."

"As long as the state pays me on time, I could care less," Rich said.

They talked about the weather and the predictions in the Farmer's Almanac for little snow.

"I hope we don't get an inch for the Olympics."

"What's the matter with you, Jake? You're all bent out of shape."

"The state always screws the natives. Look at that big whale of an arena they built right next to Hollywood. Christ, they didn't even hire locals as laborers."

"I agree," said Rich. "But you and I won't change that."

Jake finished his beer and stood up.

"Want another one?"

"No thanks. I better go. Mom's holding supper."

"Thursday at seven," Rich said. "Always good to start a job on the first of the month. Makes the bookkeeping easier, especially the way the state sends out checks. Right, Jake?" He laughed and Jake waved as he walked out the door.

After dinner, he called Terry and told her he had to work on Thursday and Friday and asked what she wanted for dinner on Wednesday.

"I can't come over on Wednesday," she said. "My mom wants to go to the mall in Plattsburgh."

"Oh," he said. "When can I see you?"

"Friday."

He didn't like it but said, "Okay."

"Sorry about Wednesday," she said. "I keep thinking about us."

"Me, too. Is everything all right?" Phones didn't cut it for this, he thought.

"Yeah. Except Friday is too far away."

"We'll make it," he said. "See you then."

He put the phone down. "Think. Think. Think," he whispered. What are you so pissed off about? He sat beside the phone and stared at the orange-darkened knotty pine walls.

Time. Where does it go? You're mad because you forgot the rent was due. You thought it was next week. Jerk. He glanced at the calendar behind him. Yup, this Thursday was the first. He'd spent money he couldn't afford, and he'd be damned if he'd take the stuff back.

His father came around the corner. "Your mother said you have a new girl friend."

"I realized the rent was due Thursday, after I spent money on supplies for the shop."

"How much are you short?"

"I'll let you know. Thanks, Dad. I can't believe I thought it was next week."

"Love will do that," his father said as he leaned against the door casing and scratched his back. "I can let you have a twenty now if you need it."

"I'm working Thursday and Friday. Till then I'll work in the shop."

"I'm going to bed," his father said. "Goodnight."

"Night."

Jake sat for a minute longer and took the calendar off the wall. From October second till Friday the nineteenth he'd been in the hospital. Saturday, he'd gone with Chad, met Terry that night, worked four days the following week, and built boxes over the weekend. This Thursday would be the first of November. It made sense on the calendar. He felt he'd had his head buried in his ass. Dumb.

He said goodnight to his mother and told her he'd be over in the morning. On the way home, he decided he couldn't do anything about mixing up the days. He'd been confused in the transition from the hospital to home.

"What is normal?" he said and closed the trailer door behind him.

CHAPTER 7

It didn't snow once in November; the air stayed cold and dry. Two small storms in December dropped six inches, enough for Jake and Terry to build a snowman in front of the trailer. The ground was white at Christmas but by that time the Olympic officials were in a panic and Jake liked to read and hear about them sweating out the possible disastrous results. Slowly, the papers kept repeating, the eyes of the world began to focus on a little town in the Adirondacks known for blizzards and cold, that only had cold this important year.

The red cedar boxes sold almost as fast as Jake could build them. He and Barney had designed, with the help of a welder, several burning irons in the shape of the Olympic insignia and on top of each box he burned in the Olympic circles. In a bottom corner he tapped in his and Barney's initials with dies from an old printing press. He liked that closeness.

He and Terry saw each other several times a week but at times it seemed the differences between them grew more important. The talked about the age distance and family backgrounds until no more was left to say. Maybe he wasn't ready for commitment.

One afternoon in early January, Jake lost his grip on a screwdriver and it gouged a jagged tear in his palm. His mother drove him to the hospital where the nurse who assisted the doctor asked Jake if he knew her daughter, Terry. Jake didn't know what to say and stared at his glue-stained pants.

"You are Jake Mason?"

"Yes ma'am."

"Do you know of any other Jake Masons?" she asked, smoothing her crisp white dress.

"No." He'd known she worked at the hospital but didn't think about seeing her there. He wanted to get up and leave.

"Hold still," the doctor said.

"Terry has invited you over to dinner several times, hasn't she?" her mother asked.

"Yes."

"How's tomorrow night? I'd like to see you under different circumstances. Terry hasn't told me much about you. Six o'clock all right?"

"Yes. Thank you."

The doctor finished stitching and Terry's mom wound gauze over his palm and around his wrist. "It'll be sore when the anesthetic wears off. Keep it elevated," she said. "Is your mother in the waiting room?"

"Yes."

She followed him out of the treatment room and Jake introduced them.

Outside, his mom said what a nice woman she was.

"Seems like," said Jake and wondered what Terry had told them – or not told them. They'd had several discussions about his going over for supper and now it looked as if Terry would have it her way.

After Jake cleaned up the work shop, he sat on a three-legged stool and rested his hand on the work bench to ease the throbbing. He and Terry both knew that if her parents found out where he lived and about his mental illness, the well-known shit would hit the fan. If she looked at the medical forms he'd filled out, she'd know the first. Terry said she hadn't told them any more that necessary about him the first month; they'd only seen each other on weekends and she simply didn't tell them where she was going. He shifted around on the stool and stared at the glow coming from the seams of the stove and the pulsating heat shimmers. He understood why they wanted to protect her – any parents would after what she'd been through, put them through. Jake couldn't imagine what her father would say or do when he went over there. Jake shook his head and smiled. "Boy, this is going to be good," he said and turned to gaze out of the frost-etched window. He imagined a headline: Banker Beats Helpless Hollywood Man over Teenage Daughter. His mother called him in to eat. Jake turned out the lights, shut the door behind him, and tried to figure out an excuse for not going.

Terry called during supper.

"How's your hand?" she asked.

"Throbbing."

"You coming to dinner tomorrow?"

Jake listened to the line noise and imagined the cold pressing the wires together.

"Are you there? Mom said I could come over and see you tonight."

"Did she say anything to your father?"

"That you looked older than what I'd said and that your mom was nice. Don't be paranoid. Dad's not an ogre."

"When you coming over?" he asked.

"We're going to eat in a few minutes. After that."

"I'll be home."

He finished his meat loaf and potatoes.

His father said, "They're going to start hauling snow. A guy who works for the town told me they need drivers."

Jake held up his hand.

"Is it that bad? You haven't worked much with Rich lately."

"You're right about that," Jake said. "I could probably do it. Probably pays good. Worth a little pain. He put his dishes in the sink. "Did he say who to see?"

"Highway superintendent. George somebody. He'll be at the garage, seven tomorrow morning. I'd get there early."

"I will. I can't make boxes with this hand for probably a week. The tourists will have to live without."

"Does your hand hurt bad?" his mom asked as she ran water for the dishes.

"I'll live. Actually physical pain is a lot easier to live with than … thanks for driving me to the hospital. I know how much you hate hospitals."

"I have codeine left from my teeth in the medicine cabinet," she said.

"Maybe I'll take one," he said and went into the bathroom.

"How many stitches?" his father asked. He was getting ready to take a shower, listening to the radio that sat on the back of the toilet. Their television had broken the week after Christmas.

"Five. It's no big deal." He swallowed one of the pills.

"Oh. I meant to tell you," his father said. "A lot of pipes have frozen lately. Pack some extra hay around the ones under the trailer."

"Chad said the same thing the other day. He told me it's the best winter they've ever had for logging, too."

"I'd imagine," his father said. "The skid roads must be froze solid and no snow to fool with." He rubbed his forehead then back along his bald head.

"I'd better go. Terry's coming over to nurse my wound."

"Awful young, Jake. Watch it. Good luck with the job."

In the kitchen his mother told him it had been nice to meet Terry's mother and how much she liked Terry.

"Thanks, Mom. She's still wearing the necklace you gave her for Christmas."

When he got to the trailer, Terry was inside putting logs in the wood box. She turned and hugged him.

"How long have you been here?" he asked.

"A few minutes. I ate fast."

"Thanks for bringing wood in. I could do it." He kissed her warm lips. "You're nice."

"It's cold," she said. "Supposed to be fifteen below tonight." He rested his arm on her shoulder and twisted a lock of her hair around his index finger. She gazed at him, a questioning look on her face.

"Let's make love," he said.

"Is your hand all right? Doesn't it hurt?" she asked.

"Not much. We never see each other on week nights."

He boosted her up into the loft with his right hand, then went out to the living room and put another log on the fire.

"Hurry. It's cold up here."

Soon after he joined her, the trailer began to rock slightly back and forth. Afterwards, all was still, and she rested her head against his shoulder. Jake rested his elbow on her hip and listened to their breathing and the crackle of the fire. "It's so good with you," she said and snuggled closer. She touched his eyebrows with her lips and kissed his nose. He rested his fingers on her shoulder and rubbed in small circles; his palm began to throb.

"Let's hope it lasts," he said and felt the codeine working in his body, making it numb and thick. In the diffused light from the living room, he watched his fingers trace lightly between her breasts and it seemed he was touching her for the first time. Her stomach felt soft and silky and the triangle of hair between her legs rose and fell slightly as she breathed. He cherished her. She'd told him he was the first one to make love to her after the child.

"You're special," he said. "Sometimes I don't want to let you in, but then you're there." He rested his wounded palm on her stomach. Heat penetrated the gauze.

"I'm glad you think so." She picked up his hand and moved it close against him. "Hug me," she said. "Oh, how I love it when you hug me." Her body relaxed after a few minutes and he felt the level beating of her heart.

She woke with a start and squeezed him. "I didn't mean to fall asleep. Was it long?"

"Not more than ten minutes." He watched her stretch and heard two of her toes crack. "Let's talk about dinner," he said as she rubbed her eyes with the back of her hand.

"Well. Mom asked me again how old you were, and I told her twenty-two." She peeked out from behind a hand to see his reaction.

"That's four years," Jake said. "What if she saw the medical forms I filled out?"

"I know," she said. "I didn't think of that until after she asked me. But four years off your age would make us four years apart. Seemed okay at the time." She shifted her position a little and bumped his left elbow. A pain flew up and down his arm. "Sorry! I'm sorry." She rubbed his arm lightly. "Better?"

"It's okay," he said. "I took a pain killer. It's working. Do you really want to lie to your parents?"

"I'm not going to stop seeing you, no matter what they say. This just makes it easier."

"What if they ask me where I live?"

She sighed. "Don't get me wrong. My parents aren't all that bad. They're just too protective." She stopped rubbing his arm and lay back. "Couldn't you say you live in an apartment outside of town?"

"Why lie? I don't like to lie." He rolled over and slid out of the loft. On the floor, he turned toward the loft and stared at her, and wanted to crawl up over her again.

"For us. Please," she said, staring at the ceiling. "We can tell them the truth after they get to know you. I'll say it was all my idea."

"You must have slept longer than I thought, either that or I drifted off, too," Jake said. It's almost ten, Terry."

"It's okay. I told them I might be late. Mom thought you were nice. They want to see who I'm spending time with." He helped her down from the loft and she started to put her clothes on. "Well, will you do it?"

"All right. If it will make you happy."

She hugged him. "I love you, Jake." The soft material of her bra rubbed against his chest as she swayed back and forth on her toes and hugged him tight.

"How late did you say you'd be?" he asked.

"Not that late," she said and glanced down.

After she left, Jake leafed through a book she'd given him for Christmas. She thought he'd like the watercolor prints of the steep mountains. He didn't even know how to pronounce the name – he thought it was Chinese; Lao-Tzu. The prints were beautiful, subtle reds and light blues behind sharp black lines, and he liked the little poems near each picture. He searched for one he particularly liked that started out 'the surest test if a man be sane.' Jake found it and settled back into the couch:

The surest test if a man be sane

Is if he accepts life whole, as it is,

Without needing by measure or touch to understand

The measureless untouchable source

Of its images,

The measureless untouchable source

Of its substances,

The source which, while it appears dark emptiness,

Brims with a quick force

Farthest away

And yet nearest at hand

From oldest time unto this day,

Charging its image with origin:

What more need I know of the origin

Than this?

Jake remembered the insanity he'd seen, been a part of, at the hospital. The dark emptiness of his depression. His own state of mind seemed better as he compared the way he was before he went in with afterwards, and now. All the questions. Involuntarily he shuddered and again heard the heavy whomp of Barney's body when it hit the ground outside the kitchen where he and his dad were laying linoleum. Why didn't he cry out? He'd fallen over five stories and never made a sound. Jake closed the book. It was like asking one of the still ponds they used to fish where its source rose from.

He hadn't been back to the graveyard since fall. It was time. He put on his clothes and went out to the car. The codeine lessened the throb, but his head felt cottony. Jake turned on the radio as he drove through tiny frost particles in the below-zero air. The Placid station was playing a bluegrass tune and Jake's feet felt heavy on the pedals when he swerved to miss a dog that chased the car. In the rear view mirror, he could see the dog standing in the middle of the road, great clouds of steam rising around its cocked ears.

The graves glistened like diamonds under the half moon. Old gravestones tilted at odd angles created strange intertwined shadows in the glare of the headlights. He shut them off and, as he listened to the music, he imagined the gravestones rose up and danced, crushing the tiny frost diamonds into dampness and then rested in perfect rows of gleaming cold granite, tired from the pent-up exertion held in for so many years. Jake rested his forehead on the steering wheel and thought, when things seem okay, they're not. He turned the radio off and listened to the even rhythm of the car engine and his own heart and wondered if he could get out and walk over to his friend's name carved into the cold stone. He remembered, "The surest test if a man be sane is if he accepts his life whole, as it is." He put the car in gear and drove the back roads. Tires crunched on the frozen slush and tears stung the corners of his eyes. He wiped them off with the gauze on the back of his hand and knew it was wrong – because he cried for himself, who was still here – while his best friend lay under a gravestone that would never dance.

The road opened up into a field and he pulled over. Ahead and to the left, all along the side of Mt. Van Hovenberg, a dull orange glow lit the bobsled run, tracing its curves against the moonlight. Jake stared at the unnatural glow. You've been hiding. The thought seemed to roll at him through the windshield and it sank into him. Hiding ever since you met Terry, and that is why you can't say I love you to her. Jake tried to steady his breathing and think calmly. His thoughts whirled like a gust of wind in dead leaves. He slapped his hand on the wheel and awful pain shot up his arm as the cut made contact with it. "I've got to beat this," he said and held his hand against the car's velvety headliner and sat still, trying to clear his mind.

He rolled down the window, put the car in gear and drove as fast as it would go, a streak of forest green, roaring on the flat frozen road. He braked hard on the first corner, almost lost it, and shifted into second. For the next several miles he drove at a crawl, then turned around in a frozen pasture and went home, thinking about when he looked over the edge of the roof where Barney fell that night they buried him. He'd seen a scramble of two by fours and pieces of sheet rock where Barney landed.

Jake got up at six, made coffee, showered and dressed. His hand was stiff but didn't throb. He planned on taking his right glove off to shake the guy's hand and keep the other one on to hide the bandages. At ten to seven he followed the superintendent into the garage. "Ever drive a dump truck before?" he asked.

"I've driven my friend's log truck quite a bit," Jake said.

"Can you split gears?"

"Sure," Jake said.

"Good. Most of the guys I've talked to think that means double clutching. You won't need it much on these loads anyway. When can you start?"

"Anytime," Jake said.

He pointed to a board on the wall beside Jake. "Take the keys to number seventeen. You can sign all the payroll forms at lunch. Pay starts at five-fifty an hour."

Jake took the keys off their hook. "Thank you, sir," he said at the door.

"Call me George," he said. "Don't horse that truck. It isn't a car race."

"I won't," Jake said and felt bad for the way he'd beat his car the night before. A big temperature gauge on the side of the garage read ten below. Most of the drivers sat in their trucks warming the engines. Each truck had a numbered sticker on the front bumper. Jake unplugged the block heater, coiled the cord on the fence like the others, then climbed up into the yellow cab and studied the gauges. The guy in the truck next to him rolled down his window and Jake reached over and rolled his down on the passenger side. "Pull the choke out halfway and the throttle just a little," he said. "Leave it in neutral. The brake is on."

"Thanks," Jake said, then did as he was told, and turned the key. The diesel stuttered and cranked to life.

"One more thing," the guy hollered over the engines. "You'll be following me and the brakes in that old bucket are touchy. Keep tapping them till you get the feel."

"Okay. Name's Jake."

"Mine's Tom," he said and touched the brim of his Cat hat. "We're loading down at the lake and hauling to a field at Van Hovenburg."

Jake pulled his Ford hat tight around his forehead, revved the engine a little and bounced in the seat. He stared at the gauges and felt like a fighter pilot. "Hot shit," he said and adjusted the mirrors. The trucks closest to the driveway pulled out onto the road and Jake pushed in the clutch, snapped the brake free, eased the gearshift into first and rolled forward. The red button for splitting gears was up; a diagram on the dash showed that meant he was in high range. He didn't want anything to do with split shifting unless it was to push the button down when the truck was stopped. He'd have to find Chad after work and ask more about it.

The trucks rolled slowly toward the lake and, once there, waited in line for two front-end loaders to fill them. They'd already cleared a large area of the five or six inches of snow. After a ten-minute wait, Jake pulled into position. The truck bounced and settled when snow fell from the bucket with a loud whomp which sounded too much like a soft body hitting dirt. Jake winced. After four bucketfuls, he pushed the red button down, waved to the loader operator and eased out the clutch. He almost stalled, gave it a little extra bit of gas and rolled forward.

He drove along the back streets, avoiding the busy downtown section. Little orange signs on telephone poles directed him along the truck route, through the fringes of Hollywood, and back onto the main route outside of town. Jake felt important in the high cab and waved to little kids on their way to school. They motioned with their arms for him to beep the horn. He was glad he didn't have to drive through the narrow main street and though he'd never considered it before, when he thought about the layouts of the road, he realized it wasn't necessary for anyone to drive through the town at all, ever. The route from Saranac Lake veered left after the ski jumps, past the road to John Brown's Grave, and missed the main road to town entirely. From all other directions the town was surrounded by wilderness, with the exception of the road that led to Whiteface and Wilmington, and that was out in God's country, too.

He scratched his head and tried to think if any other towns in the area were this way. In most of them, the main route led through the heart of town. He shook his head. No wonder everyone in Lake Placid seemed like a tourist. They are! Jake wondered why he'd never thought of it quite like that before, as he shifted down in front of the ski jumps and stared at the high towers backed by the clear blue sky.

He laughed. Who'd of ever thought he'd be paid to haul snow? Last year at this time, there must have been two feet of the stuff on the ground, more back in the woods. Jake rolled down the window and spat as he entered the straight stretch of gradual hill that climbed past the view of Marcy. He got laughing so hard he missed a downshift. The gears grated and clunked into place. "Screw the state," he yelled into the cold breeze that blew across his face. "Look at me, Barney!"

The mounds of snow near the main entrance to the bobsled run looked so out of place he started to laugh again. He hoped they had a blizzard as soon as they'd stockpiled enough. Loaders pushed the snow into high piles, and a flagman directed Jake where to back up and dump. Jake jumped down from the cab and wiped off a metal plate that explained the positions of the levers. The flagman came over and showed him; he looked half frozen, his face the color of a cooked lobster.

"Always," he said. "Always remember to put the lower lever in this position when you finish dumping a load," he said, and tapped the lever. "Otherwise the box can come up at any time." He showed Jake how to release and re-hook the tail gate, and which lever to pull up first. After the box was empty, and the levers back in place, Jake stepped into the cab and turned the heater fan on all the way.

The flagman came over and looked at the levers. "That's right," he said, and slapped the levers. "Remember. It's how guys get killed: when the box comes up and hits electrical wires."

"Thanks again," Jake said, as he popped up the red knob next to the gearshift and released the air brake. He loved that whoosh sound. On the highway he wound the truck up high in every gear, and yelled into the cold, "We're having fun now!" His and Barney's favorite saying. During the rest of the morning he grew accustomed to the truck and enjoyed it more and more. At a narrow spot in the road where a steep bank came down on one side, and a cliff on the other, he let up on the gas and tooted the air horn. The loud blast reverberated in the small space: he did it every time when a car wasn't coming. He liked driving truck. It gave him something to do, and left time to think; something, he decided, he hadn't been doing enough lately. His relationship with Terry blurred his thinking about things he had to resolve, and he didn't like this lying to her parents. At the hospital they talked about keeping busy with something worthwhile and trying not to dwell on unpleasant thoughts. He hadn't been able to do that the night before at the graveyard. Probably I should start seeing a therapist, he thought, but his dislike of contact with other mentally ill people, even in a waiting room, put an end to that idea.

Stigma. He knew it was wrong, and knew he was hiding, almost investing, in a strange way, his past, in Terry. She cared, but he couldn't cross that line of making a commitment, and that wasn't fair to her. Whenever she said, "I love you," he tightened inside like a drying nut in its shell. Oddly, he felt like he did right after Barney's death; playing a game with himself to avoid it. If he faced it head on as he should, maybe it would end up all right, but he was afraid of losing Terry, too. All this avoidance to stay away from the stigma of mental illness. He compared it to the way he felt about tourists, and he didn't want to be treated that way.

At lunchtime he sat in the truck at the town garage and tried to decide why he thought that way and wasn't sure. He and Barney always played jokes on the tourists – gave them wrong directions, let the air out of their tires, anything for a laugh. Now, it seemed, he was afraid of a similar treatment because of mental illness. He took off the gauze and put two band-aids over the top of the butterfly strip Terry's mother had put on. Through the dried blood that stained his palm, the black stitches looked like ties under one rail on the old tracks near his parents. Jake decided he had more things to straighten out than he'd thought.

Inside the garage he signed several forms, and asked George how long the job might last. "Well, now. That depends, actually," he said, and scratched at one of his black and gray eyebrows. "See, with these Olympics coming up they've dumped extra into my budget. You don't wreck that truck, and we don't get a foot of snow tomorrow or the next day, and maybe you can stay on till spring or better."

"That would be great," Jake said, already counting the money. Someone else was waiting, and Jake went out to his car, and drove to his mom's for a sandwich.

"I got the job, Mom! Can you fix me some lunch. I been driving all morning."

"Well, good." She bent over, opened the cupboard door and took out the peanut butter. "How's the hand?"

"Fine. Could you do me a favor, though?"

"What is it?" she said.

"Around five o'clock call Terry's house and tell her, or her mom, I can't make dinner tonight. We're working ten-hour days and tell her I apologize."

"I'll try. Write down the number."

"Stock piling snow," Jake said. "Do you believe I'm getting paid to haul snow around?"

"How much?"

"Five-and-a-half an hour."

"Good," she said. "Don't spend it foolish. Start a savings account at the bank." She put a sandwich in front of him.

Jake ate fast and watched the clock. Before he left, he told her maybe he could have their television fixed. He got back to work at five to one and drove the truck down to the lake and estimated five acres had been cleaned off the surface. Black ice, crisscrossed with white stress cracks glowed dully in the bright sun. The cracks seemed whiter than the snow.

He jumped when the snow hit the bed of the truck, and turned the heater fan a notch higher. He'd been thinking he didn't want to be treated differently by anyone: his parents, Chad, or Terry. Whether that meant sympathy, or extra patience. Anything. "Dammit, Barney. I wish you were here to kick my ass."

That night his whole body ached, especially his shoulders. He guessed it was from bouncing around in the cab all day hanging onto the wheel. He lay on the couch, feeling his muscles at every point of pressure, and wondered if his mom had called Terry's house. Her mom probably planned a nice supper and was pissed he didn't show up. Maybe he should get a phone.

Jake sat up when someone knocked on the door.

"Hello," he said.

His father came in and stood near the stove warming his hands. "Damn, it's cold," he said. "You got the job."

"Thanks for telling me about it. What's up?"

"Your mother wanted me to come over and tell you she called Terry's mom." He rubbed his calloused palms briskly together. "She said you shouldn't be driving a truck with your hand like that."

"It was fine," Jake said.

"Terry wants you to call."

"That's right. She doesn't have band practice tonight. Thanks, Dad. I was coming over after I rested a bit."

"You okay? You seem better."

"Getting there, Dad. Little by little. I was thinking today, some times I feel like a tourist."

"Why's that?"

"Because of the hospital, but I'm not sure. I don't like tourists."

"We can't all be natives. I read some where that the population had decreased since 1932 to about 2700 now,"

Jake got up and put on his coat and his father asked how long the job might last.

"The superintendent said he might be able to keep me on till spring."

"Isn't that something," his father said. "Stock piling snow in the Adirondacks."

Jake walked behind his father on the path, and the cold stiffened up every joint in his body. "You know truck driving is hard work," Jake said.

"There aren't many easy jobs in this country," his father said.

"That's for sure," Jake said. "Only 2700 you said. No wonder we know almost everyone."

CHAPTER 8

By the end of the week Jake enjoyed truck driving more than he'd thought possible. On Friday, after work, he stopped at the Grill; Chad came over and slapped Jake on the back so hard it hurt all the way down to his sore hand. "Just the man I'm looking for," he said. "I need a favor."

"At your service," Jake said, and coughed a little. His back felt hollow where Chad had slapped him.

"We're short a man for bowling tonight. You busy?"

Jake swallowed beer. He wanted to help out, but Terry would be pissed. They were supposed to go dancing. "What time?"

"Seven. Be done by nine-thirty, ten at the latest." Chad took a drink. "What's the matter, Jake. You married? You're never around since you started going with that young stuff."

"Okay. It's quarter-past six. I'll go home, get changed, and be right back." Jake flexed the fingers on his right hand; it had been years since he'd bowled. He slid a dime in the slot and dialed Terry's number, glad he wasn't a lefty, and could help Chad out. Terry's mom answered the phone. "Is Terry home?" Jake asked.

"Not yet."

"Could you tell her I can't come over till around ten o'clock."

"Sure."

"Thank you," he said, and hung up.

At home, there wasn't time to shower, so he changed clothes, and put on some cologne.

Before he put on his T-shirt, he washed up, and popped a zit on his forehead that had been bothering him all day. "Damn, I'm too old for acne," he said, and searched his face for black heads. He noticed the freckles on his nose seemed brighter and wondered if the sun's reflection off the snow brought them out. He combed his hair, and pushed it behind his ears with his fingers, and thought that at even with a beard, he still looked a little like his mother. The beard, an inch long in most places, had come in fuller than he'd expected.

He was halfway out of the driveway when he realized he'd forgotten his wallet. He ran in, took it out of his work pants, and stood for a moment in the silence of the trailer. He'd see people he'd been avoiding tonight. Probably Barney's brother, Paul, and others he didn't care to see. "Fuck 'em," he whispered.

At the bar he ordered a beer and shot of Black Velvet to help loosen up. The shot gagged him till he chased it with beer.

"All ready? I feel hot tonight," Chad said.

"Here. Let me touch you," Jake said, and gripped Chad's shoulder. "Maybe it'll rub off."

"Don't worry," Chad said. "If your scores are low, they'll give you a big handicap."

"They don't give them that high," Jake said.

"Let's go," Chad said.

The bowling alley was near the lake, and on the way over, Chad asked him about the new job.

Jake told him he wasn't split shifting and asked for advice.

"Try it in fourth gear first with the button down," Chad said. "When you're rolling along about forty, take your foot off the gas, pull up the button and hit the gas, but easy. Then reverse it and push the button down. After you're used to it, try it in third and second. Stay away from first, though. That's when the most pressure is on the transmission, and if you do anything wrong she might blow."

"Thanks, Chad. I like driving truck. After driving yours for all these years I trust the mirrors and know where I am."

As they pulled into the parking lot he told Chad they should get together more often.

"Seems we're both busy as hell these days," Chad said, and winked. "Lot going on."

The other two guys on the team were Chad's logging friends from Keene Valley. One brought a pitcher of beer over and Jake offered him a dollar toward it, but he refused. "I'm Bob, and this is Calvin." They shook hands while Chad bowled a practice ball that blistered down the alley.

"Think you could throw it a little harder?" Jake asked.

"Wait," Chad said, and winked. "I'm just warming up." He stuffed a wad of tobacco in his mouth and took an empty soda bottle out of the trash can to spit in.

Jake glanced around the alley. He knew most of the people, except for a few teams from Saranac Lake. Paul, Barney's brother, was two alleys over and raised his hand when he saw Jake looking his way. Jake acted as if he hadn't seen. Several weeks after the funeral Paul sold Barney's car to that red neck Curt Dixon for practically nothing. When Jake told him it was wrong Paul told him to mind his own business.

One of the guys on the other team asked Chad if he'd brought in a ringer.

Jake faced the alley, determined to enjoy the game. It was all he could do to keep his own act together without causing trouble, knowing stupidity could land him in that hospital again.

He opened in the tenth frame and ended with a one-thirty-seven.

"That's all right, Chad said. "With your handicap we might win the game."

Jake went to the bar for a refill. It took his eyes a few seconds to adjust in the dim light of the bar.

"Hi, Jake."

"Laurie. You work here?" Jake said and handed her the pitcher. She looked prettier than the last time he'd seen her in the fall.

"No," she said. This is where I practice." She laughed. "Mic or Bud?"

"Budweiser."

"You still going out with that girl? Terry wasn't it?" she asked and watched the pitcher fill.

"Yes. You still going with the bouncer?"

Her small nose turned up a little, and she grinned. "Nope," she said. "Free as a bird." She slid the pitcher across to him and winked. "Three-fifty," she said. "How's driving truck?" she asked over her shoulder as she put the money in the cash register.

"How did you know?"

"Jake. This isn't a big city. When I see someone driving one of the Town dump trucks down the road, I assume he's working for the Town." She put fifty cents change in his palm. "What did you do to your hand?"

"Keep the change, ma'am," he said and lifted the pitcher in his right hand, and saluted her as he turned, but she'd already walked away to wait on another customer, her long strawberry blonde hair waving back and forth.

He didn't do well in the second game and wondered if the beer was making him too loose. He enjoyed watching Calvin who jumped a little on his second step, took two more long strides, and released the ball in a backspin hook. Chad gave Jake a little pep talk at the end of the second game and told him to keep his shoulders square to the alley and follow-through.

At the bar Laurie was busy. In the dim light at first, Jake didn't know he was standing behind Barney's brother, Paul, who turned around before Jake could move away.

"Hi, Jake," he said, and offered his hand.

Jake looked off and tried to pretend he hadn't heard but couldn't. He stared at Paul's hand for a second, then shook it, and wanted to smash his face.

"What can I get you Paul?" Laurie asked, and Jake wondered if she knew what was going on. He's nothing, Jake told himself, and started counting, knew it wouldn't help, and headed for the bathroom. Someone had left the window open, and the icy cold air calmed him down a little. He locked the door behind him. "Get it together," he said, and washed his right hand under the tap and splashed water on his face. He dried his face on the roller towel and stared into the tiny mirror above it, gritted his teeth, and said, "Don't be an asshole! He's not worth it."

But he couldn't forget how cold Paul had been after Barney's death. Damn redneck acting as if accidents like falling off a roof happened every day to his own brother. He ought to have the shit kicked out of him.

When he came out Chad motioned him over. It was his turn.

He picked up the ball, took a deep breath, and imagined Paul's head lying on the alley in the strike zone. He let the ball fly, and every pin fell. His first strike.

"Nice going." Bob said. "Good start."

"Thanks." Jake went back to the bar for a shot of whiskey.

"It's on me," Laurie said. "Let's talk sometime, Jake. I saw what almost happened."

"What good will it do?"

"You don't know till you try."

"When?"

"I get off at midnight," Laurie said. "Pick me up. We'll ride the back roads like we did in high school."

"Let me think about it."

"See you then," she said, and started filling a pitcher.

Maybe she hadn't heard him. That first strike was the only one he bowled that game, but when it was over, he'd bowled a one-forty-nine, his best of the night.

"We may take three of the four points, old buddy," Chad said. "Have to wait till they figure your handicap."

When Jake took off his bowling shoes, his feet smelled awful, a sure sign of his bad nerves, as he knew from past experience. Outside, it was cold and clear. A part of the constellation Orion was rising above Whiteface, and Orion's sword pointed at the top. "Look at that, Chad," he said, and pointed.

"Nice night. Great logging weather," Chad said. "If the snow holds off, I'll have my best winter ever. Heh. Heh," he muttered. "And you're making money hauling the stuff." He stuffed a fresh wad of tobacco in his mouth.

"Like some of the guys say at work, 'Say farewell to Welfare, cause now I'm really screwing the State,'" Jake said.

Chad laughed and opened the car door, puffs of steam coming from his mouth.

At the Grill Jake called Terry. He didn't know she could get so mad. No. She didn't want to go out because it was after ten, and it was the second time in a week he'd stood her up.

"I'm sorry about missing dinner, Terry, and I'm sorry about tonight. Chad's a good friend. He'd do anything for me." There was a long silence over the frozen wires.

"I'm sorry". My parents have been giving me a hard time, and, well, it's that time of the month and it's Friday.

"It's not that late."

"I know. I just don't feel like it."

"Are you crying?" Jake asked.

"No. Call me tomorrow. Okay?"

"Sure," Jake said. "Good night."

Chad was at the bar, talking to Amy.

"How's the wife?" Jake asked.

"Good. Always bitching she has to work at the old folks' home. But that's natural, if it wasn't that it would be something else."

Amy placed the beer in front of Jake and took his dollar. "Thanks," Jake said, when she handed him the change.

"You're welcome." She smiled, and Jake knew if she was his wife, she wouldn't be working here. No way.

She leaned over and whispered something to Chad, her curled black hair brushing the top of the bar. From the set of her eyes, when she stood back, Jake decided she must have quite a bit of Mohawk blood. Chad laughed and she walked away.

"What was that all about?" Jake asked.

"Nothing. Let's play pinball."

Jake fished for quarters and walked over to the machine. Chad won all three games they played.

"Pinball wizard, eh Chad?"

"Nah. Want to play one more?" Chad asked.

"No thanks," Jake said. "I'm gonna go home and put some wood on the fire before the pipes freeze."

"Thanks for subbing tonight," Chad said. "We'd of been up shit creek without you."

"Let me know if you need me again."

"You bet," Chad said, and headed for the bar where Amy was sitting.

Jake went home, loaded the fire, and took a long shower. Complications. Laurie just wanted to talk, to help. But then she acted awfully friendly and she had broken up with her boyfriend. He remembered how horny she'd been in high school. They'd both been around the block since then, her more than me, he thought, if half of what he heard was true. What the hell? It might be good for my head if she wants to make it with me. Or would it?

He drove back to the bowling alley. Ice scrunched and popped under the tires, and the four-foot wide digital temperature gauge on the bank read minus twelve. The lanes were closed, and Laurie was making last call when he walked in and sat at the end of the bar. Three guys at the other end, pretty drunk, were talking to Laurie. She came toward him, and his breath caught in his throat.

"What can I get you?" she said. "I won't be long." She reached under the bar and flicked the outside lights off.

"A beer, I guess." She walked to a cooler, and he saw the outlines of her bikini underwear against the thin black pants she wore.

"Drink up," she said, to the three at the other end.

One of the guys said, "How come he gets another one?"

"He's my date," she said, and winked at Jake as she put a bottle of Bud in front of him. They finished their beers and left. Laurie turned off more lights, locked the money in a safe, then came around the bar, wiping her hands on a towel.

"So. How you been?" she asked.

"All right. Fine, actually," he said.

She sat on the stool next to him and swiveled back and forth in a half circle. "Things almost got out of hand for a minute tonight."

"You know I've got a temper."

"What good does it do to hold a grudge for so long?" she asked.

"None, probably."

"Over a year. C'mon. I think Barney's brother is a redneck louse, too. We can't change that."

"I know," Jake said.

She got up and fixed herself a scotch and soda.

"High class," he said.

"I'm on a kick for the stuff lately," she said. "Keeps me warm." She stared at him over the glass rim. "Jake, I know you don't want to hear this; you've got problems of your own, but I get so lonely these long winter nights, and all there is are jerks around here. I wanted to talk to an old friend, especially after what happened with Paul."

Jake tipped the bottle up, and let the beer slide down his throat. "You shouldn't have a hard time finding someone to keep you warm. I'm surprised. What happened between you and the bouncer?"

"The whole thing went downhill after the Professor's Mustache closed in December, and I kicked him out before Christmas." She rattled the ice in her glass and looked at him like she had in high school after they'd had a fight; she had a temper, too.

The more they talked, the more he thought about that time before Barney died. "What are you thinking, Laurie?"

"You know damn well what I'm thinking," she said. "I know you're going out with that girl you met this fall. How is that?"

"The age difference is a problem sometimes," Jake said.

Laurie swallowed half her drink. "Take me home," she said.

I'd like to. You know damn well I'd like to."

"We'll get drunk and have a party," she said. "Talk over old times." She laughed and grabbed the bottle of scotch off the back bar. "I'll bring beer, too."

"No," Jake said. "I'll share the scotch."

She turned off all the lights except one over the cash register and locked the door behind them. Orion was over the center of the lake, and he thought of pointing it out to her, but didn't.

"I'll leave my car here," she said. "Boy, is it cold."

Cars lined the main street and Jake drove slow. He didn't feel any of the booze.

. "The Olympic village," she said. "The place is really hopping." All the bars were open and doing a good business. Jake touched the brakes to let several people cross the street in front of them. They waved.

"Just like old times, Jake." She moved over and put her head on his shoulder.

It was a little more than Jake had planned, except as a fantasy. He glanced down at her shiny strawberry blonde hair and goosebumps rose on his arms. She sat up. "If this doesn't seem right to you, don't."

He turned into the side street that led to Hollywood and the trailer. "It's not like I've made a commitment. I haven't. This is unexpected. That's all."

"Let's drive around for a while," she said. "We should talk like we used to. Does it seem that long ago to you?" She rested her head on his shoulder and opened the bottle of scotch.

Sometimes it did and sometimes it didn't, he thought, and drove past the turn for the trailer, out past the graveyard. He took the bottle out of her hands and sipped it, the warmth from her lips still on the bottle's mouth. "There are so many contrasts in this town," he said, and turned the fan on the heater down a notch. "No balance."

"It's always been that way," she said. "Natives and tourists. Rich and poor. You know that. Why does it matter so much now?"

"I don't know. It's stupid, but I think if Barney hadn't been helping build a condo for some rich tourist he'd still be alive."

"C'mon, Jake," she said, and tapped his leg with the bottle. "You're not being fair to him, or yourself."

"I know. I know. I went over and over this with people at the hospital." He stopped the car on the shoulder, and she placed her hands on his shoulders and turned him toward her.

He stared into her eyes.

"There are many other things to live for, even though Barney will never be a part of them." She kissed him, and as he wrapped his arms around her, a flood of memories obliterated the time and place. She carried him away with her desire, and made it his, and somehow, he knew her need was as deep as his. He pressed her into him and moved his hands from her back to her neck and tangled his fingers in her hair.

"Wow," she said. "This is like the first time you ever kissed me. I'm having a hot flash."

"Me, too," he said, and a shiver went through him.

"Except two things," she said.

"What's that?" Jake asked.

"We don't have to move into the back seat and I'm not a virgin fighting you off," Laurie said, and glanced at him.

They kissed again, then Jake turned the car around and headed for the trailer.

When he looked at the clock on the table underneath the loft, it read seven-thirty. Laurie breathed softly, sound asleep.

The next thing he heard was Terry's voice. "Jake, I thought I'd surprise you," she said, and he heard the door close behind her.

"Oh, Jesus," he said, and then she was standing next to the loft, staring at Laurie's shape under the covers. Jake saw tears fill her eyes to the brim, then start over the edges, like that night she told him she'd had a child at fourteen. She tried to say something but couldn't get her lips to form the words. She turned around, walked to the door, and slammed it on her way out. He heard gravel spin and fly off her tires, and the horn of an oncoming car.

"Oh, Jesus is right," Laurie said into the pillow. "I'm sorry."

He put on his bathrobe, went into the living room, and smelled Terry's perfume as he put kindling on the fire and opened the drafts.

Laurie went into the bathroom and said, "I'll leave."

"Stay for a while," he said.

She came out of the bathroom and got back into bed. "My teeth are chattering," she said, and Jake watched her roll up in the wool blankets.

He fixed coffee and stared out the back window. Almost the middle of January and still very little snow. Pine needles coated with layers of frost, and the bases of the trees white. He didn't know what to think. He was numb.

It seemed to be taking forever for the trailer to warm up. He leaned on a birch crosspiece of the loft, and Laurie rolled over on her side. They gazed at each other for a long time, then she held the covers open, and he climbed up next to her naked body, and the smell of wool and her warmth enveloped him. He rested his wounded palm against her heart, surprised it matched the beat of his own.

CHAPTER 9

By the middle of the next week Jake could split shift like a veteran. The smooth motions of shifting helped coordinate his thoughts, and he knew it was easier on the truck, especially with a full load. One time he counted the number of shifts from the lake to the bobsled run, thirty-eight; no wonder his right shoulder felt so strong.

He worried about Terry, sorry that he'd hurt her, but didn't know what to do. He'd never go back to anyone if he caught them in bed with someone else. No way.

On Monday, at lunch time, he'd gone to the hospital to have the stitches removed and was relieved he didn't see her mother. The doctor said the crescent moon-shaped scar was the sign of woman, and he'd have it for life. Jake said, "Amen," and the doctor laughed, but when Jake thought about it, he took it seriously.

A desire to go away alone for a few days built up as he drove back and forth, and the mountains held his gaze more and more. The McIntyre Range behind the horse show grounds, where the opening ceremonies would be held, were frosted in pure whiteness. He wanted to climb through the frozen trees, pitch a tent with a bright blue fly underneath them, and smell the snow-fresh odors, and taste crystallized spruce gum. He shook his head and paid attention to the road. That scary feeling of knowing he didn't remember driving around the last curve raised goose bumps; he checked both mirrors.

An hour later at lunch Tom, the truck driver who'd helped Jake out on the first day sat next to him.

"Hear the news? he asked

Jake shook his head no, his mouth full of tuna fish.

"They plowed out a road over by Thousand Animals, and we're gonna haul from the landing down by the Professor's Mustache."

"Pretty steep hill," Jake said, and swallowed some iced tea.

"Crawl up and down in first low," Tom said. "It'll be sanded good."

The first trip down the steep hill to the lake was scary. Ice covered with sand. Jake wanted to jam on the brakes, but imagined sliding, and rolling the truck over and over out onto the thick ice of the lake. He pumped the brakes, and thought about unlatching the door, ready to bail out, the way he'd see Chad do on steep hills when the log truck was loaded. At the bottom, he pulled over into a cleared spot, and waited while they finished loading another truck. There wasn't much space for the big equipment to move around, and Jake hoped it took forever. He drummed his fingers on the wheel and whistled, something he hadn't done in a long time. Nice to get paid for by the state for doing nothing. He leaned down a little and gazed up the hill and could see the door of the Professor's Mustache. Down the slope of the hill he saw the humped shape of the log he fell from that first night with Terry. It seemed like so long ago. She'd helped during those first month's home, listening, believing he was healed. He'd never be able to repay her as he should.

The other truck finished loading and crawled up the hill. Jake backed into position, not far from the boat dock, and watched the loader approach with a heaped-up bucketful of snow. Another came at his truck from the other side. The truck and Jake rocked as snow thundered like an avalanche into the bed. Two more buckets and Jake started up the hill, transmission growling, gear box whining, as he increased the rpms. At the top he pushed the button down and shifted into the high range of first gear, depressed the clutch after a few seconds and shifted into high second on level ground. He met another empty truck coming in and eased over to the right, hoping he didn't find the ditch with his front right tire on the narrow dirt road. It was Tom. Jake tooted the air horn, and Tom answered with his. Jake was part of something, and he liked that. Hardwood trees cast bars of shadow across the road in the early afternoon sun. Jake strained his eyes to focus on the alternating black and white pattern. At the end of the road he waited at the stop sign for traffic. On his left, the pole the bear used to climb up, pointed into the sky, its red steel ladder rusted in the bright sunlight. He was damn glad the place had gone bankrupt. Damn tourists staring at that poor bear.

Thursday, when George handed him his check, he said, "One more week will about do it."

"Before, you said maybe there might be something else?"

"I'm working on that, but I can't promise anything. You're a good worker," George said. "Might be jobs spreading out all this snow we been hauling on the cross-country ski trails, or maybe even a job opening up at the arena. I'll let you know next week. Don't get your hopes up. Politics. Always politics."

Jake went to the bank on Friday and cashed his check. He'd saved over three-hundred dollars from his truck driving checks and another two-hundred since starting to sell the boxes in November. From the bank he walked over to the store he thought was a tourist trap, and asked Jason, the owner, how the boxes were selling.

"Real good," Jason said, and handed him a list of the sizes that needed replacing, and a check for what had been sold.

"Wow," Jake said. They'd sold nine boxes in less than three weeks. The check was for one-hundred-and-thirty-five dollars.

"People like hand-crafted stuff," Jason said. "This town has gone nuts."

Jake had known Jason for years, and noticed he wanted to take the last word back.

"I know what you mean," Jake said. The opening ceremonies are less than a month away."

Jake stopped by the bowling alley to see Laurie. The place was empty at this time of day.

"Hi. I wondered if you'd gone into hibernation this week. It's cold enough."

"No. Working and thinking, mostly."

She started to pour him a mug of beer. "No thanks. I'll have a Coke."

She dumped it out and reached for a glass. "Tell me," she said, shaking strawberry curls back from her face. "What you been thinking about?"

"Me and you..."

"And Terry," she finished for him.

"Yeah."

"That's why I didn't come by this week," she said, and put her elbows on the bar, chin on open palms.

She must have been out in the sun during the week. Her freckles, a shiny deep maroon, seemed to glow, and the tiny upward turn on the end of her nose was a little red. "Been skiing?" he asked.

"Yeah. Yesterday. They're making snow at Whiteface like never before. Great skiing. You should go."

"The crowds on the weekends are too much," he said.

Laurie stood up, stretched, and leaned on the back bar. Behind her the mirror reflected bottles, and in between them he could see the shimmering layers of her Farah Fawcett haircut, and wondered if she knew what she did to him.

"Tell me more about your thinking," she said. "I had a great time last weekend. Thought about it all week, and all those times back in high school."

"I have been, too," he said. "I'd like to take you home right now."

"I'd like to go." She smiled.

"Oh, Jesus," he said and shifted around on the stool. It felt like he had a shotgun in his pocket.

"What is going on?"

"I doubt I'll ever see Terry again," he said. "What's going on with you?"

"I'd like to keep it going. See what happens."

"One question. Serious," Jake said, and took a gulp of Coke. "Why, with all the other guys around, guys with money, college educations, cars, the whole nine yards. Why me?" She started to say something, but he held up his hand. "Let me finish. You know I'm unstable, I've been in the nuthouse, and I don't have or care if I have a steady job. I'd like to know." He scratched his beard and twirled the empty Coke glass in the wet spot on the bar.

"I want to be sure you understand this," she said. "I don't feel much different about you than when we first went out in high school. But then, as I'm sure you remember, after we'd gone out for over a year, I thought I was missing out on other things and wanted to see other guys. I was, and sometimes I'm still glad I've been around, because it helps me to know what I want, and it isn't necessarily any of those things you said before." She stepped forward and took the glass out of his hand. "Look at me. Please."

He stared into her eyes for a second, then looked past her shoulder into the mirror. "Since we graduated, I've heard more lines from guys whose only interests are in what's between my legs than you'll ever imagine. Every time I've fallen for one of their lines, I've regretted it. Maybe not at first, but eventually. And maybe I am good looking. Lord knows I've been told that enough, but to most men that also means dumb."

He saw she was getting mad and remembered how she used to bitch him out in high school. He'd started calling her his little speech maker but knew this wasn't the time to call her that.

"I don't want to get so upset," she said. "But the plain truth is that you're not like those assholes, and never were." She walked down the bar in quick short steps. "That's why," she said.

He didn't know what to say – or what to say first. When she put the glass in front of him, he looked up and smiled. "Why don't you come over after work tonight, and I'll take advantage of you?"

"Deal," she said, and laughed. "Don't get the idea I'm putting you up on a pedestal either." She leaned over the bar and kissed him, and two early bowlers walked in and whistled. She blushed. While she waited on them, he finished his Coke, and felt good all over, like they said you would in the ads. He stood up and waved.

"A little after midnight," she said, and Jake saw the envy on their faces.

He did a hop, skip, and a jump across the parking lot to his car. "Skippedy-do-dah. Yippedy-day," he sang, as he backed the car out and started home.

He ate dinner at his parents, then worked in the shop. The air outside felt warmer, and Jake thought it might snow. He built a fire with red cedar scraps and turned on the radio Barney had bought at a garage sale for two bucks. The speaker was cracked, and the first day Barney turned it on Jake said, "That's a real crackling shit radio you bought." They called it that ever since.

The work shop was neat and tidy. For each of the three different sized boxes, Jake had cut stock sizes of lumber, sanded each board and placed them in groups on shelves and under the benches. It had taken up most of his spare time when not surveying in November. All the brass hinges, screws, and latches were separated in a metal file box with plastic drawers, and all the hand tools hung in neat rows in front of the bench under the window. Jake switched on the three-foot florescent lamp. He could assemble and rub the first coat of Tung oil on two boxes a night if he kept busy. He'd quit early the night before, and now finished putting in the screws, then cut and glued half-inch diameter pieces of birch dowels into the countersunk holes behind the screws and did the finish sanding. As he placed the boards for another box into position, he glanced out the window. Tiny flakes of snow clung to the window for a second before they melted. He walked to the door and stared into the darkness. In the light from the back porch he could barely make out the flakes. He knew that if it snowed much his job would be over even sooner. Into the cold beginning snow Jake laughed, and hoped it snowed two feet. The thirty to forty-foot piles of snow he'd helped create would be worthless.

He carefully painted a light coat of glue on the face of a front board, pushed the ends of two side boards into the glue, and tightened the wood-screw clamps gradually, keeping an even tension on both clamps, and softly wiped any excess glue off with a damp white rag. It was one of the largest boxes, and measured fifteen inches long by seven wide, and four deep. These sold the best, and he thought about raising the price to twenty dollars. Jason doubled the prices on everything Jake sold to him.

He stopped working and listened when the weather came on. The announcer said two to four inches by morning, and then back in the deep freeze. Jake put hinges on another box and steel-wooled it inside and out. The red cedar grain took on a dull luster that glowed under the bright fluorescent lights; on the cover an odd pattern curved and alternated in stripes of red and white, and a knot glowed bright red almost in the center. He propped up the lid with a toothpick and put it off to the side. An hour and a half later, a second large box was ready for a coat of finish.

Jake took two pieces of plywood and laid them side by side on the bench, then rested each box on top of four pyramid-shaped pieces of wood glued to the plywood. This little device, which Barney had thought of, saved a lot of time; otherwise they could only finish the bottom and sides of a box, then had to wait until the next day when it was dry to do the rest. Smart boy, that Barney. The tiny points of the pyramid-shaped blocks were hardly noticeable after the oil had dried, and the finish steel wooled and waxed.

He covered the boxes and pre cut boards with canvas and decided he should buy more lumber soon. He sprayed the whole shop with a mist of motor oil from an old Windex bottle to knock down the dust, added more wood to the stove, and went inside his parent's house for the Tung oil while the dust settled in the shop. He started down the cellar stairs.

"Hello," his mother said, from the couch.

"It's me," he said, turned around, and went into the living room.

"Really burning the midnight oil out there, aren't you?" his father said.

"They sold nine boxes in less than a month," Jake said.

His mother raised herself up on the couch and held out her hand. "Money, money, money," she said. "I'll take some."

"Television not broke again, is it Ma?"

"No. But a color one would be nice." She laughed.

"Doing anything Sunday, Dad?"

"Guess not.."

"Can I borrow the station wagon? I'd like to buy some more lumber from Grant." While his father thought about it, Jake said, "I'd go tomorrow, but they're forecasting snow."

"Maybe I'll ride over with you. Too damn cold for anything else. "

"Thanks, Dad. Why don't you come for the ride, Mom?"

"I'll see," she said. "Not going out with Terry tonight?"

"Don't think so."

"Have a fight?"

"Sort of."

"She's a nice girl."

"Young, Ma."

"You be nice to her."

"Yeah," he said, and went downstairs.

At the kitchen door, he said, "I'm going out to finish up. Be over tomorrow."

"Good night," they both said.

Just after he closed the door to the shop, he heard a car pull into the driveway. It was after ten, and no one usually visited his parents that late. He opened the door. It was Terry. She shut off the car and got out.

"Hi," he said.

"Can I come in?" she asked.

"Sure."

"I was driving by and saw the lights," she said. "The trailer was dark."

He held the door open, and as she stepped into the warm heat, he smelled her perfume.

"Working hard?" she asked.

"Putting on a coat of finish," he said, and poured a small amount on a clean rag.

For over a minute she didn't say anything, just stared at the stove while he uncovered the boxes, flipped them over and began rubbing the bottoms.

"Those are nice."

"Thanks." He flipped the boxes over, rested them on the pyramids, Tung oiled the insides, then propped up the lids with toothpicks, and did the outsides. "Stuff smells pretty strong," he said. "Makes you dizzy." He wondered when she would start, then she did.

"I know it's over between us," she said. "I'm sad now. At first, I was angry. Angrier than I've ever been before." He heard her pushing dirt around on the floor with her boots. "Now I don't even care who it is."

Jake doubted that. He found it almost impossible to turn around and face her.

"Say something."

"You knew I wasn't sure it would work." He scratched at his beard and glanced at her, past her. "But I didn't want it to end the way it did, either. I'm sorry for that." She started to walk back and forth in front of the stove. "Please don't do that," he said.

"What?" She stared at him.

"Walk around," he said. "You're raising dust."

"I'm sorry," she said, and wiped off tears with the back of her hand. "Is it over?"

"Isn't it?" He felt like a skunk. He kept seeing Laurie as she leaned on the bar, her reflection in the mirror, and wanted Terry to leave.

Terry sat on the three-legged stool, and he finished the boxes, then picked the flashlight out of its holder and started looking for runs.

"What are you doing?" she asked.

"Looking for places I missed," he said, and, satisfied that there weren't any, switched off the light, and leaned on the bench facing her. He said, "You'll probably never know how much you helped me. I mean that, Terry. Thank you."

"I guess I knew it might not work out, too, but I can't help crying." She stood up. "Will you hug me once more?"

He went over to her. His hands were sticky with varnish, and he wiped them on his jeans. She held on tight, and he could tell by her deep breathing she was trying not to cry. She lifted her head and gazed into his eyes. "You know I love you, Jake. You've helped me, too." She took her arms from around him. At the door she said, "I told myself the other day to think of all the good memories we've made together."

When she left he sat on the stool, heard the car start, and listened as she drove off down the road. "What a shitty business," he said, and closed the drafts on the stove, shut off the lights, and latched the door. He scuffed his way home through the dusty snow, leaving a crooked trail behind him.

Halfway home, he stopped, and turned his face into the angle of the falling snow. Live a little, die a little, each day. He tried to remember who told him that and couldn't. It seemed too true.

At home he sat inside the dark trailer and listened to the fire settle in the stove.

Laurie stopped by a little after twelve and they talked for a while; she understood that he wanted to be alone.

He worked all day Saturday in the wood shop, glad for something to do. Three inches of snow had fallen, powdery stuff that would soon blow off the fields. His thoughts jumbled. He couldn't focus on any one thing for long: Laurie, Terry, Barney, Chad, people at the hospital. At times the memories tore him apart, then a calm would settle into him. The work helped, and he kept at it, though at times it was all he could do to remember what came next. In the middle of the afternoon he took a break and sat on the work bench. It was getting cold again and the sky overcast.

He stared into the seams of the stove where fire glowed and interlaced his fingers. It was just that he had lapses, but that was to be expected, wasn't it? He tried to calm his thoughts, a whirlpool, and understand his feelings. Maybe he was losing himself in these relationships, shuffling Barney behind the girls to make it easier. He didn't believe that. He was going forward, trying to live his own life without Barney. The red glow in the fire is me inside, and no one else: I am still alive. He knew that Barney was melding with the earth, like the dirt at his feet. Nothing could be done about it. He looked outside and saw a small breeze had pushed the snow off the frozen tree limbs since he'd last looked. When? No matter what changed, it soon would be spring, then summer, and fall, and over and over again.

He scuffed his feet on the floor, mixing sawdust and powdery dirt. He asked himself, who are you to question a cycle larger than any single life, and besides, maybe Barney has it better somehow. And he said out loud, "If there is a God, let Barney be with you." He shivered next to the red heat of the stove, and a sweat broke out on his forehead. Too many questions that he couldn't answer, but he knew that if there was not a God, it would be enough for Barney to be a part of the growing grass and trees. It would have to be.

He walked circles around the wood stove and felt the drafts that entered under the door over his feet, and a coolness on his face radiating from the window. In the almost three months since he'd been home, he knew he'd gotten better. Only three months. Forward, from inside out, was how he wanted to work. It was difficult. He whispered, "I'm closer to not going back."

He picked up one of the small boxes and rubbed the wood with the palm of his hand. The red cedar smell reminded him of his mother's cedar chest, where she kept wool sweaters and blankets. When he was little, she told him the cedar kept out moths. Jake touched the grain where it changed from bright red to dull white. Change, always change. Protection inside a box from flying moths who eat fabric. Jake shook his head and wondered if there were any hard-and-fast truths that never changed. He wanted a box, a truth, to protect him from death's reminders, not one to preserve them.

He put the box down. "Get on with it," he said, and stared out the window, and remembered his therapists advice. 'Follow your own best self-interests. Trust your gut feelings.' He thought, it all sounds good and makes sense, but look at all the unknowns that surface and need attention, then time to settle – more than there is time to give. He wanted Laurie, but hated to hurt Terry, who was young and loved him. For the rest of the afternoon he worked on the boxes, noticing the changing grains and colors in the wood, as if to find the answers in them.

His mom fixed his favorite dinner: roast chicken, dressing, gravy, and baby pearl onions in butter. Jake tried to eat to make her happy; he felt he'd been crying. He rubbed his eyes with his napkin, and she asked what was wrong.

"Dust from the shop," he said. "This chicken is delicious. Thanks, Mom."

When they finished eating, he helped do the dishes. His mother asked about Terry again, and he wanted to tell her about Laurie. Not yet. He sat in the living room and watched Hee Haw with his parents for a few minutes.

"Be ready at ten?" his father asked.

"That's a little early for Grant on a Sunday."

"Eleven?"

"Okay. Guess I'll go back to work."

The phone rang and his mother said it was for him. "It's not Terry," she whispered, as he took the phone.

"Hi," he said, and heard a lot of noise in the background.

"Are you busy?" Laurie said.

"No."

"Albert, the guy who runs the toboggan slide, is going to keep it open till midnight for a bunch of people at the bar who want to go. My boss says he'll close for me. You up for it?"

"Yeah," Jake said. "Might be fun."

"I'll pick you up in an hour," she said. "That's when it closes to the public."

"See you then." At home, he showered, and dressed warm. A little after ten Laurie came in and sat on the couch.

"Boy, you smell good," she said.

"Thanks." He sat down beside her. "Lot of people going be there?"

"Probably," she said. "Don't you want to go?"

"No, I do. I'd like to know what people think when they see us together."

She held his hand and rubbed the back of it with her fingers. "C'mon let's not go over this again."

He pulled his hand away and lifted a strand of hair away from her face. She stared at him, silvery red eyelashes catching the light, and he touched her cheek with the back of his hand. "I'm kind of sad today. Did a lot of thinking."

"Sometimes that's good," she said.

"Let's go slow."

"Okay." She rested her head on his shoulder. "I'm in no hurry." She paused, then, "It's so peaceful and cozy here." She lifted her head and kissed his cheek. "I think, Jake, if we try to tell each other all we can about how we feel, we'll be fine. And we'll know if we're good for each other."

"You're right." But certain things he couldn't tell her; they were his own. He hugged her. "Let's go sledding. I'll bet we can sail halfway across Mirror Lake."

Cars lined both sides of the street, and as they walked down toward the lake, they heard screams as people slid down the steep chute. Albert said hello and handed him a two-man toboggan.

Jake put his arm around her as they climbed the stairs to the top.

"I haven't done this in years," she said.

"Me either."

They had to wait a few minutes for their turn. Laurie talked to the girl in front of them, and Jake gazed out over the lake and town. Lights blazed in the Lake Placid Club windows to the right where Barney had fallen. On the left, the backsides of the shops on main street were dark. When it was their turn, Jake placed the toboggan on the flat part of the ramp and sat down. Laurie sat behind him and wrapped her arms and legs around his waist and thighs.

"Here we go," he said, and pushed the sled forward. Laurie screamed and squeezed him tight.

They dropped down the iced ramp at an incredible speed, and Jake felt his ears pop. Then they were sliding out on the clean black ice of Mirror Lake. They kept going and going, and were finally, Jake guessed, a hundred yards out when they came to a stop.

"That was something," Laurie said, as she got up. "Let's do it again."

"Try and not squeeze my guts out this time," he said.

"You loved it," she said, and hugged him, and picked him up off the ice a few inches.

"I guess you're no one to mess with," he said.

"Right." She grunted and put him down.

They rode down three more times before all the walking and cold air tired them out. On the last ride, instead of looking at the lake on the way down, Jake looked up at the clearing sky and watched the stars and clouds speed by. At the bottom of the ramp, he let out a long Yah-hoo, as they slapped onto the thick black ice.

CHAPTER 10

Jake didn't wake up until after ten o'clock. Laurie asked why he was getting up so early.

"Dad's taking me to buy some lumber," he said. "This is early?"

"I'm sleepy," she said, and rolled over.

"Laurie," he said.

"Mmmm."

"Thank you."

"You're welcome," she mumbled.

He tried to be quiet as he made coffee and got ready to go, and at eleven his father drove in the yard.

"Whose car?" his father asked, after they'd driven out of town past the ski jumps.

"Remember Laurie?"

"Yeah." He looked at Jake for a second, an eyebrow raised.

"Hers." Jake cleared his throat. "Wait till you see the snow we've been stockpiling."

His father slowed as they approached the turnoff to the bobsled run and whistled when he saw the huge mounds. "Looks like a crop of big tits," he said. "Do they need all that much?"

"I hope we get two feet the day before the Olympics," Jake said. "Those piles are for the cross-country trails."

They rode along quietly; traffic was light.

"Hand me a beer from the cooler," his father said.

Jake reached behind the back seat, rolled open the top of the cooler and handed his father a beer, then asked him to stop in Keene so he could get the Sunday paper and a cup of coffee.

In the store Jake looked through some of the Olympic paraphernalia; it took up a whole wall. T-shirts, pins, maps, hats, post cards, balsam pillows, plates, and ash trays. If he had more time he might try and sell some of his boxes in places like this and wondered what cut the store took.

In the car his father was rubbing his bald head, the beer held between his legs. He put his toque back on when Jake got in. "Wool makes me itch a little. She just washed it."

"How old were you when you lost your hair, Dad?"

His father shifted into third, and said, "About your age. Maybe a little younger. I'd just gotten out of the service and married your mother." He smiled. "That might have something to do with it. You must have noticed her nerves haven't been too good lately."

Jake removed the plastic cap from his coffee, tore a little wedge out of it and put it back on. It scalded his lips.

"What's wrong?"

"She worries too much." He took one hand from the wheel and rubbed his head. "Because you're better I'll tell you something. Both those times you stayed at the hospital I don't think your mother was far behind you. Especially this last time when she came home and said she didn't think you'd recognized her. He glanced at Jake. "Do you mind talking about this?"

"No. It's important. I'm much better."

"Good. Try and convince her. It seems that if she's not worrying about you or me, she worries about herself." He shifted around in the seat. "Maybe we both should try to show how much we appreciate her." He cleared his throat. "And love her."

"You're right, Dad. Everything's been so busy between the boxes, jobs, Terry, and now Laurie." Jake scratched at a patch of frost on the inside of his window. He hadn't spent much time with his parents, except at meals. *God, I didn't even know my own mother when she visited.* He wished he could lift the barrier against those lost days. Such confirmed blackness.

A little while later his father said, "How many girlfriends do you have?"

"I don't know. Just Laurie now." He knew he wouldn't ask about Terry but wanted to know. "Terry was too young. She is really nice, though."

"Your mother is seven years younger than me," his father said.

"I know, Dad, but I didn't think it would work out." Jake wanted to talk about something else, anything. "Chad told me Grant got a big buck last year. Over a hundred-and-eighty."

"Since the state started buying so much land the deer seem to be suffering," his father said. "They like to browse where the loggers have cut."

When they pulled into Grant's driveway, Jake, at first, didn't think anyone was home, but when he got to the door of the cement-chinked log cabin, Grant opened it, pulling up his suspenders.

"Howdy," he said.

"Hi Grant. Long time no see."

Grant cleared his throat, spat, and reached into his back pocket for a pouch of chew. "Chad was by a while back. Said you wanted some more cedar. Come on in."

Jake motioned for his father to come in, but he shook his head. Jake followed Grant in and stood by the kitchen wood stove. "Making more boxes, Jake?" Grant asked.

"Yeah. Got orders for more boxes than I got lumber."

Grant scratched his chin, and lifted one of the lids off the stove, spat inside, then added an oak slab. "When Chad was here, he said you didn't have much money, and he'd just got paid. Come with me."

Jake followed him down the cellar steps. In a back corner, beside the cider keg Grant made his hard stuff in, lay a pile of planed half-inch red cedar. "What's this? Who's this for?" Jake asked.

"Chad gave me a hundred dollars quite a while ago," Grant said, "and asked me to get it ready for you when I had time."

"But I..."

Grant stopped him. "If you don't want it, I'll keep it and give Chad back the money." He walked over to the keg and handed Jake a tin cup. "You didn't have any of this year's batch yet. Better try it."

Jake remembered the one time he'd had Grant's cider. He'd stopped with Chad, and it was all they could do to get home. Chad had told him afterwards that it was a privilege to be offered some. Grant twisted the spigot, filled his cup, and motioned for Jake to put his under.

"Chad's a good friend," Jake said.

Grant raised his cup toward the ceiling joist, and they drank. It tasted better than any champagne Jake had ever tried.

"Great stuff, Grant."

"I brought the cedar inside so it would be dry and a little warmer."

It looked like a lot for a hundred dollars. He and Barney had always bought it in fifty dollar batches. "I'd like to stay and visit," Jake said, "but Dad's waiting."

"Making syrup this year?" Grant asked.

"Plan to," Jake said. "I'll bring you over a jug."

"I've got a little bit I been saving since the last you gave me."

Jake drained his cup. That was when Barney was still alive. He patted the side of the barrel and looked at the cedar. "I don't know if I can get all this into Dad's car," he said. " He put a stack under his arm and went up the stairs carefully and saw Grant ready to lift a bunch. "I'll get them Grant."

When his father saw him with the boards, he got out and opened the back window and door of the station wagon. "Grant had these all ready," Jake said. "Chad came over and paid him and never said anything."

"Need help?" his father asked.

"Do you mind?"

His father followed him downstairs and Grant offered him a cup of cider. "It's the best, Dad."

Jake had most of the boards loaded by the time his father had finished a cup and gone upstairs with Grant to see the deer antlers.

Jake stopped to look. It was an almost perfect ten point rack, and he told Grant it was one of the nicest ones he'd ever seen, then went down cellar for another load. The cellar smelled of damp earth, red cedar, and tangy cider. Jake inhaled the pungent odors. He'd never smelled anything quite like it. Grant's worn work shoes appeared on the stairs. "Boy, it smells good down here."

"Yeah. Sometimes I get a whiff of the cedar boards upstairs. Little damp down here, though. You better start a fire and put the boards inside on stickers for a day or two."

"How long they been sawed?" his father asked.

"About a year. Planed them out a month ago. Nice not to be slogging around in two foot of snow."

Jake put the last of the boards in the car. The springs looked okay, but it was loaded. "Ready to go, Dad?"

His father came outside. "One cup of that stuff packs a wallop," he told Grant.

"It does," Grant said.

They got in the car and Grant waved from the doorway. Jake rolled down the window. "Be over with syrup, Grant. Take care of yourself." Grant nodded and spat into the snow as they drove out of the board cluttered yard.

"He's quite an old fellow," his father said.

"Wonder how old he is. Chad thinks seventy or better."

"I'd say better. He remembers my father. Been sawing lumber a good many years."

"That look like a lot to you for a hundred dollars?" Jake asked.

His father glanced into the back at the lumber. "Hard to tell," he said. "Worth more than a hundred, if it's all as good as what I saw."

"Wait till I see Chad. He hasn't got a hundred dollars to be laying out for me."

"Friends do that sometimes. He wants to see you on your feet again."

"I don't want anyone feeling sorry for me," Jake said.

"Listen to yourself," his father said. "There's a difference between feeling sorry and worrying about someone you care about."

Jake scuffed his feet back in forth in the sand on the floor. "I guess."

At his parents' house they unloaded the boards and stacked them under the benches and in a rack Barney had built along the whole length of the left wall. When they finished, Jake started a fire and straightened up the shop.

When he went inside for supper his mother was hollering at his father. "The wood stove has been smoking all day," she said. "Why do I bother to clean?"

"You probably closed the damper too tight," his father said.

"No. I didn't," she said. "It's right where you always put it."

Jake couldn't smell it. "Something bothering you?" he asked.

"I never go anywhere," she said. "Stay home and cook and clean. That's all."

"You could have gone with us. Where do you want to go?" his father asked.

"Out for a sandwich, or something."

"Just say so," his father said.

"You'd be complaining about how much it costs," she said.

"Jesus, Joany. Give it a rest."

She went into the living room, lay down on the couch, and watched television. Golf was on. Jake knew she hated golf.

"What's up now?"

"What we talked about today. She tries not to let on when you're here."

Jake went in to talk to her. "Want to eat at Kate's Diner tomorrow night?"

"No. He wouldn't go."

"I'll ask."

"No. Don't." She got up and went back to the kitchen.

Jake could smell the pork roast when she opened the oven door.

"Smells good."

His father went downstairs to look at the fire and when he came back, she told him it was time to carve the roast.

"Got some nice lumber from Grant today," Jake said.

"That's nice," she said, and stirred more flour into the gravy. She looked madder than hell.

They ate in silence, and when Jake offered to help clean up, she told him she'd rather do it herself. He looked at his father, who shrugged.

Jake heard them yelling at each other as he closed the screen door on the back porch and didn't know what to do.

In the workshop, he loaded the fire, steel-wooled the boxes, put on a coat of Butcher's wax and rubbed them till they shone. He wrapped each of them up in an old newspaper and placed them snugly in a wooden box. The smell of the new red cedar was overpowering.

Before he went home, he stepped in to say good night. It was only eight o'clock, but his mother had gone to bed, his father was asleep in a living room chair, and the house felt deserted.

CHAPTER 11

Jake sat on the couch for a long time before going to bed, listening to the wind against the aluminum sides of the trailer. Drafts pushed the candle flame around and it licked at the sides of a hole it had formed. The bad with the good: why was there always bad with the good? A good talk with Dad, then he goes home and argues with Mom. Love. Even when he was little, Jake had run outside when his parents started yelling at each other. It was worse now. Tension tired him out.

He stared through the heat waves over the stove and out the window; moonlight reflected off the dull green of his car roof. As he rested elbows on his knees and cupped his jaw in his palm, the hair of his beard tickled the edges of the moon-shaped scar. He wanted to remain alone like this for a long time.

Maybe his father was wrong. It might be winter depression, cabin fever. Why couldn't she reach out to him as he'd reached out to her so many times? Jake tried to remember any signs he might have missed and couldn't and felt selfish and guilty.

He put more wood on the fire and paced back and forth in front of the couch, listening to the new wood catch. Balance. It seemed everything balanced, and he didn't like that.

Lately, the whole thing with Terry had somehow balanced with Laurie. He'd got through that okay, at least so far. Truck driving and woodworking kept him busy and evened out the time thinking about Barney and the past. Today's good time with his father going to Grant's, and Chad's thoughtfulness, were brought into balance by his mother's problem, whatever it was.

"Damn," he said, and smacked his fist into his scarred palm, and winced. He kept reaching, trying to find something to hang on to, make sense of – to help determine what was normal, not normal. He paced and started to smash his hand into the closet door but stopped.

"Nothing is simple," he yelled, and his voice resonated against the narrow walls. "Not one thing," he whispered, and wondered why he was on the verge of tears.

He sat down at the kitchen table, tore off a paper towel from the rack behind him, and tried to calm his ragged breathing and think of ways to help his Mom. As if something magical, maybe a shadow, could blanket him and his mom, and keep them safe from whatever it was that made them feel so unstable. Vulnerable. All his questions about how people treated him, and why, rushed over him, and he knew what everyone had been thinking at the bowling alley that first night he bowled, and why Grant had been so nice today, and Jason at the store, and yes, maybe even Chad: he's been in a mental institution, be nice, he's had a rough time, he's unpredictable. Maybe it's true, he thought. They may not be far off.

The damp paper towel lay scattered in a hundred pieces on the white metal kitchen table, and he knew how his mother felt. Probably the same endless black hole opened up before her, and the longer she looked the worse it became. That's why she lashed out at anyone who tried to pull her back. They could call it depression or anything they wanted, but when you lived it, it was a black hole. Sometimes it was scary, and you tried to back away from it, half expecting another one behind you. At other times it had a smooth, warm texture that drew you in further. At its outer edges, at first, Jake remembered he saw it littered with rusted beer cans and broken bottles, and as he recovered it was bordered by green grass, a friendly place to go, but not able to stay for very long.

He sat back in his chair and tried to judge how far he was from that state, where his mother was, and how he might help. It might be very easy to go back, and as much as he hated the hospital, it represented a certain safety. No one could visit unless you allowed them to, and they didn't care if you sat and stared off in the distance for long periods of time, and more than anything else, that was what he wanted to do. No more conflicts. Yet he couldn't imagine taking his mother there or going to visit. It was hard enough to stay level without all the interference he'd been getting lately and knew most of it he caused himself.

"How much of this is fake, how much real?" he asked, as he pushed the chair out and stood next to the stove. He promised himself to be strong for his mother. He'd probably taken five years off her life, in worry over him, during the last year. Maybe this was a cause of her problems now.

He heated water and made a cup of instant hot chocolate. The picture-book Terry had given him at Christmas lay on the shelf next to the couch, and he opened it to the poem he'd marked. In the water colored painting, a tiny figure stood on the side of a sharp mountain, and Jake again read the poem next to it. After the first line, he stopped, and wondered if this was some ancient Chinese mental health book. He closed it and placed it back on the shelf and thought about that line. The word sane. Somehow, he hated that word. Sane. Insane. It was ugly, and he decided no test could determine his sanity. He'd have to reach an answer by himself.

He drank more of the hot chocolate. He could remember so many things about his mother. Taking naps with her when he was three; walks out in front of the house holding hands; hanging out laundry and helping her make those special things he liked to eat. What had he ever really done in return?

Maybe she'd come out and sit in the shop and talk while he worked on the boxes. He'd see if she wanted to go to Plattsburgh, or maybe even Burlington to shop. He put his cup in the sink and tried to decide how far in she was and think of other ways to help. How long had it been going on? It didn't seem possible she could have hidden it for long, even though she was a good actor. Then he remembered that she hadn't seemed that excited when he came home that day and told her about his new job driving truck. He'd have to ask his father more questions.

Jake climbed into bed knowing she was the source of his life, a source he would never be able to repay in full.

Sleep impossible, he sat on the couch reading many of the poems in the slim book. One helped and he read it over and over.

The breath of life moves through a deathless valley

169

Of mysterious motherhood

Which conceives and bears the universal seed,

The seeming of a world never to end,

Breath for men to draw from as they will:

And the more they take of it, the more remains.

Jake went to see her right after work the next day, and found her in bed, lying on her side, reading.

"You okay, Mom?" he asked.

"Tired," she said. "Don't worry about me."

"Can I get you something?"

"No," she said. "I have to get up and fix dinner." She sat up and pushed her graying hair back. "How was work?"

"Good. Except this is my last week. Want to go shopping in Burlington Saturday?"

"We'll see," she said. "Your father hasn't been working much lately."

"I've got a little extra from selling the boxes," he said. "We won't spend a fortune."

"I'm so tired," she said.

"I'll fix supper. What are we having?"

"Pancakes and sausage," she said.

"Rest, Mom. I'll do it."

"Thanks," she said, and lay back down. "I'll be all right."

"It's cold. Want tea or something?" he asked.

"No. Go down and fix the fire." She pulled the quilt over her and picked up the book.

Jake fixed the fire and started cooking. His father came home and asked where Joany was. Jake told him she was reading in the bedroom.

"You okay, Joany?" he called to her.

"Tired. I'll get up in a minute."

His father got a beer from the refrigerator, looked at Jake, and shook his head, then came over to the stove and twisted the cap off the bottle.

Jake rolled the sausage links around in the pan. "What happened?" he asked.

His father shrugged.

"What are you talking about?" she said, from the bedroom.

Jake and his father looked at each other, and Jake said, "Nothing. Supper will be ready soon."

She wouldn't come out to eat; said she wasn't hungry. After Jake did the dishes, he went in to see her. She told him she was tired and didn't know what all the fuss was about.

He worked in the shop till ten, cutting the new lumber into various sizes and sanding it. Maybe it was just the winter blues. He went in to say good night, but she was asleep.

For the rest of the week he drove the truck, often thinking about how much he'd miss it. The piles at the bob sled run looked like small hills. Every night when he went to his parents' house, his Mom got up to fix supper, and he did the dishes. One night his father and mother started arguing about money, and Jake left. His father was mad because she'd bought hamburger at the store instead of taking venison out of the freezer. Jake understood his father's frustration but didn't know what to do.

On Friday the superintendent handed him his last check, and Jake asked about work elsewhere. George said, "Nothing right now. People from all over the county have applications in, but I've got you on a waiting list, and we'll keep your name on our payroll until the Olympics are over in case we need a driver. Sorry. That's the best I can do."

"Thanks for everything, George. I've enjoyed working for you," Jake said, and they shook hands.

He cashed his check and bought his mom a bright blue Olympic pin at one of the shops. The town was busier than he'd ever seen it. The opening ceremonies were still over two weeks away.

He stopped to see Laurie. She was busy, and told him they were staying open till two, starting that night.

"Massage my feet later?" she said and put a beer in front of him.

Before he could answer, she'd gone to wait on someone else down the bar. A few minutes later she came back. "It's been like this all week," she said. "Where you been? I know we agreed to take it slow, but I'd like to say hello at least once in a while." She smiled and touched the back of his hand.

Jake saw some of the customers watching them in the mirror. "Mom's not feeling well," he said.

"What's wrong?" she asked.

"I'll tell you later."

"Then it's all right if I stop by after work?"

"Sure, I 'd like that."

He finished his beer, and waved goodbye when she looked at him.

Chad's log truck was at the Arena Grill, and Jake parked next to it, surprised the parking lot wasn't packed. He wanted to see Chad and thank him; he didn't feel like going to his parent's. The tension had gotten worse. Chad was standing at the pinball table. Jake ordered a beer and walked up behind him quietly. He put both hands over Chad's eyes.

"Damn you," Chad said, and kept pushing the buttons. "Cut it out. I'm about to get a free ball."

Jake took his hands away and picked up his beer off the table.

"Where the hell you been lately? All right! I got it!" He spat into the trash can next to the machine.

"I want to talk to you about something," Jake said.

"Shoot."

"I'll wait till you're finished." He watched Chad pound the ball through the spinning wheel and knock down targets. When the ball didn't quite fall into an extra-points hole, Chad jiggled the machine a little too hard, and it tilted. "Damn it to hell," he said. "That was a good one." He reached for his beer on the floor under the table and drank a quarter of it, then leaned his elbows on the table. "Want to play?"

"I want to thank you for ordering that lumber from Grant's and paying for it," Jake said.

"Oh, that's nothing"

"It's a lot to me. I picked it up Sunday. It's the best stuff we ever – I ever got."

"Did he give you any cider?" Chad asked.

"Boy, did he! Me and the old man floated home. That stuff is great."

"Grant tell you where those logs come from?" Chad asked.

"No," Jake said. "Why?"

"I cut them. Oh, maybe two years ago. They were on the edge of a swamp over near Wilmington. Biggest red cedar trees I ever saw."

"You never told me," Jake said.

"Thought I did." He wiped his mouth with the back of his hand. "I must've told Barney. He never told you?"

"No. You probably told him when he'd been drinking."

"Could be," Chad said.

"You haven't tied on a good one since you've been home, have you?"

"I did with Laurie not too long ago," Jake said. "Scotch."

"High class," Chad said. "I heard you were going out with her. Your old flame, eh?"

"I guess." Jake reached for his wallet. "I want to pay you for part of that lumber."

"No rush," Chad said. "It was pay day when I stopped at Grant's. We got to talking, and he said he'd saw that out if I wanted."

Jake handed him three twenty-dollar bills. "It's enough to keep me going for quite a while," Jake said, "I may raise my prices because of it."

"Sock it to them. Tourists are thicker than fleas on a dog's ass these days."

"I'm done moving snow," Jake said. "Unemployed as of today."

"I might be soon. Hear what they're doing to anyone with a vehicle that has over four wheels?"

"No." Jake lifted his eyebrows. "Now what?"

"They've set up parking spots in Keene, Wilmington and Saranac Lake. No unnecessary trucks in or out during the Olympics. Read it in the paper yesterday."

"How are you going to get to work?"

"I don't know," Chad said. "My pick-up is shot, and the old lady needs the car to go to work almost every day. She's trying to get rides. My log truck isn't much, but I don't trust it in a parking lot for a month."

"The bastards. "Take my car. I won't need it unless I find a job."

"No," Chad said.

"Don't give me that," Jake said. "Use it."

"We'll see if Janet gets a ride. This is one of those times being a two man show is a pain in the butt."

"Where you working?" Jake asked.

"That lot we cruised last fall. Be there two, maybe three months. Good cutting. For my sake I hope it doesn't snow."

Jake bought Chad another beer and they played pinball. Mostly local people were at the bar. Jake guessed it hadn't been discovered by the tourists.

"This machine's got more noises than a whore during full moon," Chad said.

Jake laughed. "You do all right. How's the bartender?"

After Chad beat him by a hundred-and-fifty-thousand points, Jake asked him if he wanted to play partners in a game of pool.

"Sure," Chad said, and dug in his pocket for quarters.

"I've got it."

There was a set ahead of them. Jake marked up one of his quarters with blue chalk.

"Down boy, down," Jake said. Amy was wearing tight jeans and a tie dyed tank top.

Chad shook his head. "Ain't that something?"

"I'd say something to look at, but to stay the hell away from."

"Boy, oh boy, oh boy," Chad whistled under his breath.

Jake said, "If she wears that during the Olympics there will be more action in here than at the Arena."

"You got that right."

She came back down the bar, and said, "Hi Jake. Long time no see."

"Hi Amy."

"Bud?"

"Yeah."

"Good luck, stud," Jake said. "C'mon. Our quarters are almost up.

The other game ended, and Jake racked the balls. "You shoot first," he said, when the guy didn't make anything on the break.

Chad missed an easy shot.

"C'mon, Chad."

He reached into his mouth, pulled out the wad of tobacco and spat into the basket.

The guy ran four balls before he missed, and Jake looked over the table. If he played it right, he could run the table. He put the three in the side and stopped the cue ball to line up with the seven, which he put in the upper corner. The two and the six were on the edge of a pocket behind each other. Both balls went in with one shot. He stopped to chalk up.

Chad said, "The one in the corner. Don't scratch."

Jake put the one in the corner and left himself a tight rail shot for the eight. As Jake lined up the shot, Chad said, "Don't miss."

The cue ball hit the bank and the eight at the same time and the eight dropped into the corner pocket. Chad shook his hand. "Good shooting partner," he said.

Nobody had quarters on the table, and the guys they'd beat didn't want to play again. Jake didn't feel like working in the shed, or going to his parents', or going back to see Laurie. Maybe it would be a good night to tie one on, he thought, and finished the rest of his beer.

"Give me that," Chad said. "I'm buying."

While they waited for for a refill the guys from Chad's bowling team came in.

A little later they left to go bowling, and Jake sat on a bar stool, and twisted back and forth on the swivel seat, chewing a swizzle stick. He started thinking about his mother and remembered all she'd done to help him and wished his father would try harder to understand both their problems. He stared at the bubbles in his beer as they detached themselves and came to the top. He looked up. Amy was standing there. "Are you sad?" she asked, and leaned towards him across the bar.

"Ah, no." He smelled her musky perfume and took another swallow of beer.

"You look sad," she said.

"Maybe I was for a minute. Not any more."

"Do you want to talk?" she asked.

"I guess not. Thanks." As she walked away, he forgot about what she wore. Jake thought she must be lonely and feeling like a slab of meat like Laurie said she did sometimes. Jake stared into his beer again. Like I felt at the bowling alley: shunned – people thinking about one aspect of me. He wanted to be accepted like old times. Jake smiled at his own pity. Not treated like a goddamn tourist – an outsider.

Jake felt kind of numb. He looked at the clock: almost ten. All the customers looked alike, and talked alike, except for one construction worker from down south whose voice sounded out of place. Jake listened to its rolling rhythm, punctuated by a twangy noise once in a while, and wondered if the local voices sounded as strange to the southerner. I'm still a hick, he thought, and damn glad of it. He thought of all the city slickers drinking martinis at the Holiday Inn and Hilton. The Olympics. We'll be known worldwide for a month be on TV, in the papers and magazines, and then it will be over. He sipped the last inch of beer in his mug.

Jake was still pondering over just what he wanted to do, or could do, or should do, half an hour later when Chad and the guys walked in. "Took all four points tonight, Jake, baby," he said, and slapped Jake so hard on the back it pushed him up against the bar.

"Good going," Jake said.

Amy brought beers for them, and Bob put quarters in the jukebox. Country music breezed out of the machine; Dolly Parton, 'the local "favorites," as everyone called her. Chad leaned over and said something to Amy that Jake couldn't hear, then Amy walked away.

"She turn you down?" Jake asked.

Chad winked. "Jake, I must be getting old. I've had so much fun trying that it doesn't matter so much she keeps saying no." He took a drink. "No. We've gotten to be pretty good friends."

"I'll be damned," Jake said. "Am I hearing right?"

"Yes," Chad said, and leaned close to Jake. "Keep your mouth quiet about it, too. It would spoil my image if people didn't think I was after her."

"I feel a little dizzy," Jake said, and closed his eyes. "Especially when I close my eyes."

"You need fresh air," Chad steered him toward the door.

CHAPTER 12

The next morning Jake's head pounded, and his stomach was raw. He took a hot shower, made coffee and toast, and swallowed three aspirin. "Dumb, dumb, dumb," he said, and remembered standing outside the bar, deciding he could drive, and Chad saying he shouldn't. Jake had said, "Fuck it," and threw the keys somewhere in the parking lot and started walking. He vaguely remembered spitting a gob on one of the new arena windows and laughing. Part way home he decided Chad might be lying, that he really was sleeping with Amy, but then he couldn't figure out why Chad would lie. Then Jake decided to walk to the graveyard, and soon after that he'd puked in the ditch next to someone's mailbox, then stumbled to the trailer.

He sipped coffee. "Damn the drinking," he said, and the sound of his voice made his head pound. He sat at the table and tried to think, and the dream he'd had came back to him. He was staring out a window in the condominium where Barney had fallen off the roof, when he heard something on the roof and looked up, and knowing if Barney ever fell, he could get out in time to catch him or at least break the fall. It felt good knowing that. Then Barney was falling, and Jake starts out the window, but one of his boots caught on the unfinished sill, and the next second, he heard the whomp and crack of Barney's body as it landed in the dirt, and his face was only inches from Barney's, and all he could think of was how much he hated any rich bastard who wanted to live in a condominium.

Jake got up and stared out the back window. He wondered if he'd had the dream before, but never remembered it. The snow behind the trailer was sprinkled with pine needles, bits of bark, and black soot from the wood stove. He kicked the couch softly with his toe. "This has got to stop," he said. What was it his grandfather used to tell him when he was a kid? "Think to stop and stop to think." Maybe that was why Gramp was so laid-back and mellow; he always thought things through. He sat down at the table again and sipped the warm coffee. "Stop and think." He thought of the new slab of granite that marked Barney's grave, and wondered what dead was.

"It's not only time to think," he said. "It's time to stop." The dead are gone and buried-- he didn't want to believe that – but he had to. And always will be, and nothing can be done and it's time to quit trying, and I don't want to, but I have to. Memory will have to do, and we had so many. Jake sat back in his chair and looked up. "I want to let go. I have to."

Laurie stopped by in the early afternoon. "Tied on a good one, huh, Jake," she said. "Chad dropped your keys off last night." She handed them to him.

"Thanks."

"You okay?" she asked.

"Hungover. What are you doing today?"

"Taking it easy," she said. "I've never worked so hard at bar tending in my life." She lay down on the couch, her hair fanned out on a pillow. "Someone said last night that the tourists are thicker than the number of snowflakes we've had this year. Strange idea, don't you think?"

"Lot of people around with money."

"That's another thing," she said. "I've never seen so many fifty and hundred-dollar bills."

"Why don't you go out with some of the customers?"

"You are trying to drive me away, aren't you?"

"Maybe. I saw the way the guys looked at Amy last night, and know the same thing goes on where you work. I don't like that much."

"We've gone over this before."

"I know," he said. "It doesn't make it any easier. I haven't been much good at commitments lately."

She stared at the door. "Last time we talked you wanted to slow down. Now it sounds like it's over. Is it?"

"I don't know." He wondered if she'd cry as he stared out the window.

"I won't let go that easy," she said, and got up, walked over, and sat down in the kitchen chair opposite him. "It was so good at first. I want to know what happened."

He spun his empty coffee cup around and around on the table's white metal surface. "I don't know," he said.

"Damn you don't! Tell me!" She grabbed the coffee cup out of his hands. He didn't look up and started scratching the scar and remembered the throb matching her heart beat.

"Okay," she said. "I'll tell you what I think. You want to know what I think?"

Go ahead."

"Look at me. You did the same thing with Terry, or something close. At first it was fun getting to know her, having someone around. But then you started to feel attached, and you started thinking about a commitment and you got scared, because something might happen. She might leave you." So, you pulled away to a place you think is safe." She paused. "That's what I think, and you're doing the same thing to me."

Jake didn't say anything for a minute and didn't know if he wanted to say anything.

"Damn you, Jake Mason. You're not perfect and neither am I. You've got your problems and I've thought about them." She touched his forearm. "There's always risk. If I'm willing, why can't you?"

"Okay," he said. "I'm jealous. It might be better for us if you got a different job, which I know you won't, and I understand that, but that's how I feel."

"I might if we were engaged," she said and gripped his hands.

"What?" He stood up and stared down at her. "What?" He wanted to say more but couldn't get any words out.

She stared up at him. "You underestimate a good many things," she said. "Sit down." She pointed to the chair.

His knees felt like this was a good idea.

"Remember the conversation we had a little while back, about the other men I've gone out with since we were in high school, and how I felt the same about all of them. Well, not long after that conversation I made a commitment to you and commitments don't just fly off when you want them to."

"But I still don't know why."

"Jesus, Jake, you're thick. I just told you. I'd rather take a chance on someone who is sincere and tries to figure things out than on someone who has gobs of money and is selfish." She paused. "All I'm asking is that if you want to be serious, don't run away from me. Am I getting through to you at all?"

Stop and think, Jake remembered. He gazed into her eyes, and knew he'd never seen her look so serious, or so beautiful. "I don't know. Jesus, Laurie. Engaged. Are you proposing?"

"No. I'm asking you out for lunch." She laughed. "Jake, you're letting your life go by and I think you know it won't bring back Barney." She took his hand. "If you value friendship so much you'd give up a year of your life for it, why can't you give the love you've lost to someone else?

"I don't know."

"Aren't you ever going to have a close friend again in your life?" she asked. "Is that what you've decided?"

"I'm scared, Laurie," he said. "I might lose my mind forever if it happened again."

"You're the one that has to decide," she said, and let go of his hand. She got up and turned on the gas under the tea kettle.

His hand felt warm and damp, and he rubbed it on his cheek, and said softly, "Marriage."

She leaned on the stove and said, "You are old enough."

"I can't support a wife," he said.

"Does that mean you're thinking about it," she said. "It's not an open and shut case?"

"I want to be okay, and not fight myself all the time." He rested his head on his hand. "But still--"

"Don't say why," she interrupted. "It doesn't matter. We could take all day and you wouldn't get it through your thick head. Let's leave it at this. You think about it, and I'll look for another job. In the meantime, I don't really want any coffee. Let's take a nap."

By the time he put a log on the fire she was in bed, waiting.

Jake woke up cold and alone. He pulled the covers up to his chin, and held them with both his hands, the silky edge of the wool blanket cool on his nose. She's the one that's nuts. He was about as ready to get married as he was to move to New York City. No way. He couldn't believe it. Laurie was right. Barney would never come back, and he'd never want me to give up friendship with others because of him. Maybe Laurie would understand his fears if he told her about the lost time.

He dozed off, and when he woke it was dusk, and even colder than before. The fire was almost out; only a few dusty embers showed when he stirred it with the poker. After throwing on some kindling and dry oak, he washed his face and stared in the mirror. "Some husband you'd make," he said, and stuck out his tongue. "Crazy."

His hangover was gone, and he felt bad about throwing the keys. If Chad was at the Arena he'd stop and have a Coke. Maybe he was wrong about Chad cheating on Janet. He couldn't remember parts of their conversation. "Goddamn booze is almost as bad as being crazy," he said.

The sky had clouded up and he smelled the distinct odor of snow in the air. It started before he reached the lights of the big, white Arena. Large flakes caught in the flags of the Olympic countries, and surprisingly he couldn't help feeling a little patriotic as he walked underneath them. Everything coated with white and the pure white building and flags choked him up. He stopped, leaned against a bench, and stared down the line of aluminum poles. The Russian flag caught his eye – the yellow sickle seemingly out of place surrounded by snowflakes and bright lights. As his father said, "People can bitch all they want about this country, but there's no better place to live." Jake agreed, but had a good many reasons to bitch, he felt.

The town seemed unusually quiet for a Saturday night a little more than two weeks away from the Olympics. He walked a little farther, and saw his car sitting in the parking lot where he'd left it. Chad's pickup wasn't there, and Jake was almost relieved; he didn't know that he should say anything to Chad.

On the way to his parents' house, he hoped his mother was better. Maybe she'd let him take her and Dad to dinner at Howard Johnson's. Probably not. He shut off the car and listened to the motor tick. The snow had started to accumulate on his parents' roof and lawn. Bathtub Mary looked cold and alone.

"Please be a little better today, Mom," he said, before opening the kitchen door.

"Want to go out for dinner? I'm buying," he said.

In the living room his father raised both hands, palms up. Jake walked into the bedroom. "Come on Mom?"

"I guess not tonight," she said.

"What's the matter?" he asked.

"Tired, I guess," she said.

"I think it's more than that," he said, and opened the lid of her jewelry box on the dresser. "Isn't it?"

"I don't know," she said. "I'm tired all the time, but I can't sleep."

"Are you worried about something?"

"No," she said. "My house is dirty."

"What needs to be done?" he asked.

"I'll feel better next week," she said. "Why don't you go to McDonald's' and bring home supper."

"All right. What do you want?"

"A chocolate milkshake."

"Nothing else?"

"That's enough. I'll fix some toast later."

He asked his father what he wanted, then went out to the shed and started a fire before going to get dinner.

When he got back, she wouldn't even come out for her milk shake. He poured some in a glass and brought it in to her. "You can't stay in here forever," he said.

"My back hurts a little," she said. "Arthritis, probably."

He and his father ate in the living room and watched basketball. "What do you think is wrong?" Jake asked.

"I don't know," his father said. "She likes to worry, I think."

"If it gets much worse, we should do something," Jake said. "I asked her if she wanted to see the doctor. She said no."

Jake took a bite of cheeseburger and ate some fries. "Has she been in bed all day?" he asked.

"She did a load of laundry this morning. That's about it. She doesn't want to be alone either. I'd planned on ice fishing today with Uncle Dewey but decided not to."

"I'd have come over."

"You be around tomorrow?" his father asked.

"Yeah," Jake said.

"I'll go then."

They finished eating and Jake went out to the workshop. He worked till almost midnight, cutting, joining, and sanding. He wanted to sell as many boxes as he could during the Olympics. Something told him that, in life, as in every box he made, there was imperfection, and he had to get used to it. The problem was, which ones to live with and which ones to try and fix? Lately he didn't know what was up – what was good for him – or his mother, and he wanted to find out, and a small part of him deep inside felt closer to solution than ever before.

Patience. He'd never known it very much, except when working with wood. Every box was made up of a number of measurements and angles. They all had to be correct or none of the pieces would fit together. And that took time.

All this occurred to him as he was waiting for the irons to heat up in the stove. He'd already measured and marked where the red-hot iron had to be placed on the lids of three boxes. As he flipped the iron over, and pushed it deeper into the coals, he wondered how accurate it was, or how much sense it made, to transfer what he did building boxes to life. Life sure as hell was more complicated than a box, but a box it was at times.

The heat from the stove was intense as he leaned close to see the color of the steel. He pulled on a thick leather glove, then tapped ashes off the

Olympic insignia on the sides of the stove, and carefully placed the red-hot steel on the marks he'd put on the lid and smelled the hot cedar burn.

"One thousand one, one thousand two." He counted to six and pressed the still-hot steel into another lid and counted again. Before he could do the third one, he had to reheat the iron in the stove.

He pushed a ball of steel wool into the blackened wood. When they'd first started making them, Barney had insisted they remove all the burnt wood, but Jake had been leaving some lately because he liked the effect, and Jason, at the store, liked them that way, too. One day he'd poked Jake in the side and said, "It's aesthetics, Jake, and you never know with tourists."

Now, remembering that, Jake wondered if aesthetic was the right word. Taste seemed more like it. He'd always thought aesthetics meant something more about life in general, not how you chose one red cedar box over another. Maybe we're all tourists. Didn't it say something to that effect in the Bible?

He burned-in the other box and tossed the steel outside to cool. It popped and sizzled on the snow. Across the road, in the street light's glow, he could see the snow had changed to smaller flakes and was coming down harder. He smiled. All that snow hauled for nothing. Now there was something that had to do with aesthetics.

He closed up the shop, and started to go in and say goodnight, but all the lights were off. Halfway home he remembered he'd left the car at his parents. It didn't matter; it felt good to walk in the snow.

At home he read some more of the Lao-Tzu book, and wished he knew how to pronounce the name. He tried it several ways, until he found a combination that sounded right.

He liked the tiny human figures drawn against the steep mountains and after he'd read a few of the numbered poems, leaned back against the couch, then closed his eyes. He remembered stumbling through the woods near the cemetery, tears clouding his sight, and it was as if he could watch himself banging a shoulder into a birch tree, stubbing his toe on a root, and now he knew that what had happened was something necessary, and hard, and he was glad that it was over. And now all these expectations with Laurie.

CHAPTER 13

His father stopped by at eight the next morning while Jake sat at the table drinking his first cup of coffee. "I told your mother you'd be over in a little while," his father said. "She was up and down all night."

"Okay. Did you guys have a fight?"

"I guess so. I'm not getting much sleep, either."

After he left, Jake dressed, and walked over in three new inches of powdery snow. She was at the kitchen table drinking coffee.

He touched her shoulder.

"Your father is mad at me. He doesn't know what it's like."

"Let's you and I do something today," he said.

"What?" she asked.

"You get dressed and we'll go to the mall in Plattsburgh. We'll have a good time."

"I don't know if I can," she said.

"Oh, c'mon, Mom. All you have to do is get dressed and hop in the car."

She didn't say anything for a minute. She seemed so sad and upset, and Jake wished he knew what caused it, and thought seriously that she might end up in the hospital, and he reached for her hand.

"Please Mom, maybe it will do some good to get out of the house. Try."

"All right," she said. "I'll get dressed in a minute. Will you sweep the floor? Your father says the house is a mess."

"He's just worried," Jake said.

Jake swept the floor and did up the dishes while she got ready.

"Is it cold out?" she asked from the bedroom.

"Not bad," Jake said. He went out, warmed up the car, and wiped snow off the windows. When she got in the car, she said, "Please go in and make sure the fire's all right and the stove is off."

When he came back, she wanted to know if the water was off in the sink. He told her everything was okay, and not to worry, today was a good day for a drive, and she could watch the people at the mall, as she said she liked to do when she got tired of shopping.

"I don't have much money," she said.

"Don't worry," Jake said. "I've got plenty."

He headed out of town, toward Whiteface Mountain. "Lots of people around," she said, perking up a little.

"The Olympics aren't far off," Jake said. "I'm buying you a ticket to see the pair's figure skating. No arguing."

"The paper said over sixty dollars."

"You'll probably never get another chance," Jake said.

"You don't have that kind of money, and your rent's due this week."

He braked for a sharp corner that twisted along the Ausable River. "I'll go with you."

"You're not spending sixty dollars on me. Besides," she said, "you told me you were going to a hockey game if the Americans do anything."

"Laurie said she'd pay for that," Jake said, and stopped, and wished he could take it back. He still hadn't told her.

"Laurie?" she said. "The Laurie you went out with in high school? What happened to Terry? She's a nice girl."

"I know, Mom, but her parents didn't like the difference in age between us. She's going to college next year, too."

"I still like her," she said.

"I do, too," he said.

She stared at the frozen river, and he knew she didn't like it, but at least he'd gotten a rise out of her. They passed Whiteface Mountain; the upper parking lots full of charter buses. "Look at all the people on the mountain," she said. "Think of the money they're making."

He shifted into second and went around a car turning into the ski area. The people gave the old car a funny look, and he flipped them the bird.

"That's not nice," she said.

"The hell with them," he said. "They don't care about the people who have lived and died here all their lives. To them this is all a big amusement park." He shifted into third, and the old car rolled up and down the frost heaves like a boat.

They rode through Upper Jay and headed for Keeseville. "You're feeling a little better, aren't you?" he asked.

"I guess I am," she said, and was quiet for a minute. "I don't want to be tired all the time and worry your father." She twisted a tissue in her hands. "I don't want to worry you, either. You've been doing so well. I pray for you."

"I'll be fine," Jake said. "I'd hate to see you go to the hospital."

"Oh, I'd never go there," she said.

"Don't say that. No one ever knows for sure."

"Didn't all those other people make it worse?" she asked.

"They needed help."

"But some of them looked and acted so sick when I visited you."

"They were, and probably some of them are still there," Jake said. "Actually, they helped me see how bad it can get."

"Don't ever send me."

"Don't give up. Keep busy."

By the time they reached the mall she seemed better. He didn't like going into the stores, waiting around in the ladies' department. "Where first?" he asked.

"K Mart, then Fay's. Maybe they'll have a sale on beer for your father." He parked and they walked into the department store.

"What are you looking for?" he asked.

"Maybe a pair of blue jeans, or a sweatshirt." He followed her to the women's wear section, and leaned on a carousel of sweaters, while she looked for her size. "These are nice," she said, and held up a pair of jeans for him to see.

"Try 'em on," he said.

She looked at the price tag. "Twelve dollars," she said. "Not too bad."

While she was in the fitting room, he watched all the shoppers. A woman walked by speaking French so fast at her kid he wondered how anyone could understand it. The smell of hot dogs and sauerkraut from the lunch counter made him hungry; maybe she'd eat something too. She came out with the new pants on and turned around in front of a mirror. "How do they look?" she asked. "I wonder how much they'll shrink."

"Nice," he said. "A little baggy, but probably just right after you wash them."

"I don't know," she said. "They're a little too loose in the front." She tapped her stomach.

"It's up to you," he said.

"I guess not. Maybe Penney's will have something. I like to shop there better."

"Want a hot dog?" he asked.

"I'll have a Pepsi."

"Meet me at the lunch counter when you're through."

"Okay. Be there in a minute."

He ordered two hot dogs with sauerkraut, and two Pepsi's. A girl standing in the cosmetics section had hair almost the same color as Laurie's. Marriage. She was serious, and they hadn't been going out for much more than two months. How could she be serious? The hot dog girl said, "Here you are," and he knew from her tone of voice she'd said it at least once before.

"Sorry. Daydreaming," he said, and paid her.

He put the food and drinks down on the table, and his mom walked over. "Didn't you think they were too baggy?" she asked.

"If you say so."

After he finished his hot dogs they went to Penney's. She didn't find anything she wanted. At Fay's she bought his father a case of cheap beer, and Jake kept the slip to give to the clerk at the service door when he drove around later. They went to Montgomery Wards, and he looked at tools; he needed a new chisel but decided these were too expensive for the quality. He almost bought an Exacto blade kit, but remembered the rent was due. He put the wooden box containing the Exacto knives back on the shelf and went to look for his mother, wondering how much Laurie made a week. He found his mom in the housewares section flipping through a pile of bath mats. "I could use one of these," she said.

"Get it," Jake said.

"On sale," she said. "The black one is nice."

"Can't go wrong for three bucks." He helped her slide it out from under the others.

"I'll take it," she said. "It's good to be out."

On the way home she dozed off. He glanced at her often and thought she had more grey hair than he remembered – some of them no doubt from him. All his life it seemed she placed him before herself.

When they were home, she put things away, and turned on the television. He asked if she wanted him to do anything. No. She said she'd lie on the couch and read for a while and thanked him for taking her to Plattsburgh. He leaned against the door jamb. "Mom. I don't tell you often enough, but I love you."

"I love you, too."

"I don't want you to get sick like I did."

"I won't but I wish summer was here."

"Me, too," he said. "I'm going out to the shop for a while. Just call if you want me."

"I will."

He started a fire, put pieces of cedar in a clamp, and remembered he'd left the glue in the cellar so it wouldn't freeze.

She was asleep on the couch. On the way to the shed, he brushed snow off the top of the upended bathtub. The paint had held up well. Mary's eyes stared straight ahead, and he wondered why the sculptor didn't make her look up. He reached in and touched her shoulder.

"Please help Mom. There will never be another one like you."

He went into the shed and closed the door. It was nice and warm. The box he was building didn't have one knot in it: a first. Grant must have sorted through or put this lumber aside. When they made syrup, he decided to take Grant one of the first quarts. Jake got a charge when Grant said, "Poop," about something he felt strongly about. He'd crinkle up his nose and look off to the side or at the ground and say, "Oh, poop."

He heard a car in the driveway. Too early for his father to be home. He opened the door. It was a blue Mercury station wagon. Then he recognized George, the man he'd worked for driving truck.

"Oh, there you are, Jake. Come over here. I want to tell you something." Jake walked to the car.

"How are you?" Jake asked. They shook hands. George rested his other hand on the car roof. He wore a trench coat, and Jake could see he had on a sweater and tie underneath. "I just came from a meeting with the Olympic committee," George said. "They're hiring ten janitors to work part-time at the arena. Pay's not bad: four dollars an hour. You still interested?"

"Yeah." Jake paused. "Sure."

George winked. "And you'll probably get in to all the events free when you're working. Go to the offices on the second floor near the new rink tomorrow morning at eight o'clock. They've got your name." He started to get back in the car. "Call me if there's any problem."

"Thanks a lot, George. Hey! Are they going to use all the snow we hauled in?"

"None of it, if we get six more inches of snow." He laughed. "I'm telling you, but don't say I said so. If these Olympics come off without a major foul up, it'll be a miracle."

Jake walked back to the shed. Now I'll be cleaning up after the bozos, he thought. Probably scrubbing toilets, mopping floors, and picking papers up from between the seats in the Arena. He squirted a bead of glue on the edge of a board and went on to the next one. Maybe he could get free tickets for his mother to see the skating. He'd get to see the hockey.

Not long after George left, his father drove in the driveway and walked over to the shed. "How was she?" he asked.

"Better, I think," Jake said. "We went shopping in Plattsburgh."

"Good. I tried to get her to go last week and she wouldn't."

"Guess what, Dad? George stopped by a little while ago and offered me a job working at the Arena."

"Good. That's very good," his father said. "Maybe these Olympics aren't so bad after all."

"Dad, I'll be a janitor."

"Don't knock it. You have to pay the rent." His father came over to the bench and rubbed one of the boards in the clamp. "Nice stuff," he said. "Well, I guess I'll go in and see how she is."

"Dad." His father turned at the door, his hand on the knob. "Try not to argue with her.

She's on edge. I'd hate to see her go where I've been."

His father stared at the dirt floor. It's awfully hard to live with her these days." He opened the door. "She'll be happy to hear about the job."

Jake finished gluing the box and tightened the clamps. He didn't much like the idea of cleaning up after other people.

His mom called him in for supper and wanted to know about the job. He told her he'd try and get her in to some of the skating events, and she said she didn't want to do anything illegal.

"Don't worry. I won't if it's a problem."

After dinner he started to walk home, and halfway remembered that he'd left the car at his parents' house again and went back. When he started it up, he thought about driving by the graveyard; he wanted to tell Barney about Laurie proposing, and about his new job as janitor.

He knew it was wrong, but he drove that way, and when he reached the graveyard he stopped. He rolled down the window, and it occurred to him that the feelings he had for Barney were somehow similar to the ones his mother had for him, and he for her. A willingness to sacrifice. He stared out the window at the grave, and thought, we've got to have a little more distance, Barney old friend. Everything we did is past, and I can't change it. I can and will always share the memories with myself. His breath clouded the cold night air. He shifted into first gear and let the clutch out, maneuvering the car into a three-point turn, stopping where the lights shone on Barney's gravestone. Shadows cast through the ornate steel rod fence. Let me go on living and preserve only the best of what we had, he asked, then looked up.

By seven thirty the next morning, he was showered and dressed in clean jeans and a new red flannel shirt his mother had given him for Christmas. He sat on the couch, drank his second cup of coffee, and absorbed the radiant heat from the stove. Another change today, he thought. And it may, or may not be good, but I've got to make the best of it, and I better go talk to Laurie if they don't want me to start right away.

He walked into the new Arena's main entrance to the left of the ticket windows, and scrubbed his feet on the thick rubber mat, then walked up the stairs. Probably be sweeping and mopping these fucking things soon, he thought. It was five to eight, and two people he didn't know stood next to a door with Personnel written on it in bright orange lettering. He wandered over and looked through the small windows on the doors that led to the rink. Inside, the Zamboni chugged around the ice, spraying out a fine spray of water that froze almost instantly; that would be the job to have. He turned around at the sound of keys. A well-dressed women let the others into the office. Jake followed her in, and she handed each of them a form and a Bic pen. "Mr. Jacobs will be here shortly," she said, and shuffled papers on her desk.

Jake sat on one of the plush-upholstered orange chairs and wondered who had chosen white and orange, and why. He filled out the form and put George's name down as the person who referred him, walked to the desk, and handed the form back to the lady. The phone rang, and she held one finger up while she answered it. "Yes, Mr. Jacobs," she said. "There are people waiting." Then, "Yes sir, I will."

"Go through that door," she said, and nodded toward one behind her and off to the right. The other two still hadn't finished their forms.

Mr. Jacobs, a big balding man – what hair he had left shaved off crew-cut style – stood up and squeezed Jake's hand hard. The secretary had followed him in noiselessly on the plush orange carpet. She handed him Jake's form.

"Ah, Mr. Mason," he said.

"Jake's fine, sir."

"Yes, yes," he said, and cleared his throat. "We don't rely on formality much around here." He sat down behind his large laminated teak wood desk and raised one finger in the air. "Except when it comes to running the facility and keeping it spic and span. We're on parade before the world, you know."

"Yes, sir," Jake said.

"Yes, yes. I see," Mr. Jacobs mumbled to himself, reading the job application. "George mentioned your name to me yesterday. You didn't waste any time getting here, did you? That's good."

Jake could tell he was a red, white, and blue person, and said, trying not to grin, "I'd like to help out in some way during the Olympics."

"Yes, let me ask you a few questions. Have you ever worked in a janitorial position before?"

"When I was sixteen, I worked in a gas station and the boss was strict about keeping it clean," Jake said. "He won awards from Shell Oil Company for cleanliness."

"Yes, yes. I see. That's good," Mr. Jacobs said. "Are your hours flexible?"

"Definitely," Jake said. "Any time is fine."

"Good. I'll need you to clean up after events and empty trash cans, and other things during the bigger ones. Your schedule may vary from day to day. You sure that won't be a problem?" Mr. Jacobs asked.

"Yes, sir."

"Okay. Glad to have you aboard. I'll call in one of the head janitors to show you your business. You'll be on afternoons, starting tomorrow at one."

"I'll be here."

"And remember," Mr. Jacobs said. "In sixteen days, the world's attention will focus on us. You are a part of our American responsibility to put our best foot forward. Be polite at all times. If you have any problems stop by the office."

Jake shook his hand and turned towards the door; it was all he could do not to laugh out loud. He wondered if his mop would be red, white, and blue, in the American tradition.

A short, heavy guy, Steve, showed him around the complex. First, he took Jake to a small maintenance office in the basement, gave him a ring of keys and showed him one which fit all the service closets, another for the paper towel and toilet dispensers, and two separate keys, one for each of the skating rinks. "Where do you live, Jake?" Steve asked.

"Just over the hill behind this place."

"That's good," he said. "It doesn't look it now, but we may get a blizzard, and some of the help might not get here."

They went to the old Arena built for the nineteen thirty-two Olympic Games. The hockey team was practicing, and Jake watched as a player took a slap shot from the blue line, and the goalie fielded it with his glove. My own key to the hockey rinks, Jake thought. Holy shit.

"Here are the service closets for trash," Steve said, and pointed to a double set of doors next to where a Zamboni was parked. "I can show you everything else tomorrow when you're getting paid for it."

"Thanks, Steve."

"No problem. Do your work and stay out of sight when you're not busy. You'll be fine."

"See you tomorrow."

"Yes," Steve said, and waved. Jake walked off down the corridor and heard a player slam into the boards on the rink.

It was only nine o'clock as Jake took a drive around Mirror Lake, past the Lake Placid Club. He saw David, a guy he graduated from high school with, out sweeping steps. David motioned for him to stop.

"What's up, Jake?" he asked in his high-pitched voice.

Jake rolled down the window. "Not much. Busy?"

"Oh yeah," Dave said. "Full up every night into March. I want to ask you something. You got a pair of snowshoes?"

"No," Jake said. Behind Dave he could see part of the building Barney had fallen from. "Listen. You may not believe this, but it's true." He swished the broom back and forth beside Jake's car. "A lot of South Americans been staying here. They buy all this equipment, and then don't have room to take it back on the plane, so they just leave it in the rooms. The maids have been giving me some of it to shut up, because they take most of it home themselves."

"What kind of snowshoes?" Jake asked.

"I don't know. They're pretty big." He held his hand a little above his waist.

"How much?" Jake asked.

"Oughta be worth thirty bucks," David said.

"I'll give you twenty, maybe," Jake said.

"Okay," David said. "Give me a ride around back." He got in the car and directed Jake around to a storage shed.

The snowshoes leaned against a wall. "What do you think?" David asked, and picked one up.

They were modified bear paws, only used a few times, worth at least seventy or eighty bucks. "They look all right," Jake said, and handed David a twenty. "What else you got?"

"Two pair of cross-country skis," he said.

Jake wanted a new pair of downhill boots. He'd been using the same ones since he was twelve, but he didn't see any.

"They leave any ski boots behind?" Jake asked.

"Couple pair. Here." David lifted the lid of a storage chest and lifted out a pair of white Raiche boots.

"What size?" Jake asked.

"Says ten," David said.

"How much?" Jake asked.

"What do they cost new?" David asked.

"How would I know, Dave? I don't go near those fancy stores." Jake rubbed the nicks on the inside where they'd been banged together, and said, "They're banged up a little."

"Fifteen dollars," David said. "I don't know who else would want them."

"All I have is ten," Jake said.

"Okay." David handed him the boots and stuffed the ten in his pocket. "I don't like this stuff laying around. The owners would have a fit."

"Screw them, David. It's part of your pay. Let me know if you get more."

David took the snowshoes and Jake the boots. They threw everything on the floor in the front of

Jake's car. Jake glanced over at the five story condo and wondered how long Barney had been in the air, why he'd fallen, what he'd thought. All the old unanswerable questions.

"You okay?"

"Sure."

Jake drove away and rubbed the scar on his palm against the wheel. "No more feeling sorry for yourself," he said, and glanced into the mirror. His beard had grown in fully in four months. "Go see Laurie," he said and scratched the dimple on his chin. Maybe she'd want to ski Whiteface. He could afford it now.

CHAPTER 14

Jake drove into Laurie's driveway and shut off the engine. She lived on the southern fringes of Hollywood in a pretty nice house. Not long before she rented it, they'd torn off the shingle siding and replaced it with light pink aluminum siding. But Jake wouldn't pay two hundred dollars a month rent for it, even if he could afford it. The landlord was a partner in the local contracting outfit that had hired Barney to roof the condominiums.

Jake went in through the back door. Laurie wasn't up yet, and he ran the water till it was ice cold, then filled the percolator.

She came out of the bedroom, scratching her head.

"Hi, sleepy head. Time to get up," Jake said.

"What are you doing here so early?" She wrapped her arms around him and rested her head on his back. Jake smelled the sleep she'd been in and turned around and kissed her warm forehead.

"I been up, got a job, and bought some new ski boots," Jake said.

"What job?" She stared into his eyes. "Where did you get a job?"

"At the world famous, or soon to be, Olympic Arena."

"What doing?" she asked.

He kicked a piece of dirt on the flagstone design linoleum. "Janitor," he said.

"Is that good?" she asked. "Is it something you want to do?"

The percolator started to gurgle.

"Why not?" Jake said. "It's only for a month or so."

She pulled out a chair, sat at the kitchen table, and rested her chin on the heels of her hands. He turned to the cupboard and took down cups, a shiny blue one for him, and one that said, "I'm ready for love" for her. He filled them and put hers on the table, making sure the words faced her.

"You shouldn't sit like that," he said. "It, ah, well, you know."

She glanced down the front of her robe but didn't close it. "How did you get the job?" she asked.

"George, the guy I drove truck for, stopped at the house yesterday," Jake said. "He put in a good word for me."

"Full time?"

"Anytime they need me. Though I think mostly during and after the events."

"You might be working nights like me," she said, and reached for his hand and covered it with hers. "It's nice to have you here when I wake up. I'm sorry if our talk the other day upset you. But we understand each other better. Don't you think?"

"It was unexpected, is all."

Jake stared at her back as she bent to put the milk away, her hair lying in tangles on her shoulders, and wondered if he'd ever get over the excitement her strawberry blonde hair started in him and hoped not.

She sat down again and pushed her hair back behind her ears. "I've been thinking about what I said the other day." She lifted her coffee cup a couple of inches and set it down again. "All the best things of the two years we spent together in high school seem to have picked up where they left off."

She stood up, walked over, and stared out the window over the sink. "You show me how you feel when we make love and afterwards, when you're asleep, you hold me until we're all wrapped up together." She turned to face him. "It's when you let your past problems in that you can't do anything about interfere..." She took a step toward him. "That's when I wonder what will happen to us."

Jake drank the rest of his coffee and got up to pour another cup. He said, "It's not that I don't want a strong relationship."

She walked over to where he leaned on the counter.

"I know I'm pushing," she said, "but I want us to be honest. Lately, every time we talk, I'm afraid when you leave, I'll never see you again. I'm scared, too, because I'm not sure what's best for me."

"It's been a tough year-and-a-half," he said, and wrapped his arms around her.

"I know," she said, and looked up. "I told you I'd try and understand, and I am looking for a new job, but so far, they're all temporary, and only for the Olympics. I heard about one yesterday, though, at the travel agency in town. A woman is leaving because she's pregnant, and not coming back. I'll call today."

"Do it now," he said. "I'm sorry, but I don't like guys leering at you all the time."

"I'll call now and see if I can at least put in an application today." While she went into the other room to call, Jake sat at the table, and flipped the end of a spoon around, trying to place it, each time it dropped, on a white square of the red and white tablecloth. After a few minutes she came back. "They said I could speak to someone about the job at eleven o'clock. I gotta shower and get ready. It's ten now."

"Get going," he said. "I'll drive you over."

While she was taking a shower, he went into the bathroom, pulled the curtain back and stuck his head into the steam. She jumped. "Jesus, Jake, you scared me."

"Nice and soapy," he said.

"If I wasn't in a hurry..."

"Want to go skiing after your interview?"

"Sure," she said. "I'll buy."

"No way." He put the curtain back. "I'm a janitor with a good position. I can afford it." He started whistling the national anthem, and she laughed.

"Get out of here. I have to hurry, and it takes forever to dry my hair." A few minutes later he heard the whir of a blow dryer.

While she was at the travel agency, he walked to the shop where he sold his boxes. Jason was bent over the books, while one of his workers helped customers.

Jason looked up. "Damn, these accounts are a pain. I hope your business never gets big enough that you have to do it. You been busy?"

"Some," Jake said. "How's inventory?"

"I'll check."

Jake followed him to the back of the store, and while Amos checked Jake looked out the windows facing Mirror Lake. Amos came back and stood next to him.

"Get busy, Jake. There's only a large one and two of the smaller ones in stock. Come on up front. I'll write you a check."

A middle-aged couple were looking inside one of his small boxes, and Jake heard the lady say, "Wouldn't mother love one of these?"

"What would she do with it?" the man asked.

"Put something in it," she said. "Maybe buttons or thread, or anything."

"All right," he said. "Price is reasonable."

Jake walked to the counter. Amos was tallying on the adding machine.

"Not bad. Comes to eighty-five dollars."

"Hand it over. I'm skiing this afternoon, and with the rates at Whiteface that should just about cover it!"

"You should be working in your shop," Amos said.

"I will tonight. I'll have three or four ready by tomorrow, or Wednesday at the latest."

"Good," Amos said. "I can't sell what I don't have."

Jake went to the bank a few doors down and cashed the check. When he came out, he could see Laurie, still quite a ways up the street, looking sharp in a gray-plaid wool skirt and matching jacket. She came up and linked her arm through his.

"Want to go window shopping, good looking?"

"How'd it go?" he asked, and pushed her hair back, and blew in her ear.

"Don't." She shivered. "That gives me goose bumps. It went fine. I even had an interview. It's mostly answering the phone, talking to people that come in, and stuffing envelopes."

"Well, did you get the job?" Jake asked.

"I don't know," she said. "The guy said he had two more people to interview, and I should call on Wednesday."

"Good. Let's go skiing."

They walked down the street to the car, and Jake opened the door for her. "My, this is a first," she said.

While she changed, he went home and loaded the fire, changed into long johns and jeans, and put his skis and poles in the car.

On the way to Whiteface he told Laurie that his mother wasn't doing so well. She sat in the middle and kept moving around, her pink nylon jumpsuit hissing. She wanted to know if there was anything she could do. He told her no, at least not now.

The parking lots at Whiteface were pretty full for a weekday and Jake parked in the upper lot. He hoped his bindings didn't have to be changed to fit the new boots and tried them on behind the car. The boots fit perfectly and slipped into the bindings like the old ones.

They picked up their skis and poles and walked down a steep path to the lodge. Jake stumbled along in the new boots; he always left his shoes in the car because he didn't want to pay fifty cents for a locker. He paid for their lift tickets, then they herring-boned up the short hill to the chairlift. The music of Simon and Garfunkel pulsed out of speakers on the lodge.

"Music to ski by," he said. "Nice." He noticed that the lift attendants gave her a good going over. She said hello and smiled. Her hair fanned out on her back and in front of her shoulders from under a powder blue toque. On the way up the mountain she asked if he thought he'd like his new job.

"I'll get into events for nothing," he said. "The hockey is what I really want to see."

"Not me," she said. "I want to see figure skating."

"Mom does, too," Jake said. "Maybe you can go one day with her."

"I'd like that," Laurie said.

Jake watched the people on the slopes beneath them. Every once in a while, an excellent skier moved gracefully around, past slower ones, and Jake watched their style. He'd skied only once last year, but before then, every year, and often, ever since his father had pulled him around on a ski-doo when he was six. In the last few years the cost had decreased the number of times he went; fifteen dollars for an afternoon got expensive.

Laurie touched his arm.

"What?" he said.

"Nothing. I just like to touch you."

The speakers, placed in trees and atop service buildings all over the mountain, sounded crystal clear. "They must have one hell of an amp to power all the speakers," he said. They were playing one of Chicago's old tunes, Color My World.

"I like it," she said.

"Ready to lift the bar?"

"She took her skis off the rest, and he flipped the bar over their heads. "Where first?" he asked.

"Off to the left," she said. "I need an easy run to loosen up."

"All right," he said. "You lead."

She pushed off down the mountain and Jake followed her gradual turns for a few minutes, but it was too distracting; he caught an edge, and almost fell. He skied by her on a steep section in several inches of powder on the tree line. He never had liked the man-made snow, but there wasn't much else this year. He stopped at a little rise and waited for her to catch up.

"Nice skiing, hot shot," she said. "Your buns don't look so bad twisting down the slope."

"That's why I went by you," he said, and tapped her butt with his ski pole.

"I feel good," she said. "The mountains are so clear today. Last time I skied you could barely see them."

"The ride on the upper chair ought to be beautiful," Jake said.

"Race you to the bottom," she said, and pushed off.

He waited a second and followed her, taking the middle of the hill where it was icy, and faster. He barely missed a little kid who had fallen behind a mogul, and after that, he slowed up and let Laurie win.

The ride on the second chair went to the top of the mountain, several high peaks close on the left starkly clear, and directly behind the chair, to the east, Lake Champlain and the mountains of Vermont. The sky, a bright blue, contained not one single cloud. Jake put his arm around Laurie's shoulders and stared at the rock ledges below. "Don't you have second thoughts about us?"

"Of course," she said.

Jake moved his arm from her shoulders and gripped his ski poles tightly. "That's what I thought," he said. "You were just kidding about marriage the other day."

"Listen to me, Jake. It's what I said the other day. It's not good for either of us if you keep feeling sorry for yourself about things you cannot change." She tapped his knee. "Can't you see why?"

"Yes."

"At the top of the mountain she said, "Let's ski Excelsior."

"Sounds good," Jake said.

They took off down the trail, and for fleeting seconds, Jake felt the old rhythm coming back as he turned, and the skis matched his weight and muscle direction. Laurie fell when they'd gone almost halfway, and Jake couldn't resist it: he fanned snow all over her, then helped her up and kissed her cold cheeks.

"Nice guy," she said. "Remember pay backs are a bitch. You go first."

They skied for the rest of the afternoon without a break. Jake's knees shook on the last two runs and he fell once, but Laurie didn't spin snow all over him.

"See how nice I am?" she said. "Actually, I'm so tired if I tried, I might have run right over the top of you."

"Out of shape, Laurie?"

"Usually I ski for an hour and then go in and have some brandy," she said.

"Why didn't you say so?"

"It doesn't matter," she said.

"Good," he said. "I'm still recovering from Friday night."

"Giving it up?" she said.

"Cutting down."

They skied the rest of the way down, and Jake knew he'd be sore for his first day on the job, although he had an idea that the work wouldn't be that strenuous.

Walking back to the car without his skis was like walking on air, and it was even better when he threw the boots in the trunk and put on his moccasins. Laurie said, "I'll fix steak and french fries for dinner."

"If I buy."

"Okay." She rested her head on his shoulder and fell asleep two miles after they left Whiteface. Jake tilted the rear view mirror so he could see her face. The sun caused her freckles to stand out, and she was a little wind-burned. He thought, you don't get it together soon and you'll lose her. Then he considered what might change – had to change, and a million other things -- if he was married. He didn't like the sound of that word: too permanent. And she'd probably want kids; they hadn't even talked about that. Time, he thought. I need more time.

She woke up when he drove into the grocery store parking lot. "Stay here," he said. "I'll be right back." He touched her cheek with the back of his hand.

He bought a T-bone steak, beer, Idaho potatoes, rolls, butter, and a cantaloupe. She was brushing her hair when he slid in behind the wheel.

"Hi, gorgeous," he said.

"I was tired," she said.

He sat in the tub while she fixed dinner, and the water eased the tightness in his aching legs.

As he was about to get out, Laurie came in with a pot in her hand. "Look what I brought," she said, and dumped the full pot of cold water on his head. "Payback!" she said and trotted out of the bathroom. Jake yelled, and submerged his chest and head under the warm water. Dammit, that water was cold.

After dinner they made love. "See how well we fit together," she said, and squeezed him.

"Might be because we're almost the same height," Jake said.

"Oh, I don't think so," she said. "We were the same height in high school, and we never fit quite like this. I remember when we were both virgins, and our first time.'

"I guess you're right," he said, as she rubbed his back in long up-and-down strokes. "You're putting me to sleep," he said.

"Me, too," she said.

They woke up at five o'clock and made love until light came in through the curtains.

"Oh, Jake," she said. "Has it ever been so good?"

"No." He touched the curve of her breast with a finger tip. "I didn't think I could ever feel the way I do." He rested his weight on one elbow, his face above hers. "The memories though. Laurie, I can't help it."

"Tell me what you're thinking about."

"Barney and I were kind of – I guess you'd call it soul mates – the way people meant that back in the sixties. We knew each other's moods without talking, and usually knew what the other was thinking about." He turned her chin and looked into her eyes. "It was a link from the time we were kids. When the link broke, it almost broke me."

"I wish it were me," she said. "I want to be that close."

Jake hugged her and locked his fingers together. "Can't you understand. We are becoming closer, like soul mates. Sometimes, I think, when one of us was hurting, Barney and I would have liked to have held each other like this, and once, while I was in the hospital, I dreamed I held his dead body in my arms. Believe me, I thought about that for a while."

She massaged his shoulder blades and said, "Give us a chance, Jake. A good, long, honest chance." Then she put her face into his neck and cried.

"What's the matter?" he asked. He gripped her by the shoulders and stared into her eyes.

She sniffed a couple of times, and said, "Sometimes I sense how much you lost."

They didn't say anything more, and Laurie went to the kitchen, made coffee, and brought him a cup. "Big day for you today," she said. "New job." She set the cup on the nightstand.

"Huh?" He hadn't heard a word that she'd said.

"Are you all right?" she asked.

"Fine. Thinking." He was close to something, and it bothered him because he couldn't tell if it was good or bad. He sipped his coffee and watched Laurie rummaging around in her dresser. She took off her robe and put on a pair of sky-blue underwear and matching bra.

"Having fun?" she asked.

"Maybe I'll come over more often," Jake said. "That color is the same as yesterday's sky."

"I thought so too," she said. "I wish I didn't have to wait until tomorrow to hear about that job."

"I better get going," Jake said.

"Why?" she asked. "It's not even eight o'clock."

"The store needs more boxes," he said. "I have three almost finished in the shop."

"Can I help?"

"Not really."

She'd hung his pants up to dry on a chair over the heater, and they were nice and warm as he pulled them on. Surprisingly, he wasn't that sore. She kissed him goodbye and said she might go back to bed for a while and read.

"I have a good book for you," Jake said.

"What's it called?" she asked.

"I can't even pronounce the name. I'll bring it over. It's Chinese philosophy. Good stuff."

"Call me." she said. "Maybe I'll have a new job, too."

"I will, and good luck. I'll be thinking good thoughts." He stopped at the door in the kitchen, his hand on the door knob. "I love you," he said softly, barely moving his lips, then turned and walked back into the bedroom.

CHAPTER 15

When Jake went to work at the Arena, he parked in the new lot that hung over the edge of Hollywood, and as he walked across the frozen pavement, he remembered his anger when he'd first seen this place after coming home from the hospital in October. Jake counted up the weeks. Today was the twenty-ninth of January – in fifteen days the opening ceremony would take place and three weeks later it would all be over. He'd be lucky to work a month. Then what?

He found Steve in his windowless office and he showed Jake how to punch his time card. "Make sure you always punch in, or else it's a pain in the ass to prove you were here. Let's go get you some uniforms." They walked down the long basement hallway to the heating room, and in a small office off to the side a woman took his picture for an identification badge, and he filled out a form. Steve signed it, too. The woman asked him his shirt and pant size and handed him three pairs of navy-blue pants and matching shirts. He changed when they got back to Steve's office and threw his clothes into a grocery bag. "What now?" he asked.

"When you're working, which, once the Olympics begin, will be during and after events, you'll have to keep the bathrooms near whichever arena your working in picked up and mopped, if there's time, and the garbage cans emptied. You won't be the only one working." Steve scratched his belly.

"What else?" Jake said.

"Make sure you look busy. Mr. Jacobs is a real prick about our image in public."

"Can't I watch a little if the work is done?" Jake asked.

"If you're careful," Steve said. "Look for different places to hide, behind supports, next to booths, and act like you're trying to find someone."

"Any chance the job will last after the Olympics?" Jake asked.

"Not much, but they might keep on a few."

"What am I doing today?" Jake asked.

"There was an event in the main arena last night," Steve said. "You can start sweeping the aisles between the rows on the north side, it's on the right as you walk in." He handed Jake a broom, dust pan, and five-gallon pail. "Sweep up after every aisle, so people don't track it all over."

The inside of the arena looked like an abstract flag: red seats, white walls, and blue support posts – everything else pale white ice – the center of attention. Ten or fifteen figure skaters practiced their figure routines, and Jake kept busy pushing the broom; after a while he could watch the skaters out of the corner of one eye, and sweep, too. The cement had a glossy finish and the broom slid easily over its surface. After an hour he'd finished one small section, and when he started up the steps, he saw Mr. Jacobs leaning against a pillar.

"Hello," Jake said, and dumped the five-gallon pail into a waste can.

"How's the first day on the job?"

"Fine, sir."

"Good. Keep busy. Don't get distracted," Mr. Jacobs said. "I checked a little into your recent history."

Jake looked up. "Oh, really."

"Standard procedure. I think I understand why the police had to take you off the roof of that condo. We'll keep it between us."

"Right," Jake said and wanted to run from the arena, and out of town for good. Mr. Jacobs walked away, and Jake flipped him the bird, then turned around to make sure no one saw him. A few minutes later Steve came by and told him it was time for coffee break. Jake followed him to the cafeteria and met other part-time and full-time cleaners. Everybody talked about the Olympics, and the impact they were having on the town. A few complained that they couldn't get passes to drive in from other towns; they weren't special enough and would have to ride the buses like everyone else. Jake asked what they were doing about people who lived in town. He'd damn well better be able to drive around his own town. Somebody said he'd have to check with the security office at the town hall. When they finished their break, Steve handed him his badge, and told him to always wear it when he was working.

The arena was empty when Jake started sweeping again, and the strangeness of all that space was eerie. The noise of fans hummed, and nothing else. Would his past always follow, always have an impact on his future? "Fuck this," he whispered, and stared upwards past the blue steel girders. I need something, he thought, then continued to push the broom back and forth, back and forth, not stopping to sweep up at the end of every row. Once, he looked at the ice and said, "Laurie must know about the cops taking me off that roof. I have so much to tell her," he mumbled. "How much can I?"

After half an hour, two pairs of skaters came onto the ice. Jake recognized Tai Babilonia and Randy Gardner, the American world champion doubles team from last year. A coach talked to them for a minute, while the other pair skated arm in arm.

Randy and Tai took a pose on the other end of the ice from where Jake stood, and the coach started the music. Jake leaned on the broom as they skated down the ice toward him, and Randy lifted her off the ice, holding her above his head with one hand. Jake thought she smiled at him, but it was probably for the non-existent crowd. While Jake bent down to sweep up the plastic cups, dirt, and candy wrappers, he watched them do synchronized split jumps, and a few seconds later, Randy picked her up off the ice, and threw her away from him into a spin. Jake wanted to clap. The coach looked stern as they went through the routine, and the other pair rested center ice against the boards.

The music changed, and they flowed gracefully along the ice. To slower music, he picked her up and turned around twice, before setting her down effortlessly. Jake couldn't believe his luck and looked around to see if anyone saw he hadn't been working. After the music ended, they talked to the coach and the other pair did their routine. Jake didn't think they were very good, and now he worked to catch up. Steve came in and said he was doing a good job. "We'll do something else as soon as you're finished with this section," Steve said.

In the last hour of work, Steve showed him how the bathrooms were to be cleaned and took him on another tour. "Know where you are?" he asked.

"Not really."

"In a tunnel under the road," Steve said. "It goes to the speed-skating rink. I want you to know the building in case you have to fill in for somebody else. Some other day I'll show you the locker rooms."

After work Jake stopped at his parents' house. His mother was making macaroni and cheese.

"Smells good,," he said. "How are you feeling?"

"Better, I think. Still tired," she said. "Work today?"

"I'm an official Olympic janitor." He took off his coat. "Can't you tell?"

She came over and stared at his photo. "Not a very good picture," she said.

"Guess who I saw today, Mom?" Jake asked. "Tai and Randy, and they are fantastic!"

"I mopped the floor," she said. "You didn't even notice."

"Looks nice," he said. "I'm going to start a fire in the shop. Don't really feel like it, but I'm behind."

"Dinner won't be long," she said. "Your father should be here any time."

He emptied ashes out of the stove before starting a fire and dumped them on his father's garden spot. Even though he didn't feel like working, the shop smelled so good he didn't mind. He picked up all the tools and put them in their places and raked the dirt floor. He'd wanted to spit on Jacobs when he brought that up about the roof and the cops. Jake still believed he'd had to go up there and see, look over the edge, gauge the distance, and try to imagine how awful that fall must have been. The cops didn't understand he wasn't up there to jump.

By the time he'd finished rubbing Tung oil into the boxes he'd meant to finish that morning, his mother called him in for supper. He stood by the window thinking about Laurie and Barney. A commitment to Laurie. As much as he was unsure, something told him he was becoming more committed every day. He didn't much like that word – most of the people at the hospital had been committed involuntarily.

"Are you coming?" his mother shouted.

"Be right there." he said, and threw another log on the fire, and the twisting action of his toes when he turned reminded him of the grace he'd seen on the ice.

His father still hadn't come home by the time they finished eating. "Did you and Dad have a fight?" Jake asked.

"He yelled at me this morning and I yelled back," she said.

"What about?" he asked.

"He's worried about money again," she said. "I took money from what my mother left us to pay the bills."

"What good does arguing do?" Jake said.

"He's probably at some bar," she said.

"He'll be all right."

"His supper will be cold, and I don't care."

"Mom."

"I don't. It's not my fault. I'm cooped up in the house all the time and never go anyplace."

"You went to Plattsburgh."

"First time since New Year's," she said. "I'm lucky if I go to the store twice a week, and that's usually at night."

Jake helped with the few dishes and watched the news with her. He heard the door open and went out to the kitchen.

"Am I in the dog house?" his father asked.

"Probably," Jake said. "Want macaroni and cheese?"

"She knows I hate the stuff," he said. "I'm fine."

"Joany, I'm home," he said, and sat down to take off his boots. "Working in the shop tonight, Jake?"

"Yes."

"I stopped at the bowling alley for a few beers," his father said. "That Laurie is sure a cute one."

"That she is," Jake said.

"She didn't recognize me at first. Said it wasn't that I'd gotten older, but handsomer."

"She might be your daughter-in-law someday," Jake said.

That brought his mother off the couch and into the kitchen. "What are you talking about?"

"Laurie," Jake said.

"Nobody tells me anything," she said.

"You're still upset about Terry."

"She's a nice girl," his mother said.

"I never said she wasn't."

"Laurie's much prettier, Joany," his father said.

"Thanks, Dad. You're a big help."

"Men. You're all the same," she said, and went back to the living room.

"I'm going out to work," Jake said.

His father smiled. "Laurie said to say hello, and she'd see you tomorrow."

He cleaned a space on the work bench and sat staring at the newly finished boxes. Pressure rose in his chest. Did there always, would there always be this pressure? It seemed so true that if it wasn't one thing, it was another, and on and on. Some of the reasons he missed Barney were the childish things they did, even when adults, like building a fish shanty or fixing up this wood shop. He didn't see much difference between that and how they'd dammed up the ditches in the spring or built tree houses – many of which were still used by kids in the neighborhood. They'd somehow kept all of it with them, long after they'd supposedly grown up. Barney had never quite lost his cowlick and the dimple on Jake's chin was still there underneath the beard. Jake kicked his heels back and forth.

Time. We carry the times of our childhood always. And want them back. He sat for a long time moving his legs back and forth in the warm, pungent air, and knew that he could only preserve the memories of those times; he'd never have another friend like Barney. He knew that Laurie and he were making memories like they had before when they went together in high school, and that he'd look back on them in the years to come. It might never be the same, but that didn't mean that it couldn't be as good. Love is friendship. Must be friendship.

He jumped down from the bench, his back was cold; he turned and rested his elbows on the bench and stared out the window. He dug deep within himself, and pulled up all the love he had for Barney, in a way he never had before, and tried to understand it, and knew too many things had happened to understand a friendship that had lasted for over twenty years. Maybe this was exactly what he needed to know: it could never be understood, but had to be accepted for what it had come to mean, and would always mean, even if it lasted for the next thousand years.

An odd sense of peace came over him, and his recent problems seemed nothing. The death of a friend is a monstrous loss, he thought, and stared out the frosted, dirty window, into the sparkling night.

"He loved me, too," he whispered and picked up the tools Barney had once held in his hands and went back to work.

Drops of wetness fell on the red and white silky wood, and Jake knew they were cleansing, that he was better, better able to go on, and he wasn't exactly sure why, but he knew the peace of death's acceptance could only come from within himself, and that he'd caught a glimpse of it. For a moment, he stopped work, rubbed his sleeve across his eyes, and looked up. "Oh God," he said. "Give me the patience to go on," and thought, maybe, instead of talking to myself like the therapist suggested I should talk to God.

He rubbed the dust from his hands, and carefully glued the joints of a box together, then turned the clamps tight, making sure he wiped away any excess glue that squeezed out of the cracks.

The next day Laurie stopped by the trailer at noon. She hugged him, picked him up for a second, and laughed. "Would you like to book a reservation for Borneo, sir?"

"Good deal!" Jake said. "When do you start?"

"They want me to come in this afternoon for a few hours. I can't stay. Going to tell my boss at the bowling alley and see how soon he can find someone else. Aren't you excited?"

"You bet." He held her head against his shoulder.

"Is something wrong?" She moved in front of him and stared into his eyes.

"I want this to work, Laurie. I really do," Jake said.

"I'm glad. You don't know."

"Will you stay with me tonight?'

"I'd love to," she said, "but let's go to my house. We'll celebrate. I'll try to close up early."

Jake bought champagne and Oreo's after work. When they first went out in high school, she loved to dunk the cookies in champagne. By the time she came home it was almost one o'clock.

"Boy. Am I glad that's over," she said. "My boss found someone that can start tomorrow. Let's take a bath and drink champagne in the tub."

He pulled the cellophane-wrapped Oreo's out of the paper bag. She clapped her hands. "And Oreo's! You remembered." She kissed him. "I'll start the tub."

"How was the travel agency?" he asked.

"Busy. They're trying to coordinate all these people and reservations from other countries. It's a madhouse!"

Jake tried to ignore the reference. He popped the plastic cork out of the bottle and poured some into juice glasses.

"Aren't you tired?" he asked.

"What?" She came into the kitchen wearing only a black bra and panties. "I didn't hear what you said."

"Laurie, the curtains are open," Jake said.

"It's almost one-thirty," she said, and pulled down the shades.

"Aren't you tired?"

"You know what kept me going all day?" she said. "What you said about wanting us to work. I feel the energy of a thousand," she said, and flexed her arm muscles.

"Here." He handed her a glass. "To making memories, and love," he said, knowing tonight was not the time to tell her those other things.

"And you." She clinked her glass against his. "And me. Oh, shit!" She ran into the bathroom and shut the water off.

"Almost ran over," she called. "Come and look." The bathtub had two feet of bubbles on top. "What did you put in there?" he asked.

"Good old Mister Bubble." She tested the water and took off her bra and panties. Jake went back to the kitchen for the champagne. "Bring the Oreo's, too," she said. She was up to her neck in water when he returned, her hair bright against the suds.

"Here you are," Jake said, and handed her a glass of champagne.

"Hand me a towel, please."

She wiped off her hands, and he gave her an Oreo, which she dipped into the champagne for a long time, and then she put the wet half into her mouth and sucked the champagne out of it. She smiled. "Mmmm, another," she said.

"I've seen shit-eating grins before," he said. "But none to match yours." He handed her another cookie and took off his clothes.

"How's the janitorial work going?" she asked.

"I'm really cleaning up," he said. "Make room." He eased himself into the hot water, and stretched his legs out beside her waist, reached for a towel and put it behind his back as a cushion against the cold metal faucets. Jake saw crumbs float up from the bottom of her glass and began to massage her knees in slow circles. "That's great," she said, and closed her eyes, and rested her head against the back wall. A sheen of moisture covered her face, and her skin, blushed the color of a summer sunset, glowed in the florescent light.

"Work was fine," he said.

She opened her eyes. "What did you do?"

He told her about cleaning the aisles between the seats and seeing Tai and Randy skate.

"I've seen them on TV," she said. "They're the best. I hope they win the gold."

"You look tired, kiddo," he said. When the water began to cool, he hoisted himself out of the tub and helped her up.

"I am tired," she said, as he dried her back. "Relaxed and sleepy."

"Good," he said. "We'll get all wrapped up together and sleep."

"Jake," she said, and turned around. "I love you." She kissed him lightly on the lips, and after a minute hugged her warm, damp body against his. He picked her up and carried her in to the bed.

CHAPTER 16

The next week and a half went by quickly; Jake couldn't make boxes fast enough and Laurie worked ten and twelve-hour days. She told him it was like trying to run an ant farm; everyone wanted a place to stay, and wanted her to tell them where. Money was no object: all the hotels charged a hundred dollars or more per room.

On the tenth of February, three days before the opening ceremony, Laurie came to the trailer and told him her landlord had offered her five hundred dollars if she'd move out for the three weeks of the Olympics. "I'll give you half if I can stay at your place," she said, and hugged him.

"How much do you think he'll be getting?"

"Probably fifteen hundred," she said.

"Ask him for seven."

"All right." She went home, called, then came back. She told Jake the landlord hemmed and hawed, but finally agreed.

"Good deal," Jake said. "Maybe we'll take a vacation after it's all over."

"Yay! We're cashing in on the Olympics."

"I wonder if Mom and Dad could rent their house?"

"Would they?" she asked.

"I'll ask," Jake said.

After a quick dinner with Laurie at Ruth's Diner, Jake drove to his parents' house to work on boxes. He was sick of making the same things over and over, and for a change last week he'd taken his mom to Plattsburgh again and bought a different assortment of brass- and chrome-plated hinges and catches. She had been awfully down, quiet and sad.

After an hour's work he went inside to ask his parents about renting their house. His mom wasn't too keen on having strangers rummaging through her stuff, but his dad said they could use the money – they could stay at his brother's in Essex.

"Joany," he said. "We'll pack up the personal stuff and lock it in the attic. Think of the thousand dollars."

His mother finally agreed, and Jake called Laurie to tell her.

"You coming over tonight?" she asked.

"I think I'll stay in the trailer. I'm hardly ever there."

"Okay," she said. "Call me tomorrow. Maybe I'll have found something for your folks.'

The snow squeaked under the heels of his boots as he walked to the shop. It was ten below. He threw scraps of red cedar into the fire and before long started to sweat. As he took off his coat and hung it on the back of the door, he realized how tired and run down he was.

Neither he nor Laurie had been getting much sleep; more and more of the Olympic teams arrived and they both worked longer hours. He never would have believed it, but there were twenty-four locker rooms in the arena, and he knew most of them intimately. He didn't like cleaning up sweat and tracked-in dirt. Mr. Jacobs said to him the other day, "The Olympics demand our complete attention down to the last grain of road sand dragged in."

Jake had wanted to kick one of his knees.

He heard the squeak of snow, and his father came in. "How goes it, Jake?" he asked, and clapped his leather mittened hands over the stove.

"Okay."

"I called Uncle Dewey and he said it's fine if we stay with him. He wants me to build him some kitchen cabinets."

Jake moved three boxes, ready for a coat of Tung oil, off to the side, and whisk broomed the bench.

"That money would be a godsend.."

"Let's hope it works out," Jake said, as he pushed the scraps and sawdust, mixed with dirt, into a dust pan. "This town is so crowded you can hardly walk down the street."

"They shut the main street off on Tuesday, right?" his father asked and smoothed out a section of the dirt with the sole of his work shoe.

"Yes," Jake said. "Did you get a sticker yet?'

"On Friday. They gave me a sheet with it, asking that no unnecessary driving be done. They're expecting thousands and thousands will be bussed in every day, a lady told me." Jake sprayed the air with oil. He sneezed. "Damn dust."

"How's the arena?" his father asked.

"Busy. How do you think Mom's feeling?"

"You know," his father said. "She's up and down. I never know what to expect when I wake up in the morning." He lifted the stove lid and spit inside. "I don't like head doctors, but do you think she should see one? You'd know better than me."

"Maybe. She'd have to go to Elizabethtown. That's where the county mental health place is, and they'd want to see her every week for a while."

"I don't know," his father said, and stared past Jake out into the night.

"Why?"

"People always know when things happen," his father said. "You were always worried about what people thought."

"It's a sickness, Dad. Like having an ulcer or something." He knew damn well his father didn't want all Hollywood saying the Mason family was nuts, and he didn't really blame him.

Talking about it brought back all he'd gone through when he came home last fall.

"Most people don't think of it that way," his father said.

"I'll talk to Mom about it tomorrow," Jake said. "She always thought my doctor did a good job."

"You never went back like they told you."

"I had enough of people telling me what I needed to do. I'm fine."

"But still," his father said.

"Don't worry, Dad. The doctor's a nice guy. He knows I'd come for help if I needed it."

His father turned to go.

"The boxes look real nice," he said. "Good night."

Jake leaned on the bench after he left and tried to remember the last time his father had given him a compliment. His mother's illness was a strain his father had to live with, and Jake wished he could do more to help, but knew that mental illness had to run its course. Depression was like going down a mountain at night. You were never really sure of the trail, and you wanted to get the hell out, all the while hoping that someone would come along and take you by the hand. Jake stared out the window, part reflection, part snow and trees. No one had taken his. The blackness he'd looked into had fully taken him over his second time in the hospital, and he'd lost those four days. But afterwards, his mind had leveled out, and he'd begun a slow, spiraling, wobbly ascent, up to, at first, the edges of the awful blackness, and finally, farther and farther into the open. He didn't like remembering; he'd shut it off, shuffled those thoughts to the back of his mind. His mother hadn't given up hope on him, and made it clear she never would. She'd seen him at his worst.

He started to work on a box. Tiny steel particles rose into the light as he smoothed the Olympic circles on the lid. When he came out of the time he'd lost, he was sitting in front of the television. A Yogi Bear cartoon was playing, and when Jake smiled, an attendant walked over and asked him if he felt any better. Jake had shaken his head, trying to unclog the blanket that still smothered it, and stared at the attendant, realized where he was, and lowered his eyes. He heard the ranger bitching out Yogi for stealing food, and from that day on he improved. They sent him to group therapy and let him go outside.

The hospital was huge. Buildings of different vintages, sizes and shapes, hooked together or standing alone, on a piece of land, Jake estimated, at least fifty acres, bordering the St. Lawrence River. All the buildings had tremendously high ceilings, and Jake hated the ant like affect they produced. He estimated the ceilings reached to the height of three stories, nearly as high as the Lake Placid Club condos. An attendant told Jake the buildings were designed when it was believed the lofty heights allowed the mind's bad thoughts to disperse more easily.

He wiped off the Olympic insignia and uncovered the third box. He couldn't stop remembering it. The first time he went into the hospital the drugs they gave him made him crave candy all the time, but he didn't have much money, so he chewed sticks of Juicy Fruit till they lost their sweetness.

One day he'd gone to the little store for the patients and bought gum and a candy bar, then took a different way back to his building. He walked by a small stone building with bars on the window, and a guy about his own age stuck his hand out. "Help me," he said. "Help me. I don't belong here. I didn't do anything!"

Jake walked closer, scared and nervous. "Why are you in there? Are you alone?" Jake asked.

"I've been here for a week." His hands gripped the bars and he pounded his head against them. Jake turned away. "Tell them to let me out!" Jake felt sick and bent over with pain in his stomach. He spat out his gum and walked away. What kind of place is this, that they'd lock someone up in a stone building with bars?

He went back to the ward, and wanted to tell someone about it, but didn't dare; he wanted out, and from that day on did everything they told him to, thinking he could heal himself at home. Wrong. Again.

He sprayed more oil in the air, threw wood on the fire, put a quick coat on the boxes, and walked home to the trailer. The fresh air tasted free, and he thanked God he didn't have to spend the rest of his life in that hospital. He'd asked a nurse one day how long some of the people had been there. She told him some had come when they were in grade school and would never leave. "Poor lost souls," she said. "All we can do is try and make them some sort of home here." After that he was more understanding when someone ran away if he said hello or swore and called him names.

The snow scrunched under his boots and he whipped his arms back and forth to keep warm. The brush and small trees, snarled like barbed wire, reminded him he was free, but also, that he could have stayed there forever if his mind hadn't somehow righted itself.

At the trailer Jake unzipped his coat and held his hands to the fire, wondering again how much of this Laurie needed to know.

The next morning, he called Laurie from his parents' house. She told him that none of the

Realtor's and all the rentals were handled by them – were renting apartments in Hollywood. "Of course, they don't call it Hollywood," she said. "They wait until you tell them where the house is, and then say they can't rent all they have now and take your name."

"Shit," Jake said.

"I have a few more places to call," she said.

"How come they rented yours?" he asked.

"I guess it's not in Hollywood."

Jake knew she was right but wanted to throw the phone against the wall. "I'll tell my parents," he said.

"Coming over tonight?" she asked.

"I don't know what time I'll get out of work, and the boxes need finishing."

"Is something wrong?'

"Tired, I guess," Jake said.

"Can I come over? Maybe I can help."

"I'll call," he said.

"Bye, hon," she said.

He talked to his mom about seeing his doctor in Elizabethtown.

"Well, maybe," she said. "It's a long way to go."

"Dad or I can take you. It would only be once a week, at most."

She twisted her hands together and gripped them tight. "I don't know," she said, and stared out the window over the kitchen sink. "The front porch is a mess. That's your father's job, but he yells at me for it. Some of your things are out there, too. I'm too tired to think," she said. "And I can't even enjoy reading anymore." She tapped the edge of her wedding ring on the sink.

"Can it hurt to see the doctor one time?"

Her head fell forward, and he thought she might cry.

She said, "I'm afraid of how your father will feel about it."

"He wants you to get better," Jake said. "We talked about it last night."

"What did he say?" She stared out the window as if waiting for it to break.

"He said it was okay if you see my doctor. He's a nice guy."

"I want it to be over."

"It takes time," Jake said. "You didn't get sick overnight, and you have to give it some time to get better."

"People will think the whole family is crazy." She came over and sat down next to him. "I'm sorry, Jake." She put her hand over his. It was cold and dry.

"I love you, Mom," Jake said, rolled his hand over, and squeezed hers.

"I know," she said. "I know you father loves me, too, but he doesn't understand."

"We'll get through this and you'll be better when spring comes. You've got to try, though."

"Okay." She squeezed.

"Good," he said. "Don't give up."

Jake called the doctor at eleven and luckily caught him between sessions. The doctor wanted to know how Jake was doing. He didn't ask why Jake hadn't come for follow-up therapy and told him he could bring his mother over the next morning at ten.

"Tomorrow at ten, Mom, and don't sit around worrying about it today. You know how much that doctor helped me."

He kicked the few inches of snow with the heels of his work boots as he walked to work.

Everything looked dirty and cheap in Hollywood. It pissed him off that the Realtor's wouldn't rent the houses, but he understood. It seemed impossible to him that he was working at the white elephant on top of the hill. Its brightness hurt his eyes as it came into view, and the sun shone brightly on the flags that fluttered in a light freezing breeze.

"I'm a hypocrite." He entered the tourist world, and thought of his mother, curled up in bed, unable to enjoy her favorite pass time, reading.

He punched in and asked Steve what he wanted him to do.

"Bathrooms," he said. "These people are hogs. We cleaned them at ten this morning, and I just walked around and they're filthy again."

Jake filled a mop bucket with steaming water and checked a cleaning cart for supplies. "You'd think they'd have a little respect, Steve. These bathrooms are in the gaze of the world. On display." Steve looked up. Jake winked, and they laughed.

For the first three hours Jake cleaned bathrooms and told people where the nearest usable one could be found. By four o'clock he felt like a jug of the blue disinfectant they used for everything: toilets, sinks, floors, walls. He stared at the back of his arm to see if it was blue.

"What next, Steve?" he asked, as he put the cart away and emptied the mop bucket. "Take a break. To hell with what the world thinks."

A second later Mr. Jacobs came around the corner rubbing his pudgy hands together. "Hello, boys," he said. "You been cleaning bathrooms, Jake?"

"Yes, sir."

"Good job. I just did a tour of the place." He spread his arms out wide. "Magnificent! I want every person that comes in here to feel like this building has just opened for their personal inspection." He brought his hands together in a loud crack. "And today it does." He turned to go and started shaking hands with people passing by in the corridor, like an ambassador, asking them how they liked Lake Placid, how long they were staying, blah, blah, blah.

Jake and Steve listened till he was out of earshot.

"That man is a bigger asshole than all outdoors."

"You got that right," Jake said, and wondered if Jacobs checked on all his employees for a black mark to use against them.

"Okay if I putz around in the arena for a while?"

"Sure," Steve said. "Take a check on the trash cans."

Jake stuffed trash bags in through his belt loop and walked to the arena.

When he inserted his key into the lock of one of the doors, several people asked if they could go in and sit down. "Sorry," he said, and closed the door in their faces. Couldn't they read? Signs on the doors read, Closed Practice Session. No Visitors.

He wandered around the top row of seats and when he was near center ice, stopped and leaned against a pillar, ready to look into a nearby garbage can if Jacobs came around. Six skaters glided and spun on the ice. A girl started the music to her program and began it in a dazzling spin. The music gathered a slow momentum, and she spun and danced down the length of ice once, then a second time leaping to touch her outspread toes.

The other skaters moved out of her way as she turned and danced, glided a split second, then did a triple toe loop at mid-ice. Jake shook his head in disbelief. She couldn't be over fifteen. He wanted to be closer, and started down the aisle, watching her, but acting like he was looking for trash between the seats.

The music slowed to a waltz, and Jake wished he knew more about classical music. Her hand and head movements interpreted the music as she glided forwards, sideways, and backwards, her legs carrying emphasis. It seemed to Jake, magic. The music picked up and Jake watched her speed down the ice, bouncing and swaying with the new rhythm. She leaped, spun, and caught the edge of a skate, but didn't fall. She glided back to center ice, spun and spun, arms over her head, then down at her sides as the music dwindled away.

Jake realized he hadn't done anything resembling work since she'd caught her skate edge and walked back up the stairs. He walked around flipping the lids of trash cans. At the further end of the arena, he peered at the smaller practice rink through wire-enforced glass. Through the tiny-shaped diamonds of wire glass, he watched skaters practice their figures. A young guy pushed off on one skate and started around one of the larger circles of a figure eight etched into the ice. When the first circle was almost complete, he turned around, and propelled himself once more to complete the figure eight, never once leaving the lines on the ice. Finishing the first figure eight, he turned to face forward again, and entered another figure eight, much smaller, inside the large one.

Jake walked back around the arena and did a tour of the building. In the old arena, hockey players from Switzerland were practicing, and from where Jake stood behind the glass boards, they looked like Vikings. Jake hoped the Americans beat them. He'd read the other day that the American team wasn't much more than a pick-up team from universities across the nation. Jake hoped they were wrong. He'd watched the Russians practice for a few minutes the week before; their faces full of a mean self-confidence as they slapped the puck back and forth and yelled in words that, to Jake, sounded primitive.

In the office Steve told him he could go home and asked if he wanted to work overtime the next day, then take Wednesday off for the opening ceremonies. "That's where everyone will be," he said. "Not much to do here."

"Sounds good," Jake said, and punched his card. "See you tomorrow."

That night at supper, he told his parents none of the Realtor's would rent in Hollywood. "It doesn't matter," his father said. "You didn't want to leave anyway, did you, Joany?"

"I guess not," she said. "It was a lot of money, though."

"Well, I've got good news," his father said. "The business manager at the Club asked me to work full time. At least for the next two months, and maybe more. So we couldn't have rented anyways."

"Good deal."

"I start eight-hour days tomorrow," his father said.

"I'll take Mom in the morning," Jake said.

"What?" he said and looked at her.

"You didn't tell him, Mom?" Jake asked.

"He got here just before you did," she said.

"You're not going into the hospital, are you?" his father asked, alarmed.

"No. "She's going to see my doctor in Elizabethtown tomorrow morning."

"Oh."

No one said anything. It was as if somebody had tented a dark wool blanket over the kitchen table.

"I hope they help," his father said. He reached out to touch her and stopped. She got up and cleared the table.

"Can you take her?"

"Sure," Jake said. "And on Wednesday, Mom and I are going to the opening ceremonies."

"Good."

She ran water for the dishes and Jake helped clean up. He touched her shoulder and told her not to worry.

The boxes, lined up neatly on the bench, glowed when he turned on the light. He steel-wooled, sprayed oil and was rubbing on the final coat when someone knocked at the door.

"Are you in there?" Laurie asked.

"Come on in," he said.

She came in and stood next to him. "Can I help?" she asked.

Jake handed her a piece of cheesecloth and she folded it into a square like the one he was using. He reached under the bench for a bag that contained a finished box that needed a coat of wax, then handed her the can of Butcher's wax. "Put on a very light coat."

"Sorry about the renting," she said.

"I figured as much," he said.

"So sorry," she said.

"It's not your fault." Jake finished the box he was working on and put it aside. "I'm taking mom to see my psychiatrist in the morning," he said.

"Is it that bad?" Laurie asked.

"No, Laurie. It's not that bad," Jake said. "She needs help Dad and I can't give her, that's all." He traced the insignia on a box. It felt a little rough and he applied another, thicker coat of wax. "The people that have misconceptions about mental illness are the ones that need help." He stopped working and stared at her. "Say something."

"I didn't mean it negatively," she said. "No one ever likes to go to any doctor for anything." She kept polishing, pushed one of her nails into a joint to remove the excess.

"Dad's afraid people will think the whole family is nuts, after what I've been through and now Mom. It sucks."

"Not everyone thinks that, and the ones who do don't matter," she said.

"You've never been on the receiving end and I hope you never are." He burnished the hinges and the front latch. "I take that back," Jake said. "You should have an idea of what it's like from going out with me. You must see the odd looks and sense the questions people have."

She started to say something, but he held up his hand.

"'He's been in a nuthouse. Why would she want to go out with him? She can do better than that and on and on. Don't you worry about it happening to me again?"

"Yes," she said. "I worry about what I'd do. Can't you see I love you and think we can get through any bad times? Everyone has bad times."

He started polishing the insignia again. The wax filled in the tiny gaps and it felt much smoother. "I'm glad you're honest. Love can blind a person. Like mine did for Barney."

She pushed her hair back. "I can't compete with that."

"You don't have to."

"Good," she said and kept polishing.

Jake knew her temper and put his hands on her shoulders, turning her to face him. Her face glowed with almost the same color as her hair and she took a couple of deep breaths.

"It's not fair for you to compare me and Barney."

"Okay. I'm sorry. It's how my mind works." He stacked the waxed boxes, towels between each one to protect the finish, and checked the ones he'd recently finished with Tung oil, then covered the bench they rested on with a piece of canvas.

"What next?" she asked.

"What else? More boxes." At the bench under the window, he pulled precut pieces off the shelf underneath. "You still want to help?"

"Sure," she said.

He handed her a sanding block made from a small piece of two-by-six and placed a cover for a large box between two quarter-inch pieces of plywood nailed to the bench.

"What's that do?" she asked.

He'd nailed them all over the top of the bench; one set for each of the different length of boards that he used. "It was Barney's idea," he said.

She began to sand, and he told her to always go with the grain, then he started on one of the side pieces. A light red-pink dust filled the air and Jake hoped it didn't get into the fresh wax or Tung oil, but he didn't have time to wait for them to completely dry. He threw more wood in the stove and opened the window an inch. Above the rasping sound of the sandpaper he said, "It's nice you're here, Laurie. It's the first time anyone has helped me."

She showed him the board. "How's this?"

He ran his fingers along the smooth surface. "Fine. Do the other side, then I'll show you how to sand the edges and the ends."

"I was thinking the other day," she said. "Maybe I talk too much."

Jake kept sanding and took a close look at the grain, blowing sawdust out of the way.

"About what?"

"I know it scared you when I talked about marriage and it petrified me that I'd messed everything up."

"It shocked me," he said and blew sawdust from a scratch, then sanded it out. "I didn't have the faintest idea." He stood up and pushed at the lower muscles in his back. "I'm scared too, sometimes."

"I respect your commitment to Barney."

"It can be a weakness, too."

"I don't know."

"What do you mean, you don't know? I've logged in almost two months at the hospital because of my inability, or whatever you want to call it, to deal with losing my best friend."

"I look at it differently," she said. "To me it's proof of the kind of person you are. That friendship meant life, and when it ended a part of your life did, too."

"You're right about that," he said.

"Show me how to do the edges," she said.

He handed her a one-inch block and told her it had to be kept perfectly flat on the edge as she drew it back and forth. "No rounded edges," he said. "I'll knock a little bit off the corners later."

Jake closed the damper on the stove and said, "Most of me died for a while."

"You've gotten better," she said.

He picked up another board and decided to tell her about the lost time. "I can't remember part of when I was in the hospital this last time."

"Maybe it was part of the healing process."

Jake listened to the crackle of the fire for a moment, then said, "Sometimes it seems like ten thousand years since Barney's been gone, but at others it seems like yesterday."

She scratched her head. "Sometimes I feel like that when I think of the time between high school and now. Painful, but probably necessary."

"I want to forgive your past. and that helps my ability to make a commitment. We both may be stigmatized in this town and because of that I wonder about us," he said, then, "Let's say goodnight to my parents, if they're still up."

His mother was bent over reaching for something in the refrigerator when they came in. She stood up. "Hi," she said. "It's been a long time since I've seen you, Laurie."

"Hi, Mrs. Mason."

"Want a piece of cake?" she asked. "Call me Joany."

Laurie looked at Jake. "I'll get it," he said.

"No, sit down," she said. "Take your coats off. It's cold out, isn't it?"

"We need more snow," Laurie said.

"Yes. Isn't it terrible for the Olympics?" She put two plates with pieces of cake on the table. "Now, what can I get you to drink? Milk, coffee or tea?" she asked.

"Milk for me," said Jake.

"Me, too, thanks," said Laurie.

Jake hadn't seen his mother so perky in weeks. Not since Terry had been around. She wanted to know all about Laurie's new job. Jake went into the living room and talked to his father for a minute. They'd woken him from a nap. "I guess there won't be much cake left," he said.

"It's real good," Jake said. "How do you think the new job will go?"

"It's work." Then, "Hi Laurie," he yelled.

"Hi, Mr. Mason."

"Laurie help you in the shop?" his father asked.

"Yeah. She did all right." Jake went back to the kitchen and finished his cake and milk, put the dishes in the sink and asked Laurie if she was ready to go.

"Sure," she said. "Six-thirty comes early. I'm glad to see you again, Mrs. ... Joany."

"Me, too," his mom said. "Come more often."

On the way home, Laurie told him what nice parents he had.

"Mom's a good actor," Jake said. "Might be good if you came to dinner some night."

"I'd like that," Laurie said. "I should have gone to your parents before this. You must worry about her."

"I do," Jake said. "Your confidence in me helps."

"Stop for a second." She wrapped her arms around him. "I'm so happy with you. Sometimes I wish we'd never broken up in high school."

"That's one thing I have learned. Going back is impossible; all you can do is keep the memories, and they fade, too."

"It doesn't hurt to wish once in a while," she said and touched her nose to his.

"You still smell like red cedar," he said.

"I wonder why."

The next day on the way to the doctor's his mother told him she didn't think she needed to go, but once it was over and she was back in the car, she told him what a nice man the doctor was and she hadn't minded talking to him at all.

He had given her a prescription for an anti-depressant, and they stopped at the Elizabethtown drug store to have it filled. It was almost impossible to get to a drug store, or anywhere else, in Lake Placid, especially since they'd closed off the main street.

When he dropped her off at home, he told her that he wouldn't be over for supper because he was working late, and she should be ready at noon tomorrow for the opening ceremonies.

At work, he cleaned the bathrooms and then was assigned to the locker rooms and didn't finish them until ten o'clock. He called Laurie from a pay phone at the arena and told her he was going home to bed. On the way out of the arena, he picked up some free literature about the Olympics. Outside, he stopped under a street light. People, he thought: all kinds of people – natives, tourists, millions watching on television. Today at the mental health clinic, he'd felt like a visitor, judging the other patients in the waiting room. At the hospital he'd been accepted. Roles and reversed roles – love and being loved. Into the salt-grimed cement Jake stared and groped for something, like trying to find a lost wallet in a dark alleyway. And he knew Laurie could help, if he'd let her, that she was his best chance.

He walked away from the arena and dropped the colorful Olympic folders to the ground, then turned and reached for one. On its front, a figure skater twirled in a blur of speed, one hand held high.

CHAPTER 17

During the night, two inches of snow fell, dusting the ground and trees with a layer of whiteness that reminded Jake of the confectionery date rolls his grandmother used to bake. He slapped the snow off the car with the back of his mitten. Pace, he thought. Pace. That pamphlet said the speed skater and biathlon skier needed to pace themselves. He needed that. Lately, the whirl of action caught him up like a beer can caught in the churning snow pushed by a snowplow down the road. A dusky blue-beige sky, close to the earth, made him want to stop everything, and go away and sort out his mother's depression, his contrary feelings about the Olympics, his relationship with Laurie, and the deeper thoughts in himself he'd glimpsed lately. He slapped the car roof, and a circle of snow blew away. "You're fine," he said, but didn't know for sure how long the juggling act could last.

He started the car, and as it warmed up, wished he hadn't shut the alarm off at nine and slept till eleven-thirty. His mother probably wondered if he was coming.

She had on her coat when he came into the kitchen.

"All ready?" he said. "The eyes of the world are on Lake Placid today."

"It's a nice day."

Jake drove the back way out of Hollywood and came down the road past John Brown's grave. In grade school a teacher took his class to see the old homestead and grave. He couldn't understand why they had to stand behind a barrier and peer into the rooms. It all seemed fake. He and Barney had gone outside and played on a huge boulder near the grave.

"Wonder what old John would think of this," Jake said.

"What?" she said.

"John Brown. The abolitionist. You know."

"Sorry," she said. "I wasn't listening."

In front of them, the Olympic torch soared fifty feet, the McIntyre range its backdrop. A security officer eyed the sticker on Jake's car, and motioned him into a parking lot adjacent to the ski jump. "Look at all the people," his mom said, and twisted the rear-view mirror to fix her hair.

"You're beautiful, Mom." For a second, he saw her as another person might; her brown hair streaked with gray, and her cheeks slightly fallen as she tapped powder on them from a plastic pink compact. "Will you be warm enough?" Jake asked. "There's a blanket in the trunk."

"I'm fine," she said.

He re-adjusted the rear view mirror, and it came off in his hand. "Damn," he said, and stared at the spot where the metal had broken.

"I'm sorry, Jake."

"It's not your fault," he said. "I'll find another one."

"Look at all the flags," she said, as they walked across the street. Many of the people around them wore mink or raccoon coats, or expensive, full-length down parkas. His mother's camel coat looked shabby, and he pulled his toque down further over his ears.

People wandered all around the big field, and an orchestra could be heard tuning up in a newly constructed amphitheater. He held his mother's arm as they stepped up the bleachers and remembered then that Terry was supposed to play.

He thought people were staring at them and knew how foolish it was to think so. Many sat with steaming cups in their hands, and he searched for a concession stand to buy his mother a cup of coffee. He sat close, as if to protect her, but she seemed oblivious to it, and stared as if trying to absorb it all.

"I love to watch people," she said.

"Lots of them here." Jake counted the number of people in an estimated twelve by twelve area of the bleachers and started multiplying across. "If they fill the bleachers, there might be twenty thousand people here," he said.

"That many!" she said.

"You don't remember the 32' Olympics, do you?" he asked.

"I was a little girl," she said. "All I remember is my mom taking me to watch Sonja Henie, and afterwards I wanted lessons, but my parents couldn't afford them."

Jake spotted a cluster of people around a concession truck. "Want coffee?" he asked.

"Okay." She reached for her pocketbook.

"I'll get it. Anything else?" He stood up.

"No."

"Excuse me, son."

Jake turned around. It was an elderly man in a black wool coat.

"I couldn't help overhearing. Would you mind getting me and my wife a cup? The bleacher steps are murder."

"Sure," Jake said. "How do you like it?"

"Black is fine," he said, and reached for his wallet.

"Pay me when I come back," Jake said.

Jake stood in line and bought four cups of coffee, three black, and one with extra milk for his mother. One of the orchestra members blasted away on a trumpet nearby. It sounded awful. Then he saw Terry standing next to other band members. He wished her to look up. He wanted to walk over and say he was proud of her, but she didn't look his way and he pushed plastic tops on the Styrofoam cups, and carried them stacked, two in each hand.

After he handed out the coffee the man held out a five-dollar bill, and Jake refused to take it. "Come on now, young man. I appreciate you waiting on us old folks," he said.

"You're welcome, and a thank you is enough," Jake said.

"Well, thank you then."

They could see the athletes unloading from buses off to the left, and the bright colors of hot-air balloons filling dotted the airport. Jake had heard there were twenty-five of them.

"I wish we owned a good camera," his mother said.

"We can cut pictures out of magazines," Jake said. He sipped the scalding coffee, and watched the steam move around in its blackness.

"My dear young man."

Jake wondered where in the hell this guy was from but turned around and smiled.

"Are you from here?" he asked.

"Yes," Jake said. "We live in Lake Placid."

"Perhaps you could help me then. My wife and I are from Switzerland, and our present accommodations are not to our liking."

"Where are you staying?" Jake asked.

"At present, in Wilmington. We're forced to take buses and standing in the cold to wait for them is difficult, at best. Might you know of a place in Placid available?" he asked. "We've called, but it seems everything is taken."

"How long are you staying?" Jake asked.

"We have a flight scheduled out of Montreal next week" Jake looked at his mother and didn't know what to say. "How much are you paying now?" Jake asked.

"A hundred-and-fifty dollars a night, meals included," he said. "I'd pay more for a spot nearer the Olympics."

"My parents have an extra bedroom, but it's probably not what you're used to."

"My good man," he said, and rested his gloved hand on Jake's shoulder. "I didn't always wear expensive coats or drive a Mercedes. I'm sure my wife and I would be comfortable at your parents. Is it close to the arena?"

"Within walking distance," Jake said.

"Oh, my. Gertrude, did you hear that?" he asked his wife.

"Much better," she said.

"Mom, what do you think?" Jake said. He leaned close to her so that they couldn't hear.

"You'll have to ask your father," she said. "Be a shame if they had to leave because of the buses."

Jake turned to the man. "I'll have to speak to my dad, but if you want to see where they live, I'll take you over after this, and give you a ride back to Wilmington."

"Wonderful. It's so considerate of you."

Jake heard his wife say something, but only caught the word 'provincial'.

His mother touched his arm. "They're ready to come in, it looks like."

Underneath, and behind an arch with the Olympic logo across it, the various colors of the Olympian teams were forming into solid groups. Jake couldn't stop thinking about the money his parents might be able to make. What luck, he thought, and hoped his father would think so, too. The high school bands played as they marched to a middle section of the field, then the orchestra in the amphitheater played, and the Olympians filed in. The colors impressed Jake most, but even they seemed artificial against the new snow, and mountains in the distance. A breeze pushed the flags out straight, the governor welcomed everyone, and the torch was officially lit. Mittened applause was lost in the wide-open space.

"Are you warm enough, Mom?" Jake asked. "It'll only take a minute to get the blanket."

"If you don't mind," she said.

Jake excused himself down through the bleachers. He wasn't interested in speeches by dignitaries. Away from the crowd, it seemed like any other afternoon; the sporadic applause seemed far away. He opened the trunk, shook out the dusty blanket, and refolded it. He hoped Terry was happy.

When he returned, a flag ceremony was in progress on the skating rink of the infield. His mother looked cold, and he wrapped the blanket around her shoulders, then tucked it under her legs.

"Thanks," she said. "I saw Terry."

"I'm glad she's part of it," Jake said. "She helped when I first came home."

The teams paraded around an oval and waved to the crowd. As the ceremony drew to a close, thousands of balloons were released, and the hot air balloons drifted off from the airport. Colors of every hue sprinkled the mountains, and everyone applauded. Jake turned to the man. "Before we leave, I want to say one thing," he said. "We live in the poor section of town and it's not very fancy."

He looked at his wife. She raised her eyebrows, and he sighed. "Perhaps we'd better not. You see, we usually spend our winters in a warm climate. Maybe we'd better go back overseas. Thank you for your kindness," he said, and offered his hand.

Jake lifted the blanket from his mother's shoulders and folded it up. She was stiff from sitting, and he held her elbow as they descended the bleachers.

"I'm so glad we came," she said. "Something to tell the grandchildren."

"Tomorrow the games start," he said, and wondered if Laurie had gotten tickets for the Giant Slalom the following Tuesday. He hoped to sneak away from work once in a while and see some of the speed skating tomorrow.

"Those people were very nice," his mom said.

"The old guy was, but his wife seemed kind of snippy."

"The cold is hard on people not used to it," she said.

"I guess."

Jake dropped his mother off, and halfway home remembered he had to deliver the finished boxes and turned around. The main street was closed off. Jake found a canvas knapsack of his father's, wrapped each box in a grocery bag, then tied the leather thongs on the knapsack tight.

As he passed the arena, he wondered if the bathrooms were clean, and what a little sulfuric acid would do to the toilet seats. He knew what several drops had done to one of his text books in high school. The parking lot off to the side of the old arena was full of buses, and he heard a bus driver tell one of the Olympic hostesses, dressed in red, that his bus schedule was all messed up, and that some of the people he'd picked up had waited over an hour in the below-zero weather.

Flags hung limp along the crowded streets, and people moved in and out of the shops like little wind-up soldiers in colorful parkas. Others crowded around Olympic pin-seller tables on the sidewalk. Jake hurried through the crowd. Everyone looked at everyone else, or in the shop windows, and no one seemed to be in a hurry. On one corner Curt Gowdy stood signing autographs. He seemed much taller than Jake had imagined from TV.

He felt hemmed in and pushed through faster than the crowd was moving. It wasn't a street anymore, but a wide promenade for people to watch one another, and put themselves on display. He heard every kind of language he'd ever imagined and saw different facial structures of every race. Jake felt like a tourist in his own town; nothing seemed familiar with the street closed off, jammed with people.

"Hi, Amos. What a zoo!" Jake said.

"The cash drawer is full, Jake, and the boxes are selling well," Amos said. "More stock?"

"Yeah," Jake said. "Three more."

Amos checked his record sheets. "I've sold eighty dollars-worth since you were in." He handed Jake a fifty, a twenty, and a ten.

"Cash, Amos?"

"Sure. You don't think I'm paying the state all they want during this, do you?"

"I wouldn't," Jake said.

"I jacked the prices on every box ten dollars," Amos said. "Money is burning a hole in these people's pockets. Keep busy. We'll sell all you make." Amos turned to answer someone's question, and Jake left. He stopped, and leaned against the front of the bank, watching the people all bundled up in bright parkas and expensive boots. They seemed disembodied. Faces peering out of scarves and hoods into other faces or shop windows. The air was filled with the buzz of conversation, and the shuffling of feet on dirty snow and frozen pavement. Tourists. Maybe I am one.

Jake walked to a steep flight of stairs that went down to Mirror Lake. Here it was less crowded, but the noise and yellow shine of rented ski-doo's filled the air. He walked along the edge of the lake, kicking four or five inches of snow in a fan at every step. An invasion, he decided, it was like a goddamn invasion. What did all these people know or care about the Adirondacks, except that it was pretty, and the Olympics were here. Olympic Games. The games he played at work, the games the Realtor's played with housing, the games Amos played in the shop. Those were the real games: the game of money. And what were the athletes there for? Nothing else, Jake decided, than to be better than the Russians. That's all everyone talked about. The Americans. The Russians. A competition for world politics on the athletic level: the reds against the red, white, and blue. Superpowers. The other countries were pawns filling the chess board as interest.

He sat on a log frozen into the ice on the shore, and anger kept him warm. He wondered what the athletes thought, and remembered the talk, when the decision was reached that a black man from Louisiana or Texas had made the bobsled team over a local boy. The natives all thought it was politics to show that Americans weren't prejudiced. It was common knowledge the local boy was just as good or better.

Jake stared across the lake at the five story condo where Barney fell, the sunset reflected in its picture windows. The urge to move off into the woods gained strength. He saw the crowds of people as gobs of motion with no memory, but knew each person lived in their individual worlds. He wanted to know if they hurt as bad as he did at times, if they kept trying to find something deep inside that made sense and put it all together. And he hung his head and stared at the ice he'd uncovered with his feet. Its opaqueness reflected some thoughts, absorbed others. And he remembered a Thoreau quote from high school that really clicked: "The mass of men lead lives of quiet desperation."

He looked up at the sound of boots on snow. A Chinese man was taking his picture, his wife beside him. Jake heard the shutter click and the automatic rewind squeal. The man walked over and offered his hand.

"You don't mind?" he asked.

Jake stared at him, then his wife.

The man let the camera swing free on its strap, and with his hands described a circle. "You fit," he said.

Jake stood up and started down the shore. "Wait, please," the man said. Jake turned. The man held a pencil, and a small pad of paper. "I send you copy. You see."

He told him his name and address. "Make it an eight by ten," he said. The man smiled, pocketed his little book, and walked away, his wife following a half step behind, and Jake was ashamed for saying that.

Jake sat on the log again and tried to see himself through the camera. He smiled and shook his head. "I fit all right. Like a snowstorm in the tropics." He scratched his beard and thought about Laurie and what the future held for them. For the next three weeks she'd stay with him. He ached for something, and he didn't know what it was. The discomfort of not knowing fuzzed his head up like a bad hangover, and he stood and started to walk directly across the middle of the lake. I'm missing something, he thought, and for the first time realized it wasn't Barney; it was something in himself he had to fit together. Jake stopped and wondered what the water looked like under the thick ice. He stomped his foot, and the snow rayed out. Black ice and the lightning bolt of a crack appeared in front of his boot. He stopped the urge to get down on his hands and knees and peer into the jagged white, closed crack – dig into it with Barney's knife. He knew it was chance that when he removed the snow in a puff of air from his stomping it uncovered a crack, but to make sure, he stomped around the ice in a circle and exposed more black ice, sometimes with tiny air bubbles trapped inside, but only the one crack. He saw himself through a camera again and laughed as he danced around like some crazy skater doing figure eights.

Out over the ice he heard someone calling his name, and a figure approached.

"Jake? Is that you?" Laurie shouted.

He waved his arms and started to walk towards her. She must be on her lunch break.

"Did you lose something?" she asked. "I thought it was you, but I couldn't tell."

"Horsing around," he said, and looked back towards the openings between the buildings, half expecting to see a crowd staring.

"What are you doing out here?" she asked.

"Are you kidding?" he said. "It's impossible to move in that crowd. I've seen enough people today to last a lifetime."

She wrapped her arms around one of his. "How were the opening ceremonies?"

"Colorful," he said. "Crowded. Let's run away and build a cabin."

"I'm ready," she said.

They started back to the shore. He held her close, but she was like the people he'd seen in the crowd. Layers of clothing hid all but her face, and he couldn't think clearly. He tried to listen as she talked about work and bringing some of her things over to the trailer.

"I guess I'm tired," he said.

"Thank God this only lasts three weeks,," she said. "It wears on you."

"I'm afraid, Laurie."

"Of what?"

"I keep looking for something I can't find."

"We'll look together," she said, kicking the snow ahead of them. She stopped and rested her head on his shoulder. "You're so far away sometimes I don't know what to do, and that scares me."

"I should tell you some things."

"Me too.," she said, and looked up. "Are you better off with me than you would be alone?"

"I want to be," he said. "Usually, probably. I'm close to something. It's like the ice stops us from seeing the water, but it holds us up, too. I can't explain it." He stared at her strawberry hair where it lay in tangles outside her knitted hat.

"You want it both ways," she said.

"What?"

"You want to stand on the ice and be able to see through the water all the way to the bottom."

"Maybe you're right. I think if I can understand why Barney died, I'll understand everything else."

She polished the ice with the bottom of her boot. "Don't you see how impossible that is?"

"What else?" he asked. "Be like them? A crowd of lost souls who don't even know why they're here?"

"You're not God, Jake. You can't understand everything any more than you can prove why Barney isn't here anymore."

"I've dealt with that," he said.

"No. I'm sorry," she said. "I don't think so."

"Why?"

"Many of the answers you're looking for are not find able. Even if you chopped a hole in the ice, you wouldn't be satisfied with the little bit of water you would see. You'd want to keep chopping until there wasn't any more ice, and then you wouldn't have anything to stand on."

Jake started walking.

"That's the part of you I love: the will to find and make the peace you want so badly, but I'm afraid it might destroy what we have, and maybe even both of us in the end."

"I know I'll never have all the answers. Even to the day I die, but I won't stop looking, and I disagree. I'm not trying to be God, but I am trying to understand myself. And I think I know why I reacted so strongly to Barney's death. He looked toward the condo. "Love," he whispered.

She stopped and stared at the snow. "No wonder. Being there when he fell, going up on the roof the day he was buried. It's no wonder it's been so hard."

"And hard on you and everyone else I know. I wonder if it's not meant for me to understand his death. But it is possible to understand why I reacted the way I did."

"Can I fit?" she asked.

"Yes," he said. "Because I know some day you and I will both die, too, and the way we talk to one another means something, and always will if we try hard enough."

She stopped, and hugged him, and lifted him off the ice, and when she put him down, they kissed as they had the first time they went out, some time ago. And he thought after so much time had passed maybe there was a way to make mental illness a success story. As they hugged he vowed not to let the mental anguish of pain have the last word.

CHAPTER 18

They walked back to the trailer after dinner at his parents on Sunday night. He had worked extra hours every day at the arena since Thursday and finished eight more boxes.

"Damn the state," he said.

"It's a mess," Laurie said.

"It's a wonder some old fart hasn't frozen to death waiting for a bus,"

"You should hear the phones ring, and listen to the people complain at the agency," she said. "They either want their money back or they want us to send them a taxi."

"They're covering up, too," Jake said. "Reporting no one has missed an event. Shit! A busload arrived yesterday in time to see the last twenty minutes of a competition at the arena, and no one would refund their money." Jake waved his arms in the air. "You should hear my boss. He's having fits. Half of the workers are late every day, and some refuse to wait in the cold. They don't understand why they can't get passes to drive in."

"It's in all the papers," Laurie said. "The Olympic committee is blaming the whole thing on the state. But the way I understand it, they deserve all these problems. They're the ones that asked the state in the first place to help them with transportation."

"You'd laugh to see my boss," Jake said. "He says it's a blemish on the games. He said the other day, 'We are ridiculed in the eyes of the world forever.'" What an ass!"

"Does he really say these things?" she asked.

"Honest. It's all the workers can do not to laugh in his face." Jake opened the door of the trailer.

"Nice and warm in here," she said. "Cozy." She took off her mittens, hat and coat, and put them in the closet. "Tell me, Jake. How do you like shacking up with me?"

"Terrible," he said, and put more wood in the stove. "It's awful."

"You better watch it, or I'll kick you right into that stove,"

"We've hardly spent any time together," he said. "You leave before I get up and we're never here much at night."

"Think of all the money, Jake. I've got over a thousand dollars in the bank. More than I've ever had."

"I've got eight hundred," he said. "What will we do with it all?"

Laurie put her arms around him, and said, "Actually, I'd like to buy a piece of land out in the woods some place."

"Okay by me." Jake put on his gloves and went outside to the wood pile and Laurie opened the door when he started back, his arms piled with wood. He dumped the logs into the wood box and made another trip.

"Want some coffee?" he asked, after she shut the door.

"No. I want you." She tapped him on the nose with a finger. "You. You. You," she said, and traced his features with her fingertips. "You have the cutest nose. It's all I could conjure up the other day." She parted his beard. "And there's that dimple. You know I haven't seen that since we started going out." She kissed him. "I saw and talked to so many people lately, I couldn't even remember what you look like., My ears ring for hours after work."

"By Friday it should be quieter," he said. "That's only five days."

"I'm glad your Mom and Dad got to see the pairs figure skating today, although your mom was pretty disappointed Tai and Randy didn't skate. It's terrible he got hurt, and in a practice session."

"How did Mom seem to you at dinner?"

"You can tell she's trying hard to show she's okay."

"I think so, too. She's got to keep trying. That's what I tell her all the time." Jake took off his coat and asked her if she'd gotten the tickets for the Giant Slalom on Tuesday.

"Yes," she said. "My boss was a real pain about it, and they didn't cost him diddly. He buys them in lots of fifty."

"How much did he charge?" he asked.

"Nothing, but he wants me back by one."

"I have to be at work, too," Jake said, and sat down on the couch. She sat beside him.

"Laurie, " he said, "Why do people get married?"

She sat up a little straighter and pushed her hair back.

"I'm not sure I know what you mean," she said.

"Is marriage an announcement to people?" he asked. "Is it a contract of faith between two people? Or something like that?"

"Both those and more," she said. "To me it's a public and private promise that links two people together forever. Even after they're gone, it remains."

"I like having you here," he said. "Even though we don't see much of each other, it's nice to know this is where you live."

She rested her head against his shoulder. "I like it, too," she said.

"Good!" he said. "When do we get married?" He jumped up and danced around the trailer. It swayed and rocked from side to side and the windows rattled.

"Jake! You didn't even ask me!" He bounded over to her from the kitchen table.

"I'm sorry," he said. "It's my first time."

He rested on one knee and put both his hands in hers. "Will you?" he asked.

"Will I what?" she asked.

"Oh, come on."

"It's my first time, too, and I won't live my life with you saying you never asked me."

"All right, Laurie," he said, and tightened his grip on her hands. "Will you marry me?" A tear fell from his right eye, and he saw she was crying, too. She squeezed his hands and stared into his eyes.

"Mr. Mason," she said. "Meet Mrs. Mason. By asking, I'm already your wife."

Jake opened a bottle of wine, and they toasted. They talked about everything, drank to happiness, went to bed, made love, and talked some more. At three o'clock, when Jake came back to the bedroom after checking the fire, she was asleep. He stood next to the loft and studied her for a long time and pictured her when they went together in high school, and then, as she would look years older. He wanted to reach out and touch her but didn't want to wake her. The reasons she loved him, and he her, were right, he knew, but he'd resisted them, and tried to find a reason for not following the truth. He rested his head on the birch cross-piece of the loft, and listened to her easy breathing, smelled the musky scent of their love making. The past is passed, he thought. I'm living in the here and now with her, and we'll make it because we want to, more than anything else. He closed his eyes and drifted off, then woke up, his cheek on the parchment-like bark, and saw how fragile Laurie's reddish-white eyelashes were in the light from the other room. We are each other, and we'll have to take care of each other.

He climbed up in the loft, over her, and under the covers. She rolled over in her sleep, put a leg and arm around him and sighed. A wash of peace settled into him. He closed his eyes and placed his scarred hand on her stomach.

Twenty minutes later he woke up: rested and full of energy. He looked at the clock and started to bounce up and down on the bed, making the trailer sway from side to side. "Wake up, Laurie! We're getting married!"

"Jake, it's four o'clock in the morning," Laurie said.

"Aren't you excited?" he asked. "Wake up. How can you sleep?"

She propped herself up on her elbows against the pillows.

"You're something else," she said.

"I'm something else? You're something else," he said. "You're the one that proposed a month ago."

"That's right," she said. "I had you in my clutches then."

He pinned her elbows to the bed and bit her neck. "Who's in whose clutches now?"

"Jake! Don't bite me," she said. "You'll leave marks." She tickled his ribs and he rolled away.

"I can't sleep," he said. "I don't want to."

"I can tell." She rolled on her side, drew her knees up, and stared at him. "We're going to be fine," she said.

"Damn right," he said, and put his hand on her hip outside the covers. "We can talk. If we can always do that, it'll keep the dark times away. You helped me the other day on Mirror Lake."

"We've always tried to talk. Sometimes I regret those years we were apart after high school, but I guess that time taught me what I want. And need."

"It will always take time for me, Laurie, for everything. To let the bad fade away and the good seep in."

She touched his cheek with the back of her hand, and said, "I think a part of your memories of Barney have made you stronger in many ways.

"I know I didn't deal with his death very well," Jake said.

"You expressed the loss you felt honestly," she said. "That is not a weakness, it's a testimony."

"You don't know what it was like at the hospital," he said.

"Tell me," she said.

He rubbed her hip bone in small circles with the palm of his hand. "I literally lost my mind," he said. "I told you I couldn't remember. I didn't even know my own mother." He rested his head against the pillow. "A fall into blackness that lasted and lasted."

"Is that what you were looking for in the ice the other day?" she asked. "An answer? A way out?"

"Something like that," he said. "All the stuff going on with Mom and the crowds of people confused the order I have to keep inside."

"That's why you were scared the other day," she said. "You were trembling when we came off the ice."

"I was petrified that if I lose it again I won't ever come out of it." He stared into her eyes.

She leaned against him, and said, "We'll be stronger together."

"I know, but I don't want to use you for that. It has to come from me."

"What?" she asked.

"The strength. It's a kind of peace inside that helps me struggle with the blackness that seeps in. Mom feels it from time to time and she doesn't know what to do."

"Tell me what to do and I'll help," she said.

"I'm not sure you can," he said.

"Don't I?" she asked.

"Of course," he said. "But it's like a candle in a drafty house. You can cup your hands around it to stop the wavering, but you could never stop up all the drafts that create the wavering," Jake said. "You couldn't hold your hands there all the time, either."

"I'm strong. " she said. "Stubborn, too."

He tweaked her nose. "And pretty, and proud, and a hundred other things I don't deserve. That's why I'm not letting you get away."

"Good," she said.

"You help me in ways words will never tell."

"That sounds nice," she said. "Hug me." He hugged her, and through the little window above the loft saw the dim light of false dawn chasing off the night and thought of the chances she was willing to take with him and promised to do his best by her. God help me, he said to himself, then whispered, "peace lies within."

"Jake? Is it time to go to work yet?" she asked.

"No. Rest," he said. "I'll tell you when."

That day at work Jake hid as much as he could from the crowds, cleaning locker rooms and bathrooms between events when they weren't being used. He sat in a stall for an hour reading the Daily News, his cleaning basket between his legs as a table. He smiled every time someone knocked on the door. He'd slept for a few hours after Laurie went to work, but not enough. On his coffee break he called her, and she put him on hold. After a few minutes of muzak, he was ready to hang up, and then she came on.

"I can't talk long, Jake. Did I dream last night?"

"No," he said.

"I'm dead tired," she said. "This place is a zoo. People are here from all over the world, and they want to extend their stay if our hockey team has a chance at the gold, but no one's willing to put down a deposit on the tickets or the hotel rooms until it's a sure thing."

"Tell them tough," Jake said. "I won't be home till one or so."

"Why?" she asked.

"I have to clean up the arena, and the game won't be over till after eleven."

"Wake me up," she said. "I'll have slept six hours by then."

"Okay, Mrs. Mason," he said.

"Good-by, husband."

Jake ate dinner in the cafeteria and listened to everyone argue about the state's transportation foul-up. Steve asked him why he looked so tired, and Jake told him he'd been up most of the night, after he'd asked his girlfriend to marry him.

"Hey, listen everyone!" Steve said. "Jake's engaged!" Everybody clapped and congratulated him. Steve told him he could take a nap in his office and went off to work.

Jake rested his head on the desk and dozed off. He woke when he heard a key in the door. It was Mr. Jacobs.

"What are you doing in here?" Mr. Jacobs asked.

"Got a little stomach ache," Jake said.

"Well, you should go home. We can't pay you to sleep. We've got enough foul-ups as it is."

"Yes, sir."

After he left, Jake rubbed cold water on his face. In the main arena he emptied garbage cans and watched the United States beat Romania seven to two. It convinced him they had a shot at the Russians if they kept playing as well. He smiled and went to ask Steve if he had any aspirin. Jake told him about the big boss finding him asleep.

Steve said, "Screw him."

"That man is impossible. He bitched one of the girls out for not having her identification badge on straight. Do you believe it?"

"I guess," Jake said.

Steve leaned back in his chair. "How about these Olympics, huh? The Americans are stealing the show, between Heiden taking the gold every day, and the hockey team's winning streak."

"You bet," Jake said. "Send the Soviets home with their tails between their legs."

"There's an outside chance the Americans will meet them in the medal round, they say," Steve said. "I'm not sure how it works."

"The arena will rock if they do," Jake said.

Jake and six other guys swept out the arena. It wasn't until after one that they punched out. The cold air woke Jake up. He had to admit that although he and Chad called the arena the white elephant when he first got home, it did serve its function well. Everybody praised it, but none of them saw the poverty behind it in Hollywood. Jake kicked a frozen chunk of snow that had fallen off someone's fender, and almost broke his toe. "Yeow-chh!" he yelled, and his voice startled him. He wondered if he'd ever be comfortable with all the contrasts of this town.

Laurie woke him up at eight and said they should leave by nine for Whiteface.

All right," he mumbled. "Coffee."

"It's ready, your lordship." He drank it as he sat on the couch in his underwear. Laurie had already taken her shower and was wandering around in a bra and panties.

"Married life I all right," he said, and gave her a wedgie when she walked by.

"Jake!" she said. "Get in the shower and get dressed." She snapped her underwear back in place.

"You shouldn't parade around like that," he said.

"I don't like clothes," she said, "and it's so nice and warm in here. Like I like it."

He stood up and gave her a hug. "You smell good."

"Thanks," she said. "Please get ready. I'll probably never have a chance to see the Giant Slalom again, or Phil and Steve Mahre."

Jake showered, trimmed his beard, and drank another cup of coffee while getting dressed. "What's the thermometer say?" he asked.

"Twenty," she said. "A heat wave."

They made it past the checkpoints by Jake showing his arena badge and explaining that he was assigned to Whiteface for the day. Laurie had to show her ticket. One state official told Laurie she should be riding a bus, not riding with a state employee.

"Good Lord," Jake said, once they passed the final road block. "You'd think we were gonna kill somebody."

"It's a farce," she said. "They're trying to make up for all the screw-ups last week."

Jake tried to drive around the worst of the frost heaves, but it was impossible. The old Ford rose and fell over them, and Laurie hung on to the front edge of the seat.

"This thing rides like a boat in rough waves," she said.

"Imagine what it's like in the back of those buses," Jake said. "This car's been good to me."

Open water in the Ausable River sparkled in the sunlight, and water crashed around, over big boulders in rapids that never froze. Jake stared at the river until Laurie touched his leg.

"Good fishing in this section," he said.

"Did you catch any?" she asked.

"Huh?" he said.

"You are so far away sometimes," she said. "I don't know what you're thinking."

"Day dreaming."

"Are you happy?" she asked.

"Very," he said.

"Me, too." She rested her hand on his shoulder.

"Isn't life wonderful?" he said.

"You!" She slapped his leg. "You're such a smart ass. I haven't had it easy, you know."

"Who has?"

"After we graduated, you went off to college," she said. "That's when my parents got divorced."

"I know, you wrote me."

"I didn't tell anybody the whole story," she said.

Jake slowed down for a frost heave and remembered the letter. She seemed to accept their divorce, and her parents never seemed to be on great terms, even when he and Laurie were going out.

"I never told you why they stayed together as long as they did," she said.

"I guess not," he said.

"They both loved me, and agreed to stay together, but only till I graduated," she said.

"When they finally told me that, it made me feel sick and guilty." Jake heard her voice break and glanced at her. She'd stuck her chin out and was fighting to hold back the tears. He reached a hand out to her, but she moved to the passenger side, and stared out the window.

"How come you haven't told me about this before?"

"I keep telling myself it doesn't matter and try to believe that I've been fine all these years since it happened, but it's not true." She stomped her foot on the floor. "I don't want to tell you this, not now."

"We talk about my problems enough," he said.

"Jake, you don't know what it was like. By the middle of summer, they were divorced. My father left, and by fall Mom had gone back to Buffalo. She wanted me to go with her, but I wouldn't. I had a job as a waitress and thought I could make it."

"You did, didn't you?" he asked.

"Sure. In a way," she said. She wiped her eyes. "Come sit next to me."

She slid across the seat. "Try to imagine what it was like," she said. "I was eighteen, and every joker I waited on stared at me like a piece of meat or made a pass at me. I was alone, Jake. Living in a cheap apartment, sleeping half the day away, feeling sorry and stupid, and I didn't know what to do. You were the only guy I'd ever slept with, and I knew all these guys wanted one thing."

Jake gripped the wheel tighter, and watched his knuckles change color. Why was she telling him all this now? "Laurie, does all this matter to what we have?"

"It might," she said. "I can't kid myself about marrying you. Neither should you. We've both done things we regret. They make us what we are."

"If you're about to tell me you started sleeping around," he said, "I already knew that."

"You did? How?" she asked.

"I came home on vacations. I talked to people. You know how small this town is," he said. "Like most people know I've been in a nuthouse."

She stared out the windshield and tears, streaked with mascara, rolled down her cheeks. "I wasn't myself then," she said. "I was alone, and I hated myself."

Jake put his arm around her and pulled her into his side. "Relax," he said.

"No," she said. "There's something else."

Jake tried to relax his hand on the wheel. "Tell me," he said.

"A lot of times when you talk about Barney's death, and what it's done to you, it brings back the empty feeling I had when you and I broke up, and then you went away to college."

Jake started to say something.

"Let me finish first," she said. "You may think there's no comparison to what happened between us and Barney's dying, and that it wasn't a big deal when we broke up. And I'm not forgetting that it was my idea. But later when I saw the way other guys treated me, and the way my parents fought, I wanted you more and more, and the loss meant more to me than I ever expected. That fall, after my mother left, I think I had a nervous breakdown. I can't even remember parts of it. Like you don't remember."

"But you changed," Jake said. "You dealt with things."

"I grew callouses, Jake, like you get from slinging shit all day. I quit sleeping around because I knew what people thought and I started going out regularly with big guys who beat the hell out of anybody who bothered me."

"Jesus," Jake said, and wanted to bang his head on the steering wheel. He pulled into the High Falls Gorge parking lot.

"We're gonna' be late," she said. "I didn't mean for this to come out all at once."

"No. It's good it has." He turned off the key. The roar of the water filled the air, rising up from the gorge below. He could imagine what people were saying when they saw them together. There goes the crazy man and his whore. He knew he was being unfair.

"Two questions," he said. "Did you sleep with a lot of guys from town or were they from out of town?"

"Mostly guys that came into the restaurant, that I saw later in the bar after I got off work."

"Okay." He stared across the river. "Did you ever sleep with Barney?"

"What? Why?" she asked.

"Did you? The truth."

"No. We didn't hang out in the same places. Does it matter?" she asked. "Do you want a list of names?"

"No. I'm sorry," he said and opened the car door and walked to the bank's edge. Water fell off into the gorge and a fine mist above formed the bars of a rainbow that disappeared into the cold ledges below. He shook his head from side to side and instead of putting his hands in his pockets, he let them tingle in the cold air. I should have crawled into a snowbank and died that winter after Barney was buried. Nothing goes right. Nothing! Even when I think it is, it turns to shit.

Laurie came up and stood beside him.

"I'm sorry, Jake," she said. "I should have left it alone."

"Oh no," Jake said. "It's right to bring it up. I had you wrapped up in a beautiful box with a white bow on top."

"Did I destroy it all?" she asked.

"No," Jake said and kicked a stone off the gorge's edge. "It takes two to do that."

"I knew this had to come up," she said. "And it should have sooner."

"You can't do anything about your parents any more that I can do anything about Barney. We can feel sorry for ourselves, and I think we're both pretty good at that in one way or another." Jake picked up a stone and threw it across the narrow gorge. "The other stuff I knew about, maybe not the extent of it, but I'd heard."

"We're missing the race," she said.

"What time is it?" he asked.

"My watch is in the car." She went to get it.

Jake leaned down, picked up a handful of the pea gravel and heaved it high in the air, watching it fall from sunlight to rainbow to shade and into the clean, white foam. Frozen sunlight, he thought.

"It's five of ten," she said.

He walked over to the car and lifted her up on the fender.

"We've both got the same problem," he said. "We don't deal with emotional pain very well, and we keep on caring when we can't do anything about what's happened."

"Marriage may not be our only choice," she said. "I think it's the best one. That is if you're not going to dump me."

"No." Jake grabbed her by the ribs. "And you know why?"

He touched her under her chin.

"We care enough to try and understand each other and each other's problems." He put his arms around her. "We must both believe peace lies within us."

CHAPTER 19

They rode up the mountain on the chairlift and listened to the announcer give the names and times of the racers as they came down the mountain. The slope Jake and Laurie had skied on not long before was crowded with people cheering the racers down the hill.

"Let's climb up near the starting gate," Jake said, and stepped off the chairlift.

Walking in the man-made snow was like wading through corn starch, and Laurie hung onto his arm for support.

"Looks like a stampede," he said, and pointed to all the footprints in the snow. People pushed against the orange plastic catch fences all along the course and some had climbed the trees. Jake bent down, and helped Laurie get on his shoulders when the announcer said Steve Mahre was in the starting gate. The crowd went wild. Jake edged closer to the snow fence, and Laurie yelled that he'd started. Jake couldn't see much. He held onto her knees and tried to keep his footing in the mushy snow. When Mahre went by the crowd noise hurt Jake's ears, and after he'd skidded around the corner below them, the noise subsided. They listened for his halfway-mark speed. He was slow.

Jake took another glance at the starting gate, then turned and started to walk down the mountain with Laurie still on his shoulders, but almost fell.

"Let me down," she said. They walked down the length of the course, stopping at different places to see the racers go by. "It's not as exciting as I thought it would be," she said. "Hard to see."

When the race was over, everybody tramped down the mountain. On a steep part of the slope, instead of walking, one group of young people lay on their backs, heads pointing downhill, and slid on their slippery nylon ski jackets to the bottom. "What the hell?" Jake said.

"That's dangerous," Laurie said. "Someone will get hurt."

They stood off to the side and watched. Some of them really got moving on the steep parts of the hill. One guy, about Jake's age, and a little overweight, slammed into the back of a middle-aged woman, and Jake heard the woman ask him what kind of an asshole he was why didn't he act civilized! Jake laughed so hard he had to grab hold of Laurie to stand up.

Two members of the ski patrol skidded to a stop near them and announced through a bull horn that everyone was to clear the slope and walk down the sides.

"What time is it now?" Jake asked

"Noon," she said.

"I guess we'll make it to work on time. I'm sure glad we didn't pay thirty bucks a ticket to see that."

In the car, Laurie said, "Jake, I know how close you are to your parents, but have you ever thought of moving?"

"Out of Placid, maybe," he said. "Out of the Adirondacks, never. Why? You want to move?"

"I don't know," she said. "So much has happened lately. Best of all, we're engaged." She paused and touched his shoulder as he started the car.

"I don't know where we'd go, or how we'd make ends meet," he said, and backed the car out of its spot.

She walked with him to work, and when they stopped to rest in the middle of a hill Jake pointed to the Arena ahead and Hollywood behind.

"Have you ever heard that Alcoholics Anonymous slogan?" she asked. "Something about the patience to change the things you can, and accept those you can't?"

"Why can't it be changed? They've pumped millions to show that a small town in the mountains can host the world for three weeks."

On top of the hill, he stopped and stared at the mountains, and wanted to be sitting with Laurie under a tree in the snow, a small fire in front of them, and a cozy tent behind.

"I'm late," Laurie said. "See you tonight." She kissed him and smiled. "C'mon, Jake. They'll be over soon."

"Right," he said, and watched her walk down the line of flags, and tried to imagine how he would suffer if he never saw her again. And what would she think if he went back to the hospital? The stability he'd been working on ever since last fall was crumbling, and yet seemed to be rebuilding, too, and he wasn't sure of the end result. He stared into a pass between the mountains and tried to shut everything else out. Then, that out of chaos success was possible.

He heard someone banging on the plate glass windows behind him and turned. Mr. Jacobs stood on the second-floor landing, and when he was sure Jake saw him, he lifted his wrist and pointed to his watch. Jake walked toward the building and nodded. With a broad sweep of his arms, Jake took in the arena, flags, speed-skating rink, and smiled up at Mr. Jacobs. Mr. Jacobs smiled, took out his handkerchief, and wiped a smudge on the window, then waved for Jake to come in.

That morning Heiden had won his third gold medal. He and the hockey team were all anyone talked about. Jake couldn't keep straight who had to beat whom, to finally win the gold, but today one of the workers told him it was almost certain the Russians would play the Americans on Friday night. That night when he punched out, Jake asked Steve about work Friday night if the big game took place.

"Jacobs said no overtime," Steve said. "State cut him off cold. How many hours you have in by then will decide it."

"I'll sneak in if I have to," Jake said.

"Don't tell me about it," Steve said. "Jacobs is on the prowl like a bobcat these days."

On Thursday night, after work, Jake walked over to Mirror Lake and watched Heiden receive his fourth gold medal. He wandered the outskirts of the crowd and stared at the stars. At the end of the ceremony, they shot off fireworks. Everyone oohed and ahhed, and on the way home, he heard the crowd inside the Arena cheering at the hockey game and was glad he didn't have to clean up. He started down the hill, stopped, and turned around. He hadn't seen Chad for days. He might be at the Arena Grill.

Jake walked inside, and saw him next to the pinball machine talking to a tourist. Amy poured him a draft and asked where he'd been hiding. She had on more clothes than the last time he'd seen her. Chad came over. "Where you been, you old dog?" he asked.

"Busy cleaning up after tourists," Jake said.

"You don't come around anymore." Chad spit into an empty beer bottle. "How's the job?"

"It sucks," Jake said.

"Who said quite a while back that they'd never work for the bozos?" Chad asked.

"Got to live."

Jake glanced at his fifty cents change on the bar, and remembered he still owed Chad money. "Let me buy you a beer," Jake said. "Drink up." Chad chugged the rest of his beer and put the mug on the bar. Jake chugged his and placed his mug beside it. The beer tasted good. He paid Amy for two fresh ones and took forty dollars out of his wallet. When Chad wasn't looking, he slid the money through the handle of his mug.

"What's this?" Chad asked.

"I should pay you interest," Jake said.

"Oh, that's right." Chad stuffed the bills into his shirt pocket. "I saw Grant the other day," he said.

"How is he?" Jake asked.

"Pretty good. Wanted to know if you were making a killing selling them boxes."

"I'm rich," Jake said. "Laurie and I are engaged."

Chad fell back against the bar. "You're what?" he said, and spilled beer on his pant leg. "You're not kidding, are you?"

"Nope," Jake said.

"You old son-of-a-bitch," Chad said. "Congratulations."

"Thanks." Jake took a long swallow of beer.

"I knew she'd quit the bowling alley," Chad said. "You living together?"

"Her landlord rented her house for the Olympics," Jake said. "We are till that's over."

"I'll buy the next beer," Chad said. "I don't know what your plans are, but Grant wanted me to ask you something. He needs someone to help in the sawmill two days a week this spring and summer." Chad spat into the beer bottle. "You interested?" he asked.

"Long drive," Jake said.

"Something else, too," Chad said. "The farmer where I'm working stopped me the other day, and said he remembered you talking about making maple syrup," Chad said, and took a drink. "Hey, you know, this might work. He wanted to know if you'd help him. I guess he was talking to your uncle who told him you could stay at his place if you wanted," Chad said. "But you're getting married. I'll be a son-of-a-bitch."

"I wonder if Laurie could find work over there," Jake said.

"Not much going on in Essex," Chad said.

"I don't know that Dad will make syrup this year," Jake said. "He's working full-time at the Club."

"Do you want to move?" Chad asked.

Jake rubbed moisture off the side of his glass. "I think so, Chad. Too much going on here."

"This might be a good chance," Chad said. "Between you and me, I think that old guy has money, and he might take you on as caretaker after syrup season is over."

"You think he might?" Jake asked.

"I can't say for sure," Chad said. "Go talk to him."

"I think I will," Jake said.

They played partners for a few games of pool, and the tourists smiled as Chad moved around the table in his green work pants, tobacco-stained T-shirt, and pine-pitch blackened hands. Jake saw some of them grimace when Chad spit in the trash can against the wall. Chad winked at Jake.

"Sometimes I miss on purpose," he said. "Watch." He walked over, spit, and hit the side of the bucket, and Jake saw one girl look like she was going to puke.

Jake slapped Chad on the back. "Nice going," he said.

By midnight the bar was so crowded it was almost impossible to get a drink or walk around. He and Chad leaned against the bar, giving anyone that got too close a dirty look.

"Amy looks like she's wintering well," Jake said.

"I guess," Chad said.

"What's that mean?"

"She has problems, too."

"Such as?"

Chad didn't answer right away, and Jake wondered if he would.

"Such as she has to have an operation. Remember the last time we talked, and I told you my friendship with her might mean more than sex?" Chad looked at Jake over the top of his mug while he drank. "You didn't believe me."

"No. I guess I didn't. What kind of operation?"

Chad put down his mug and faced Jake. "Cancer, Jake. Goddamn cancer. I wasn't going to tell you."

Jake watched Amy behind the bar, as pretty as ever. "When is the operation?" he asked.

"Two or three weeks. She hasn't told her husband yet. You and I are the only other people that know."

"Tell me what I can do."

"Maybe come around a little more often."

"Sure."

They talked for another twenty minutes. Chad told him he stayed every night and helped her close. He wanted to tell Janet but wasn't sure she'd understand.

Later, outside, Jake felt sorry he'd misjudged Chad. "What an asshole I've been," he said up into the cloudy sky.

Even though it was after midnight, people were still out wandering around. Jake sat on a park bench underneath the flags and stared toward the mountains he couldn't see. His mind wouldn't focus on one thing before it jumped to the next. He remembered how happy he'd been to come home from the hospital, along with the fear of what other people thought of him. Then meeting Terry, and the conflicting emotions he'd had about her hauling snow, Laurie, the arena job, Mom's depression, his engagement, and Chad's fooling around and how wrong he'd been about that.

He remembered the gray squirrel when he cruised that lot with Chad; its bushy tail had twitched and snapped when it came close, and then it ran away and hid behind a log, and then came back even closer, ran up a tree, around and around, climbing higher. He'd stayed as still as he could, trying to predict where it would appear next. Lately he'd been running around like that, not really knowing what to do, not taking the time to think. How close was he really to Laurie? Why did so many things bother him that he knew he couldn't change or fix?

He tried to remember the changes the mountains went through from season to season, from day to day – sunshine, snow rain – and he couldn't hold their shapes clear. He pushed his feet into the frozen, salted snow, and cursed himself.

Laurie had said he wasn't God, but that didn't stop his wanting to know what would help him understand himself. He kicked the snow hard with his heels and hit the cement base of a flag pole. Pain shot up his leg, and the bottom of his foot numbed. "I'm stupid. That's what it is," he said, and bent forward, elbows on his knees. Why can't I accept the things that are good, without always testing them from every angle, and asking why? Why? I let Barney's death drive me out of my stupid-assed mind, and have I learned anything? He clasped his hands together and wondered if he was sorting things out or making them worse. The thoughts kept running, refusing to focus, as he stared into the dirty snow. You have learned, but things are still so complicated you can't see it or won't. They wouldn't be so complicated if you didn't ask questions no one has the answers to – except God.

This is crazy, he thought, and leaned back on the bench. Take Laurie and get away from this town. We'll do it together. And if I go back to the hospital – so be it. He smelled the beer on his breath, then heard the shuffle of people behind him. The fucking drinking didn't help either.

Laurie was putting wood on the fire when he opened the door. He told her about the possibility of living in Essex. She smiled and hugged him tight. "I want to make a new start," she said.

Before they went to sleep, he said, "Let's not sit around analyzing it. It's enough that we're together." He hugged her and whispered, "I love you, Laurie."

"Thank you."

He got up at seven with her, and by eight he was on the way to Essex. Mr. Farnsworth invited him in and commented on the length of his beard since they'd seen each other. He told Jake he hadn't made syrup last year because he couldn't handle the gathering or cut all the wood by himself. "Putting it up in jars isn't as easy without my wife, either." Mr. Farnsworth walked over to the kitchen wood range and stirred the coals. "I couldn't pay you much," he said.

"My problem, Mr. Farnsworth, is that I'd need a place to stay. I got engaged not too long ago." The old farmer scratched his head, stood in front of the stove a moment longer, then walked to the window. He pointed with a crooked finger. "Down there, in them spruce trees next to the brook, is a cabin we used to use in the summer some. You could maybe fix that up. It ain't much, though."

"Okay if I look it over?" Jake asked.

"Go ahead."

Jake put on his coat and walked across the field. Set back on a gradual bank next to a small brook, a two-room log cabin rested on piles of stones at each corner. Jake opened the door, and let his eyes adjust to the dimness before going in. He guessed it measured eighteen- by-thirty-two. A wood stove sat in the center of the main room, and a ladder led to a loft.

Off to the left was a small kitchen, and he wondered what Laurie would think. Through a window over the porcelain sink he could see an outhouse.

He walked around the outside. The roof looked good and none of the windows were broken. He went back inside and climbed the ladder to the loft. He couldn't see any place where it had leaked; it smelled dry and dusty. Cobwebs and mouse turds were everywhere.

Jake closed the door gently. He could see it all cleaned up with a braided rug on the floor and curtains in the windows.

He asked Mr. Farnsworth if he knew of any work for Laurie. He didn't, but said he'd ask around. "Be nice to have you young people here," he said. "Lonely sometimes without the wife."

He pointed his curved finger at Jake. "She wouldn't have allowed you to live together unless you was married, but it's okay by me, so long as you're engaged."

"We'll be married soon," Jake said.

"Good," Mr. Farnsworth said. "People talk, you know."

"How much would you pay me a month?" Jake asked.

"Two-hundred is as high as I can go," he said.

"What would you want me to do?" Jake asked.

"Be pretty much full-time during sugaring " he said. "After that, help put in the corn, and haying later on. You'll have plenty of time to fish and hunt if you want."

On his way home, Jake kept shaking his head. It was too good to be true, and he caught himself asking a lot of questions. "Take it as it is," he said. "He wants somebody around the place to help out and keep him company."

Jake stopped at Grant's and told him he'd like to work a couple of days a week after sugaring. Grant acted pleased and said, "Fine, fine," then, "poop," and offered him a glass of cider to close the deal, and Jake's feet floated over the pedals on the way home.

The streets of Lake Placid were packed. Jake made it to work on time and started in on the bathrooms. Two more days of this and I'm outta here, he thought. Mr. Jacobs made it official that afternoon. All the extra help would be done on Sunday, after the closing ceremonies.

The place buzzed with talk about the hockey game. One of the workers told him the scalpers were selling tickets for two hundred dollars each.

At three-o'clock during break everyone was betting on the game. Most of the workers didn't think the Americans could beat the Russians, and one of the full-time employees said he'd give two-to-one odds that the Russians would win. Jake asked if he'd bet a hundred dollars. The guy stared at Jake and everyone quieted down. Most had been betting five or ten dollars.

"Sure, wise guy," he said. "I'll be glad to take your money."

They shook on it. Mr. Jacobs came in. He said, "Everyone that's due to get off at six, can you stay? Forget what I said about overtime." Jake and the others nodded.

"Thank you," Mr. Jacobs said. "The world's eyes are scrutinizing us closer than ever before." He rubbed his hands on his suit jacket and walked out mumbling.

Jake called Laurie. "What time will you be finished?" he asked.

"By six, I hope."

"Stop by the Arena," he said. "Maybe I can get you into the hockey game."

"How did it go today?"

"Pretty good," he said. "I'll tell you later."

Jake walked over to the old arena. The Russians were loosening up. He wandered around checking trash cans and tried to put a hex on them. When they'd finished, the Americans came on the ice, and Jake thought they looked nervous.

By five o'clock the Arena was fuller than he had ever seen it, and the buzz of excitement made it seem warm enough to melt the ice.

When the puck hit the ice at the opening face-off, the stanchion Jake leaned against shook and vibrated as everyone rose to their feet screaming. The Americans, dressed in white with red and blue lettering, looked like kids, compared to the older Russian team in their dull red uniforms.

The Russians scored first, and the crowd moaned, and sank into their seats. The Russians were much more sophisticated in handling the puck, particularly on defense.

The Americans scored, and Jake thought the woman next to him was going to pee her pants. She jumped up and down and screamed so loud it hurt his ears. At the end of the first period, each team had scored another goal. Very few people left during the intermission. Jake wandered around and checked to see if Laurie was there yet. He found her waiting outside the main doors.

"They won't let me in." she said. "I want to see it."

"Follow me," he said. He walked up to a state policeman at one of the doors. "Excuse me, sir. Mr. Jacobs asked me to take this lady to the press booth."

The officer looked them over, and said, "It'll never happen again. Go ahead."

He and Laurie stood at the top of the seats near center ice. When the Russians scored the go-ahead goal in the second period, he thought he was at a funeral. Someone yelled, "Get their red asses," and faces turned in that direction, then the crowd livened up. Jake was so tense before the third period he had to force himself to relax and breathe regularly. It was as if all of America was on the line. Nothing counted if they didn't win.

It was almost impossible to talk. Jake grabbed Laurie's hand, and worked his way down to the glass at ice level. He pounded the glass with his fists every time the Americans went on the offensive. With two-and-a-half minutes left, he saw an American slide past a Russian defense man next to the far boards, stop dead and shoot. Jake knew it was in before it touched the net and wanted to jump over the barrier. He was almost crushed by a surge of people moving forward. The game was tied, and the concrete rumbled beneath his feet. He turned and saw ecstatic faces chanting, "U.S.A., U.S.A., U.S.A." Laurie was easy to find. She was several people away, and grinned when he looked at her, then gave him thumbs up.

Jake thought both teams would play defensively, with less than three minutes left, but the Americans played like it was the opening period. The Arena was like a vast tank of adrenaline, all focused on the players. When Eruzione put the puck into the net in the final seconds, Jake almost lost consciousness; he saw gray and leaned on the people around him for support. Laurie moved closer and reached a hand across several people to grab his. The game of the century was over, and the crowd stayed on its feet and cheered for another fifteen minutes, but after a while Jake was conscious of nothing but Laurie's hand.

CHAPTER 20

White spirals of wood emerged from the tree and fell to the snow. Jake reversed the bit and brace and blew a puff of air into the hole. A drop of sap seeped out; he tasted its sweetness on the tip of his finger. White, thin clouds touched the peaks of the Vermont mountains, and the sky above him was so blue and bright it hurt his eyes to look at it. He reached into the galvanized bucket for a spout and tapped it into the tree with a ball-peen hammer; its ringing echoed through the woods. He hung a bucket on the spigot and adjusted it to rest level.

The first drop appeared and plopped into the bottom of the bucket with a twang. Jake moved from tree to tree, careful to avoid boring near the lighter colored circles inside the gray Bark the dead spots from years past tapping. He was glad there wasn't so much snow that he had to wear snowshoes, like other years he remembered.

As the sun set over the Adirondacks, he climbed out of the sugar bush, and sat on a sun warmed ledge on top of the hill. They'd known Laurie was pregnant when they left Lake Placid two weeks ago. The small wedding ceremony with his mom and dad, and Chad and his wife, was exactly what they'd wanted. When Jake told his mother after the ceremony that she'd be a grandmother soon, she'd cried and hugged him, then placed her hands on his shoulders and smiled.

"That will make me very happy," she said. Jake watched as she turned to look for someone, his father.

After Jake told him, his father shook his hand, then covered Jake's hand with both of his.

Jake gazed off toward Lake Placid and remembered rubbing her still flat stomach the night before as light from the kerosene lantern flickered off the rough log rafters. She'd fallen asleep before he could tell her how much he loved the peace and quiet, and her.

Before the sun completely set, Jake headed down the hill, and checked the buckets as he went along. The ones most recently tapped were almost empty; the ones he'd tapped that morning were half full, and the buckets he'd hung the day before, up and down the brook near the cabin, were full, some running over. He hurried to gather them before it was too dark to see.

THE END

ABOUT THE AUTHOR

Timothy Strong holds a master's degree in English and Creative Writing from Binghamton University, where he was mentored by Larry Woiwode. Tim's poems and short stories have been published in the Alabama Review, the Mississippi Review, Blueline, False Grief and the Awakenings Review. An entrepreneur, he owns and manages the BirchBark Bookshop, offering over 75,000 used and rare books. He lives in the foothills of the Adirondacks.

NOTE FROM TIMOTHY STRONG

Word-of-mouth is crucial for any author to succeed. If you enjoyed *Tourist*, please leave a review online—anywhere you are able. Even if it's just a sentence or two. It would make all the difference and would be very much appreciated.

Thanks!
Timothy Strong

We hope you enjoyed reading this title from:

BLACK ROSE
writing™

www.blackrosewriting.com

Subscribe to our mailing list – *The Rosevine* – and receive
FREE books, daily deals, and stay current with news about
upcoming releases and our hottest authors.
Scan the QR code below to sign up.

Already a subscriber? Please accept a sincere thank you for
being a fan of Black Rose Writing authors.

View other Black Rose Writing titles at
www.blackrosewriting.com/books and use promo
code
PRINT to receive a **20% discount** when purchasing.